A SWING AND A MISS

He shrugged, blew her off. "I don't care what you spend. The furniture means as little to me as my game meant to you today."

She stood silent for longer than he liked, as if fitting missing pieces into a puzzle. She had no business trying to figure him out.

"Later, Keely." He nudged her toward the door.

He jerked off his sweatshirt, in need of a shower. He tugged on the drawstring of his sweatpants, realized she hadn't budged. "Staying for the show?"

She shook her head. "It's Memorial Day Weekend. I'm taking two days off. The Rogues play at home. You'll be around for the dogs. I'm going back to my apartment."

Back to her place? He'd allowed her into his life, only to have her cut him out?

Expecting her to leave, he dropped his sweatpants. One step toward the shower, and an unexpected slap on his bare ass spun him around.

"Congratulations on your win," Keely managed, blushing. "Isn't that what jocks do? Slap rear ends to celebrate?"

"You're not a jock." Psycho stared at her, finding it hard to believe she'd smacked him.

The sting of her slap had shot straight to his groin. Nothing outside of sex was going to appease him now....

MORE PRAISE FOR KATE ANGELL!

DRIVE ME CRAZY

"Kate Angell takes the checkered flag with this romantic race."

—*The Midwest Book Review*

"A light-hearted romance packed with adventure and laughs, *Drive Me Crazy* is a definite keeper, and I'll be looking forward to more by Kate Angell."

—*Romance Reviews Today*

"*Drive Me Crazy* is a fresh, original, and entertaining romance that is unputdownable."

—Harriet Klausner

"One fast, sexy ride for any reader...a unique blend of comedy and the paranormal...If you as any reader like your romance hot and sexy with a wacky twist, then this book is for you!"

—*A Romance Review*

"Hot, sexy, and funny to the last page."

—Romance Junkies

"A keeper!"

—Reader to Reader Reviews

CURVEBALL

KATE ANGELL

LOVE SPELL NEW YORK CITY

To Sue-Ellen Welfonder—
we are great friends, animal lovers,
and most importantly, you totally get the
Winged Monkeys from The Wizard of Oz.
Curveball *is for you.*

LOVE SPELL®

June 2007

Published by

Dorchester Publishing Co., Inc.
200 Madison Avenue
New York, NY 10016

ISBN-10: 0-505-52707-3
ISBN-13: 978-0-505-52707-3

The name "Love Spell" and its logo are trademarks of Dorchester Publishing Co., Inc.

Printed in the United States of America.

Visit us on the web at www.dorchesterpub.com.

ACKNOWLEDGMENTS

Debbie and Ted Roome, you are my Naples, Florida family.

Stella Brown, the perfect neighbor. I appreciate you proofreading my manuscripts.

Ashley Stevenson, we have Scrappy and Angel in common. And a love of great books. Life is good.

Marion, Paul R., Judy, Kristin, Grace, Paul, Max, and Mary, my Fargo, North Dakota family.

Always, I'm grateful to my editor, Alicia Condon, for her guidance and enthusiasm. You make me a better writer.

CURVEBALL

WELCOME TO
JAMES RIVER STADIUM

HOME OF THE RICHMOND ROGUES

Starting Lineup

25	RF	Cody McMillan
18	C	Chase Tallan
11	3B	Jesse Bellisaro
21	CF	Risk Kincaid
7	SS	Zen Driscoll
15	1B	Rhaden Dunn
44	LF	Ryker Black
1	2B	James Lawless
51	P	Chris Collier

PROLOGUE

"What the hell were you thinking?" Guy Powers, owner of the Richmond Rogues, was addressing the Bat Pack, the top power hitters in Major League Baseball. His gaze shifted among the players seated on the other side of his desk. Right fielder Cody "Psycho" McMillan, third baseman Jesse "Romeo" Bellisaro, and catcher Chase "Chaser" Tallan, all slouched in tan club chairs, arrogance and pride personified. Not one of the men showed an ounce of remorse.

Powers slammed the *Virginia Banner* atop a growing stack of newspapers. Headlines glared back at him. Big and bold and block-lettered.

Psycho wastes no time getting in swing of things.

Richmond brawlers take to the field.

Powers shoved himself forward in his brown leather chair. He rested his elbows on a massive claw-footed oak desk. Pursed his lips. His tone conveyed pure disgust. "Media Day. Photogra-

1

phers, journalists, television, and radio. A chance to hype the season ahead, and instead you fought, showed your asses."

He shuffled the newspapers, snagged one from the bottom. Ruffled the pages. Read, "Sportswriter Emerson Kent's column, *Press Box*, claims player egos have grown larger than the national pastime." He creased the newspaper, returning it to the stack. "I tend to agree with her."

"Kent's column is a joke," Psycho snorted. "She should return to the society section. The lady writes as much about the players' haircuts, tight butts, and the restaurants we frequent as she does about runs batted in and who stole second."

Powers's nostrils flared. "Emerson draws women readers. Women who fill one-third of the seats at James River Stadium."

"Emerson went out of her way to make us look like jerks," Psycho complained.

"She didn't have to go far today." Powers's gaze was now as hard as his reputation in the National League East. "You screwed up."

All around Powers, the room bristled with hostility. Standing in an arc behind his desk, publicist Catherine Ambrose, team manager Tim Rhodes, pitching coach Danny Young, and team captain Risk Kincaid all glared at Psycho as if he'd committed the crime of the century.

In Powers's eyes, Psycho had. An hour into interviews and photo ops, the right fielder had taken batting practice, showing off for the press. Powers's latest acquisition to bolster the bullpen had been on the mound. Left-hander Chris Collier had thrown some major heat.

Heat that gunned down Psycho. The fastball clocked at one hundred miles per hour caught the right fielder on the hip. Spun him around and drove him to his knees.

The press and the executives had cringed.

Trash talk erupted between the two men. Loud and profane. Collier had claimed it was a wild pitch. An accident. Psycho swore the pitcher had thrown to maim him.

Animosity shot between home plate and the mound, soon spreading among the other team members as well. The ballplayers spat and glared. Clenched their fists. The atmosphere darkened as the men primed themselves for a fight.

The head trainer ordered Psycho off the field, instructing him to ice his hip. Psycho had blown him off. His ego on the line, he'd taken a stiff practice swing, once again facing down Collier.

The press stood on the sidelines, wide-eyed and taking notes as quickly as each could write or relay play for television or radio broadcast.

Collier was smoking, pleasing the crowd with his changeups. Then came a slider.

Psycho whiffed. Couldn't buy a hit. Dark determination glazed the power hitter's eyes as he dug in, edging home plate.

Collier fired a sinker. The ball spun, dropping suddenly as it reached the plate. Psycho couldn't jump back fast enough. A guttural hiss escaped him as the ball slammed into his instep.

Media sympathy surrounded him until Psycho threw down his bat, tore off his batting helmet, and charged the pitcher's mound, bent on retaliation.

Chris Collier dropped his mitt, and stood his ground. Psycho threw the first punch, and then all hell broke loose. Romeo and Chaser jumped off the bench and the bullpen emptied. Players took sides, and fists flew.

A fight captured by the media. A publicist's nightmare. Catherine Ambrose would be hounded by the press the entire season. Powers made a mental note to send her a bottle of Tylenol. Extra-strength.

Catherine did an exceptional job in public relations. No one thought faster on her feet or spoke with more authority, continually bending over backward to downplay the team's behind-the-scene disputes and nasty divorces. She stood between the players and the press to keep the Rogues's name as polished as their World Series Trophy.

Unfortunately for all concerned, today's on-field fiasco could not be buried with the obituaries.

Powers ran his hands down his face, focused fully on Psycho. "You broke Chris Collier's nose. His vision's distorted. He won't start the season opener."

"Start Cooper Smith or Roan Ginachio. Both have more talent than Wimbledon," Psycho stated as he crossed his ankle over his knee and rubbed his bandaged and deeply bruised instep. Had the ball caught him an inch higher, it would have shat-tered his ankle.

Wimbledon . . . Powers shook his head. His lat-est acquisition had taken a whole lot of ribbing since his arrival. Collier's sharp features, white-blond hair, light hazel eyes, and lean frame made him look more like a tennis pro than a baseball player. Psycho had tagged him Wimbledon, just to be annoying.

For some reason, Psycho and Collier had hated each other from the onset of spring training. The fight today was the culmination of weeks of taunting, aggression, and bad blood.

Powers listened as pitching coach Danny Young ripped Psycho a new one. "Media Day tar-gets trades and new acquisitions. Collier was to throw a series of pitches, show his heat."

"His *heat* struck me twice," Psycho reminded Young.

"It was an accident. Collier was about to apolo-gize when you stormed the mound."

"Apologize, my ass. The man has a rifle arm and precision timing. One wild pitch, I might be-lieve. Two"—Pyscho shook his head—"the man threw to take me out of the game."

"You crowded the plate," Young openly accused.

"Like hell I did."

"You did." Team captain Risk Kincaid backed up Young. "Roger Clemens in his prime would have nailed you."

"Clemens I would have excused," Psycho snarled. "Wimbledon deserved what he got."

"No remorse, Psycho?" Powers raised a brow. His silence said it all.

Romeo and Chaser nodded their agreement.

Behind the Bat Pack, their sports agent, Cal Winger, shook his head, disgusted by their behavior. Winger had represented the three players from their first appearance in the majors. He'd grown gray trying to keep them in line. And quite bald. Frown lines bracketed his mouth. He looked ten years older than his present forty-five.

Powers still had a full head of dark hair. He'd be damned if the Bat Pack would drive him to either hair dye or plugs. Or an early grave. They'd already caused him an ulcer.

There would be no fighting in his organization. Not as long as he owned the team. His starting pitcher was out for the count. Which left the bull pen lean.

Powers scooped his rubber stress ball off the desktop. He squeezed it so hard his fingers pressed his palm. The tension slowly left his body.

He wanted to be calm when he leveled his punishment on the Bat Pack. Clearing his throat, he spoke with the authority of his position. "Psycho, you're the most fined and suspended player in Major League Baseball, both on and off the field. You disregard rules and fair play. You're arrogant and self-centered, and a total pain in the ass."

Psycho's eyes widened in a *who, me?* expression.

Keeping his voice even, Powers tallied, "Four black eyes, five split lips, two dislocated shoulders, and a bruised kidney resulted from the fight. In the midst of the fray, Romeo slammed into Emerson Kent and knocked her down. Her suit jacket was ripped and her slacks grass-stained." Powers cut his third baseman a look. "She's new to sports. I don't want her harboring ill-will toward the Rogues. A personal apology and the purchase of a new outfit are in order. Understood?"

Romeo slowly nodded.

Powers lowered the final blow. "The Bat Pack will be suspended one game for each man or woman injured."

"Sit the bench for thirteen games? Son of a—" Psycho swore a blue streak. "I'm more at fault than Romeo and Chaser. Suspend me, let them—"

"Walk?" Powers shook his head. "They should have held you back, not joined the fight."

"This totally sucks, Guy." Psycho was the only player on the team who called Powers by his first name.

"It's about to suck a whole lot more. You'll be fined for fighting. I'm talking six figures."

Psycho's jaw went slack. "You can't—"

"I can, and I will," Powers assured him.

"Trade me."

"Definitely an option." An option Powers would never execute. No other player breathed baseball as Psycho did. The right fielder was a feared contact batter and base stealer. He consistently drove in ninety runs from the leadoff position. His leaping catches on defense had frequently robbed an opposing player of a home run.

He'd slammed into the cement wall so many

times, chalk outlines similar to those drawn around a dead body decorated the outfield perimeter. Each one was a testament to his dedication to the sport. He had six Golden Gloves and had been voted onto the 2006 National League All Star team.

Powers pushed his chair back from his desk, stood. He met Psycho's gaze squarely. "Keep your animosity off my field."

Every muscle in Psycho's body tightened as he leaped up. "Might want to share that advice with Wimbledon as well."

Powers watched the Bat Pack leave his office. All strut and swagger. Young men flanked by fame and fortune and a lack of repentance.

Once management had departed, Powers sat alone. He'd done what he had to do. He'd taken the Bat Pack off the roster. Richmond fans would not be happy. The Rogues had gone four years without a Divisional Championship. Five years had passed since they'd won the World Series. Richmond wanted another trophy as much as Powers needed control over his team.

His Rogues lacked unity. He blamed the salary cap and off-season free agency for the dissension. Only six of his original starters remained. The newcomers crashed the park with attitude and their own sense of self-importance. An importance that the Bat Pack resented. Captain Risk Kincaid had gone out of his way to build team spirit, but the Bat Pack had pulled the welcome mat.

The three power hitters stood alone. They had each others' backs. And no one else's.

Powers faced Opening Day with rookies and second stringers. Not a good way to start the new season.

His heartburn flared like a blowtorch.

ONE

Cody "Psycho" McMillan's doorbell rang, the tones playing thirty seconds of Tom Petty and the Heartbreakers's "I Won't Back Down." Barefoot and bare-chested, his jeans unsnapped, he jabbed in the code to disengage his security system. After hearing three clicks and a beep, he opened the heavy oak door, then leaned negligently against the jamb.

"Cody McMillan?" A slender woman with delicate cheekbones and a dimple in her chin stood outside. Her deep blue gaze was as cautious as it was curious.

His eyes narrowed. "Who's asking?" He lived on the outskirts of Richmond, in a gated historic district. Yet time and again fans and groupies landed on his doorstep. Her car wasn't parked in the driveway, which meant she'd walked onto his property. Walked, or climbed the stone wall surrounding his Colonial. The lady didn't look like a rock climber.

The afternoon sun struck her from behind as she stood beneath the columned portico, surrounding her in a halo of light. Dressed in a wrinkled blue suit and worn-down heels, she looked like an angel down on her luck. He glared at her darkly. "You're trespassing."

She took him in, from his narrowed eyes and naked chest to his bare toes. She blinked twice, then said, "I'm here on business."

"Insurance, encyclopedias, vacuum cleaners—I'm not buying."

"I don't do door-to-door. I'm here to offer my services."

"Do those services include your sweet mouth?"

Her lips parted, and her eyes went wide.

Crude and rude, he'd rendered her speechless. He was acting like a jerk, but didn't give a damn. Since he'd been suspended from the Rogues, he'd lit into anyone who'd crossed his path. This woman had picked a bad time to *offer him a service*.

She swallowed hard, took a step back, only to catch one navy pump on an uneven brick. She wavered, nearly lost her balance.

His reflexes sharp, Psycho snagged her wrist, righted her. He noted her smooth skin. Delicate bones. He ran his thumb over her palm. Soft, but sweaty. She was nervous.

So nervous, the black leather portfolio pinned beneath her arm slid down her side. Heat colored her cheeks as the broken clasp flew open and a map of Richmond, a blank notepad, and a box of tampons landed at his feet.

11

Psycho hunkered down beside her. Blushing profusely now, she quickly scooped up the map and notepad. He handed her the box of tampons. Closing the portfolio, she got to her feet, ran one hand over her hip. The skirt pulled tight against her hipbones, the fabric worn thin at the seams. A row of staples hemmed the skirt to just below her knees. She wasn't dressed for success.

"I'm Keely Douglas, from Gloss Interiors," she introduced herself.

Gloss Interiors? Who was she kidding? Psycho crossed his arms over his bare chest. Studied her. Her portfolio was empty of prize-winning photographs and decorating plans. He was not in the mood to be played.

"I've met with three interior designers today. I wasn't scheduled to speak with a fourth," he stated.

"Your secretary worked me in. A last-minute appointment."

She didn't give up. "You spoke with Mrs. Smith?"

She looked relieved. "Yes, Smith, that's correct."

Busted, sweetheart. Psycho had a financial adviser and a sports agent. An attorney on yearly retainer. A part-time pet sitter. But no secretary. He rubbed his knuckles along his stubbled jaw. Wondered how much rope it would take for her to hang herself. "Mrs. Smith didn't mention you," he said. "She's old and forgetful. After this incident, due to be fired."

Keely looked horrified. "Please don't let her go

on my account. I may have written down the wrong day and time."

"Maybe you did." He took a step back, one hand on the door, ready to close it.

She didn't take his hint to leave. Instead, she straightened the lapels on her blue blazer, along with the decorative gardenia pin that drooped over her right breast. Teacup breasts, Psycho noted. He preferred a handful.

"Have you already contracted with a design firm?" The woman was persistent.

He shook his head. "I've yet to commit."

He never would have begun the project if the Daughters of Virginia had not badgered him to restore Colonel William Lowell's childhood home. A home Psycho had purchased without ever considering its heritage. All he cared about was that the Colonial gave him privacy in a world where everyone wanted a piece of him. The estate now stood in near ruins after having been gutted by an ambitious previous owner who never got beyond the demolition stage.

No matter those who came before him, the Daughters blamed Psycho for the Colonial's distressed state. They demanded he restore its integrity. Their weekly visits, letter writing campaign, and constant phone calls had prompted him to start the restoration.

Unfortunately, his contact with architects had proven disastrous. Their vision of his home was much different from Psycho's own.

Not one of the reputed designers had impressed him. Once they identified him as a Rogue, they'd seen him as the Bank of Psycho. A man with limitless funds and little taste. Not one of the decorators asked him what he wanted. Each told him what he needed.

Their designs resurrected the Classical American Style, complete with carved moldings, mullioned windows, and plaster ceiling medallions. Lacquered walls and stenciled floors. Their discussion of antiques had drawn his yawn.

He'd seen enough fabric swatches and hand-painted Chinese-patterned wallpaper to last him a lifetime. All he wanted was to restore enough history to the Colonial to get the Daughters off his back. It was late afternoon. His priorities lay in a workout, a run, and reflection on his suspension. Not dealing with Keely Douglas.

"Do you have a business card?" he finally asked her. "I'll have my secretary give you a call. We can set up an appointment for later this week."

She bit down on her bottom lip, looked up at him with those deep blue eyes. "My schedule is full. It would be weeks before I could work you in."

Yeah, right. Psycho didn't believe her for a second. "We'll connect next month, then."

She looked so disheartened he almost gave her thirty minutes of his time. Almost. The cavalcade of Cadillacs creeping down his driveway drew his attention to the Daughters of Virginia and their untimely visit. Didn't these women have anything better to do than uphold their southern pride?

"Shit," Psycho swore beneath his breath as one car door opened and the first of four Daughters stepped out. The president, Rebecca Reed Custis, led the way. The women marched on the house with the precision of Confederate militia. All silver-haired and dressed in gray linen suits with platinum Daughters of Virginia brooches pinned at their throats. He half expected them to shoulder rifles and bayonets.

"Mr. McMillan." Rebecca offered Psycho a tight-lipped, cultured greeting.

"Hello, Becky." He kept his tone casual.

She looked him up and down, shuddered. "Don't you own a shirt? A pair of shoes?"

He scratched his bare belly, then jammed his hands in his jeans pockets. The worn denim pulled low on his hips. So low the *Stands on Command* tattoo at his groin was visible. "I'm a nudist, Bec. I could have answered the door with my bat and balls showing."

She paled at the thought. "We've come to see what progress you've made on the Lowell House."

A silence settled as the Daughters stared him down. The atmosphere was as combative as a battlefield prior to the first shot. He needed a delaying tactic—

"Mr. McMillan has hired my design firm—" Keely Douglas's voice rose from behind the matrons. "We've spent the afternoon together, exchanging ideas. I was just leaving when you arrived."

15

The lady should have been long gone. Psycho felt immediate relief she'd chosen to linger. She'd saved his butt. "Keely Douglas of Gloss Interiors, meet the Daughters." Psycho introduced each one.

Rebecca looked down her nose at the young blonde and sniffed. "Your firm is not recognized by the Richmond Historical Society."

"My heritage interested Mr. McMillan more than my experience." She modestly dipped her head. "Keely Douglas *Lowell*. Fifth-generation grandniece to the colonel."

Psycho stared at Keely, as transfixed as the Daughters. *Grandniece, my ass*. Rebecca Reed Custis could trace the lineage of every Confederate leader who'd fought in the Civil War. Lowell's family tree didn't include Keely Douglas. He waited for the Daughters to chastise Keely for defaming the Lowell name.

Rebecca turned on the designer, studied her so closely that Psycho pressed between the women and moved to Keely's side. "Problem, Becky?" he asked.

"She's illegitimate," Rebecca stated.

Keely sighed, her shoulders slumped. "Embarrassingly illegitimate," she confessed. "My heritage lies with Marshal Cutter Lowell, Colonel William's brother. Marshal had relations with a tavern wench in 1862, and the bastard side of the family was born."

"Good heavens!" Rebecca slipped a lace handkerchief from her gray clutch purse and fanned her face. "A blight on the Lowell name."

A blight called bullshit, Psycho thought.

"Marshal could never measure up to William," Keely said, so sincere she made Psycho blink. "The colonel was a man revered. William Lowell graduated from West Point without demerit. He possessed every virtue of other great commanders without their vices."

"Mary Chestnut, the Richmond diarist, called him 'the portrait of a soldier,'" Rebecca praised.

"He bore himself with remarkable distinction. Erect as a poplar with his shoulders thrown back," Daughter Helen Adler Paine commended.

"Lowell was dignified and cordial. His aura of infallibility drew the unconditional trust of his soldiers." This from Daughter Olivia Morris Tuthill.

"My family has an original oil painting of Lowell on his warhorse Ranger." Keely spoke with reverence. "He's impeccably dressed in his Confederate uniform, projecting unconscious dignity as both soldier and gentleman."

The Daughters were immensely interested in the oil painting. They wondered which master had created the work, deciding it must be Winslow Homer, and Keely concurred it was.

Psycho couldn't believe his ears. The lady had stones. Keely stretched the truth like a rubber band that would eventually snap her in the ass. He shot her a warning look, which she totally ignored.

"Though I'm not outright related to William," Keely humbly continued, "I do have a very personal interest in retaining the history and American spirit of Lowell House."

"Would you return the colonel's painting to its rightful place above the mantel?" Rebecca inquired of Keely.

"If Mr. McMillan so wished."

"Definitely my wish," Psycho said.

Debate ensued as Rebecca quietly consulted with the Daughters. Keely didn't appear the least bit fazed that they spoke behind her back. She looked calm. Downright serene. Her thickly lashed blue gaze shone clear. Her lips curved in an unconcerned smile. She gave nothing away, as if lying was second nature.

Psycho often lied to get himself out of trouble or to get a woman into bed. He made promises. Broke them. He had to admit Keely knew how to twist words to her benefit. Damn impressive.

Several minutes passed before Rebecca once again faced Keely, interest in her eyes. "Tell us your plans, Miss Lowell. How do you envision the restoration?"

Psycho shook his head. Keely was no more a Lowell than he was. Yet she'd penned her name in their family Bible. On the bastard side.

Allowing the Daughters and Keely entrance, he crossed to the fireplace, which was big enough to swallow a Volvo. He watched as Keely took in the twin staircases to the second floor and the large landing at the top, along with the stretch of center hallway that led straight through to the back door. She looked oddly in her element among the rotted wood, chipped plaster, and sagging ceilings.

"In every renovation, my design firm retains the history of the Colonial while unobtrusively modernizing the home," Keely began.

"How much modernizing?" Concern pinched Rebecca's lips.

"Only as far as updating the plumbing and heating systems. The lighting and appliances," Keely returned.

"How many Colonials have you renovated?" Psycho asked, just for the hell of it.

Keely met his gaze squarely. "Enough to know you'll need a respirator to breathe life into your home."

"Well put, my dear," Rebecca applauded.

Psycho couldn't believe Keely had won over the Daughters. The women had hounded and chastised him for months. Yet the mere mention of her being Marshal Lowell's illegitimate grandniece, and the suggestion that she possessed an antique oil painting had landed Keely in their good graces.

She'd also inserted herself into his life without his permission. Psycho didn't like anyone to have the upper hand. Though she'd saved his ass, it was time to put her in her place. Just so she knew where she stood with him.

Pushing himself off the fireplace, he sauntered toward Keely. "Take us room by room and lay out your plans." He put his afternoon run and workout on hold. "I'm damn curious."

Keely sighed. "We've all ready discussed the restoration at length. Surely you're tired of the conversation."

"Never tired," he returned. "I want the Daughters to be certain I've hired the best possible designer."

"The remainder of our afternoon is free." Rebecca spoke for the group. "With the recent death of my dear husband, I've time on my hands. A short tour of the house would be delightful."

"Let's tour," Psycho agreed.

Keely Douglas inwardly cringed. McMillan's expression told her she had no wiggle room. Hard and intimidating, he knew she'd lied about her heritage and the oil painting. He'd yet to discover she didn't know the first thing about design. She hoped to keep him from making that discovery.

Keely needed this job. At twenty-seven, she still didn't know what she wanted to do with her life. She was considered an adult, but without a grown-up job. She'd been both a waitress and a dog walker. Ticket taker at the movie theater. She'd sliced bread at a bakery. No employment had lasted more than six months. She wanted a job that ran a full year. Her rent was due. She didn't want to be forced to live out of her grandfather's station wagon.

Renovating a Colonial couldn't be all that tough. She loved history, found the Civil War fascinating. When a close friend employed by Tashika Designs mentioned that the most infamous Rogue in Richmond baseball planned to have his Colonial restored, Keely had taken a chance. She'd parked her car a mile from the guard gate and snuck in when the guard conversed with one of the Colonial Hill residents.

It hadn't been hard to pick out McMillan's home. It was architecturally challenged. A total eyesore with chipped cornice trim, two crooked windows and missing bricks. She'd researched the Colonial inside and out. Had spent a chunk of her last paycheck on architecture books covering the period.

She'd bluffed her way through much of her life. Fabrication came as naturally to her as breathing. Envisioning the Colonial fully restored, she propped her portfolio against a dark, pine-paneled wall and entered the formal living room, left off the entrance hall.

After a dozen steps, Keely slowed. Her eyes went wide and her jaw slack as red and green Christmas lights blinked their welcome. The décor was complemented by dark green lawn furniture and an electrical cable spool functioning as a table. A wooden sign hung on the wall above an enormous home theater television: A GOOD FRIEND WILL COME AND BAIL YOU OUT OF JAIL, BUT A BEST FRIEND WILL BE SITTING NEXT TO YOU SAYING, "DAMN, THAT WAS FUN!"

Through a scarred wooden portal leading into the dining room, she caught sight of a dismantled dirt bike on a tarp smudged with grease. Every drawer of the nearby Craftsman tool chest stood open. Dirty rags littered the floor. The scent of oil was overpowering.

Her smile broke, and relief settled bone-deep.

Any redecorating would be an improvement over the way McMillan now lived.

More confident, she informed the Daughters, "On our first meeting, Mr. McMillan and I discussed the living room. He confided that his favorite season is autumn, when the sun glistens off the trees surrounding the house. We agreed the room should be decorated with that warmth. Glazed yellow walls that glow like aged maple leaves on an October afternoon. All highlighted with sage, burnt orange, and russet red."

"I'm an autumn as well," Rebecca piped up, pleased.

Keely glanced at the man she'd labeled "fall". Too masculine to be handsome, he radiated a raw intensity that intimidated her. Enigmatic eyes, a deceptively casual stance. She had a hunch he was a ticking time bomb.

"Mr. McMillan wants authenticity rather than reproduction," she pressed forward. "A camel-back sofa in apricot velvet, chintz-covered slipper chairs, and oriental carpets."

"A fine rosewood piano," Rebecca chimed in.

"An antique secretary. One with scalloped pigeonholes and paneled doors," Helen Adler Paine suggested.

Charlotte Maitlan Moss swept her blue-veined bejeweled hand toward the double-sashed windows, now covered by bedsheets. "Sheer inner curtains beneath tailored swags."

"A tea caddy," added Olivia Morris Tuthill.

"Definitely a tea caddy," McMillan muttered darkly.

"Perhaps a tall-case clock by Simon Willard," Rebecca put in enthusiastically.

"Mr. McMillan's already placed the clock." Keely motioned the Daughters toward the entrance hall. There, she pointed to the wide landing at the top of the twin staircases. "He'd like the grandfather clock centered between a row of newly constructed windows."

"Impressive," echoed the Daughters.

Keely moved to the east staircase. "Mr. McMillan also suggested a tri-corner table bearing a silver tray, holding candlesticks and an oil-burning lamp," she said straight-faced. "Something that would call to mind a time when candles were carried upstairs to light the way to the second floor."

"A lovely idea." Rebecca looked at Psycho with new respect.

The man remained silent.

Climbing the first step, Keely let her imagination go. "Polished hardwood floors, a low fire burning in the hearth . . ." She ran her hand over the banister and paused. "Teeth marks on the newel post?"

"Mr. McMillan's dogs," Rebecca informed her. "The black mongrels have chewed the history right out of the house."

"They're Newfoundlands, Becky," McMillan said denfensively. "Six months old and full of themselves."

At this mention of the pups, loud barking drew everyone's attention down the center hallway to the back of the house. Trailing McMillan, the Daughters marched out the rear door with Keely on their heels.

Her eyes widened at the sight before her. Two of the biggest dogs she'd ever seen had broken from a fenced run and now romped playfully about a small cemetery, set back from the house.

"Boris, Bosephus," Psycho called to the Newfies, who totally ignored him.

"Those animals are as undisciplined as their owner," Rebecca huffed.

Undisciplined *and mischievous*, Keely noted as Psycho jogged across the lawn toward the dogs. The man was fast, but the pups were faster. He didn't reach them in time. To everyone's horror, one dog lifted his leg on a headstone, while the other started digging at the grave site. His front paws scooped like a bulldozer. Chunks of grass and dirt went flying.

Rebecca gasped, swooning. "That's the Lowell Family Cemetery!"

Keely caught the matron's arm, held her upright.

Helen Adler Paine shuddered. "Colonel Lowell must be rolling over in his grave."

Keely watched as Psycho grabbed one Newfie by the collar, only to have the second pup escape. "Boris!" she called out, hoping to draw one of the dogs toward the house, and away from the graves.

She drew him all right. One hundred pounds of

drool loped across the yard in her direction. Boris had no brakes. His front paws struck her chest and knocked her to the ground. He sniffed her crotch, then slobbered all over her suit and licked her cheek. He had the worst puppy breath on the planet.

Beside Keely, Rebecca hyperventilated. Scrambling to her feet, Keely snagged Boris's collar and held on tight. It wouldn't take much for the Newfie to drag her across the yard.

From the corner of her eye, she saw that Psycho had penned Bosephus and was coming after Boris. He took charge of the pup with one hand, then patted her down with the other, checking for broken bones.

He probed her shoulder, her clavicle, and smoothed down her lapel. Her heart skipped when his fingers brushed her breast, then swept over her grass-stained skirt. His palm curved her hip, swept her butt. Lingered a moment too long on her left thigh. He skimmed dirt off one calf, traced a new ladder in her nylon. Then met her gaze. "You hurt?"

Not hurt, but downright tingly. There was nothing caressing in his touch, yet she felt aroused. Her nipples peaked and warmth filled her belly. "I'll live."

"Miss Lowell was attacked." Rebecca came to stand beside Keely. "Those animals scared the life out of us."

"There's a leash law on Colonial Hill," Olivia Morris Tuthill informed him. "We're appalled those black beasts run free."

25

"The boys have learned to flip the latch. I need to get a lock," Psycho said as he led Boris to the pen.

"Miss Lowell," Rebecca said with southern dignity. "We would understand if you no longer wish to work for Mr. McMillan."

Psycho McMillan. His reputation and news of his suspension had preceded her visit. Commentary on every radio and television station reported him wild and impulsive. A man on a short fuse. He'd fought his own teammate. It had taken the strength of six men to pull Psycho off Chris Collier.

As he came toward her now, his dark gaze narrowed. She took him in. Unruly black hair, bruised hip and foot, and raw male swagger. He'd yet to snap his jeans. His *Stands on Command* tattoo was still visible.

Naughty, notorious, and an avowed nudist, he was like no man she'd ever met. He both scared and attracted her. The attraction won. She would take her chances with him and his Colonial.

She cleared her throat. "I appreciate your concern, Rebecca, but I've never backed down from a challenge. I will return the house to its noble heritage."

Admiration shone in the older woman's eyes. "The colonel would be proud." With those words, the Daughters picked their way across the lawn and departed.

The moment they were out of sight, Psycho turned to her. He rolled his shoulders, dug his hands deep into his jeans pockets. "You saved my butt. Got the Daughters off my back."

"They want their heritage preserved."

"Can you make it happen?"

"I can try." He hadn't officially offered her the job. "Am I hired?"

"Against my better judgment. You've no experience."

"Allow me to decorate the entrance hall and living room," she bargained. "If you're not satisfied, I'll walk."

"If I'm not satisfied, you'd better run."

"I'll also train your dogs," she suggested to sweeten the pot.

"They've been kicked out of two obedience schools."

"They need hands-on discipline. How long have you had them?"

"Long enough to build a run and learn they can flip a latch." He raked one hand through his hair. "My brother recently separated from his wife. She kicked him out of the house and forced him into an apartment with no room for the dogs. I took them off his hands. They're playful and clumsy. Tend to be wild."

Wild, just like their master. "I can handle them."

"Question is, can you handle me?"

"Handle you *how*?"

"I'm a nudist. I like being naked."

She'd bet he looked good nude. "Whistle a warning before you enter a room."

"I'm not a nice guy," he told her straight out. "I flip off the world. Play by my own rules. I hear son of a bitch more often than my name. I tend to piss people off. I'll tick you off too."

"Maybe I'll tick you off first."

One corner of his mouth curved. "Maybe you will."

There was a moment of silence before she shuffled her feet. "Guess I should be going."

"Guess you should." He rolled his tongue inside his cheek. "I'll be at James River Stadium tomorrow. Call my secretary for a key to the house."

She hesitated. "Mrs. Smith, right?"

"If she doesn't answer, I keep an extra one taped to a brick beneath the second window to the left of the front door."

She scrunched up her nose. "You don't have a secretary, do you?"

"No more than you have an oil painting of Colonel William Lowell on his warhorse Danger."

"Ranger," she corrected.

"Stretch the truth all you want with the Daughters, but be straight with me."

"I'll work on it."

"Work sky blue, sun yellow, and outfield green into the interior design," he said. "I'm pure summer, sweetheart. Not an autumn."

TWO

Jesse "Romeo" Bellisaro mentally relived Media Day. The fight had been unavoidable. His collision with Emerson Kent, totally inexcusable. In all his thirty-three years, he'd never purposely hit or knocked down a woman—even though retaliation had been justified when he was eleven and a jealous Sylvie Davenport punched him on the school playground. All because he'd shared his Milky Way with Avery Jane Carmichael. The first girl in his sixth grade class to wear a bra. Sylvie's birthstone ring had cut the corner of his right eye. He still carried the scar.

Sylvie had been the only female ever to hurt him. On the whole, women loved Romeo. He loved them back. He kissed, stroked, and took them to bed as often as was humanly possible. He enjoyed buying them gifts, taking them on expensive dates, making them feel desirable.

He could always find something special that set each one apart. Soft skin, pretty eyes, a good personality, a nurturing nature, a love of sports or politics.

He drew women with a wink and a smile. He liked to flirt and tease. Liked to fill the ladies with as much lustful yearning as he felt in their presence.

He'd known a lot of lust in his lifetime.

It was now five o'clock. The exact time the receptionist had told him Emerson Kent would be leaving the *Virginia Banner*. Housed in a building older than time, the *Banner* occupied the top five of the twenty floors. The majority of the reporters had passed retirement age. Emerson was the first new blood in a decade. The first to write a sports article for women, and make it to syndication.

Romeo planned to charm the sports reporter into a new outfit, as well as writing a nice article on the Rogues.

He'd circled the block twice and found parking places nonexistent. Engine running, he double-parked his Dodge Viper behind a sporty BMW Z4, then focused on the main entrance to the building. People slowly trickled out. Mostly men. He waited and waited. No sign of Emerson Kent.

Two minutes after six and she appeared. He recognized her immediately. Feathered chestnut hair, her signature red-framed glasses, and a cocoa-brown pantsuit that didn't hide her curves. Her leather briefcase was her only concession to the fact that she worked in a man's world.

Her strides purposeful, she walked directly toward him. He tracked her movements as she rounded his car. Disregarding his smile, she jabbed a finger from his Viper to the Beemer. "You're blocking my car."

So the hot little ride belonged to her. He'd have taken her for an Avalon or a Lumina, not red, sleek, and convertible. He wondered how often the woman went topless. If she let the wind muss her hair? Threw caution to the wind? "Didn't know that was your car."

"Now that you do, pull up so I can back out." She retrieved her car keys from a cigar box purse.

She hadn't given him a second look. *Major put-down*, he could hear Psycho and Chaser chuckle. A first for Romeo.

Swinging his car door wide, he unfolded himself from the driver's seat. Emerson jumped back, frowned. He'd nearly taken her out a second time. She took him in, from his long-sleeved white shirt rolled up his forearms, down to his dark jeans and black Pumas. Her eyes narrowed and her lips pursed. The air between them cooled.

She didn't like him. The thought struck him square between the eyes. Left him uneasy.

"Romeo Bellisaro." He went with a formal introduction.

She was slow in taking his hand. A quick connection and release. "I know who you are, but not why you're here."

"I came to apologize for backing into you on the sidelines during Media Day."

Her green gaze sharpened behind her red frames. "You *slammed* into me. Knocked me down."

31

"I would have helped you up if the player I was fighting had backed off an inch."

"Ryker Black *was* in your face."

"Our fight went beyond the Psycho-Collier skirmish. It gave Black an opportunity to pound me for smiling at his girlfriend."

"Must have been some smile."

"Harmless, but Black read it as a sexual invitation."

"Was that your motive?"

"I don't mess with other men's women."

"I guess Black saw it differently."

"He's gone dumb and blind over some Hooters chic. He doesn't trust other men near her. Black's an ex-marine, served his country out of college before signing with the Rogues." He ran his thumb over a split lip. "Man has a wicked hook. The fight should never have reached the sidelines."

"You got in one good punch."

"You saw?" The fact she'd noticed pleased him. "I blackened his eye."

"You're lucky he didn't mess up your pretty face."

His pretty face. The bane of his existence. "Black can be intimidating."

"I've heard he chews pitchers up and spits them out."

"Leaves only bones."

She smiled then. And Romeo fell to her smile. He'd never been affected by the simple parting of a woman's lips, yet Emerson Kent struck him harder than Ryker Black.

Her green eyes held humor. Her cheek a dimple. Her mouth was perfectly formed, he noticed. To him, the slight gap between her front teeth was a total turn on.

He stared so long, her smile faded. She tapped her watch. The band was fashioned with curved sterling silver spoons, and it sported a wide Roman numeral face. "It's late."

"You have plans?"

"Plans to eat dinner and work on an article for Sunday's paper."

"What's the article about?"

"A column predicting the pennant races."

Romeo hated reporters and their predictions. "Rogues are a safe bet."

She shook her head. "Not this year. The Bat Pack's out of the rotation for thirteen games. The Rogues have always banked on their power hitters."

"Others will step up to the plate," he said with more assurance than he actually felt. "Rhaden Dunn and James Lawless have power."

"Both are hitting weak, .226 and .215 respectively for the spring. They need support. The only player with plate power is Risk Kincaid. He can't carry the team."

"Our bullpen—"

"Is lean," she said, cutting him off. "Tendonitis in his elbow could sideline Cooper Smith. The stress fracture in Roan Ginachio's back could end his career. Psycho took the only pitcher with promise out of the game. Chris Collier will be sitting the bench until his vision clears."

"What about Jason Maseratti?"

"No speed. No command. Last season he walked eighty-six batters in one hundred forty-two innings."

Romeo shifted his stance. "Thought you wrote about players, their dates, and dining experiences. When did you start quoting stats?"

"I flew to Fort Myers and watched spring training."

She'd been in Florida? "I didn't see you with the media hounds."

"I bought a ticket and sat in the stands."

"How many games?"

"Six. No one played harder than the Bat Pack. You took preseason as the real deal. Set the standard for Opening Day, until Psycho took out his own teammate before God and the press."

"Chris Collier threw to maim. Psycho had no other recourse."

"Fists are always the answer." She nodded toward her car, bent to open the door. "I need to leave."

Kiss off. He could picture Psycho's and Chaser's wide grins. They'd be loving the fact that Emerson Kent wasn't into him.

"I hoped to buy you dinner," he said to her back.

She looked over her shoulder. There was a

flicker of surprise in her green eyes. "Reason behind the invitation?"

"So I could take you shopping afterward and buy you a new suit. The one you wore on Media Day got torn and grass-stained."

She turned slowly. "Guy Powers sent you to pacify me."

Heat crept up Romeo's neck. "He made the suggestion; I acted on it."

She stared at him, openly assessing his offer. "What color was my ruined suit?"

Color? "What does it matter?"

"On the sidelines with other reporters, I'm one of the guys. I don't expect to be treated any differently. If you'd knocked down Albert Timmons, would he have gotten a meal and a new pair of pants?"

Timmons . . . reporter for the *Richmond Times*. Emerson's chief competitor covering Sports. And a thorn in every player's side. Short and wiry, the man would elbow his grandmother in the gut to get a story. More than once, he'd shown up in the Rogues locker room, as excited over a loss as over a win. Albert rubbed the players' noses in their mistakes. The man was mean-spirited. Took cheap shots.

"Timmons wouldn't have gotten even an apology."

"Let it go, Romeo." Her car door clicked, and she eased it open.

Damn! He'd noticed Emerson on the sidelines, had checked her out just like every other member of his team. Romeo had liked what he'd seen: an attractive, no-nonsense woman who fit into a man's world and held the respect of her peers.

There was a heartbeat of silence before he raked his hand through his hair and said, "Red blazer, white blouse, and navy slacks. When I first saw you, I appreciated your sporting our team colors. Your hair was braided. Navy pumps." He paused. "Media badge on your left breast."

Her eyebrows arched. "Pretty detailed for a man posturing for the press."

"I never posture," he corrected. "You were the only female on the sidelines. I gave you a second look." He always noticed how a woman dressed. From suits to panties, he complimented them down to nothing but skin.

"Jewelry?" she tested him further.

"Hoops at your ears, and as for a necklace"—he lowered his gaze, took in her breasts—"classic gold chain with a cross nestled in your cleavage."

"Lucky guess."

"Lucky breasts." A lazy smile spread across his lips. "I own Bellisaro Americano, a sports bar at Riverside Mall. We can dine in privacy. Make it a working dinner if you like. We can talk World Series."

She hesitated. Her reluctance confused Romeo. Women asked him out as often as he requested dates. Psycho and Chaser would be laughing their asses off over Emerson's indecision.

"I owe you a new suit and I'll toss in a pair of shoes," he added for good measure.

"I'd prefer a gift certificate."

"I'd prefer to be there for your selection."

She blew out a breath. "As long as we make it quick."

"I don't do quick." He cured her of that notion. "Time spent with a woman is best enjoyed slow."

Returning to his car, he pulled forward. Once she'd backed out and was behind him, he eased into traffic. He kept a close eye on her in his rearview mirror, not wanting to lose her in rush-hour traffic.

His heart slowed when he ran a yellow light and she chose to stop. After that she disappeared in traffic, and he wasn't sure she'd even show until she pulled into the parking lot twenty-seven minutes later. He released a breath he hadn't realized he'd been holding.

She'd had him wondering . . .

He jumped out of his car, went to meet her.

"I stopped for gasoline," she explained, her laptop in hand.

Gasoline *and groceries.* He caught sight of three brown bags on the passenger seat. A loaf of bread, bottled water, and a roll of paper towels were all visible. Emerson Kent had hit a convenience store while he'd sat in his car and counted the minutes.

She hadn't been in a hurry to meet him.

There'd been no breathless giggle or kiss to his cheek. No reaching for his hand. No brush of her body.

Damn disconcerting.

There was silence between them as they crossed the parking lot and entered the sports bar. Two feet inside the door, Romeo was recognized. And mobbed. So much for privacy.

He shot Emerson an apologetic look as requests for autographs multiplied. Autographs were as much a part of professional baseball as playing the game. He'd never turned a fan away. He signed place mats, napkins, unpaid bills, and T-shirts. Two female fans kissed him. One on the cheek, the other full on the mouth. With a hint of tongue.

Ladies slid their phone numbers into the pockets of his jeans. Their fingertips stretching toward his sex.

From behind, the scrape of a tapered nail along the waistband of his jeans warned of someone checking to see if he wore boxers or briefs. He twisted slightly. No need to flash his bare ass.

Thirty minutes shot by before the crowd thinned enough for him to locate Emerson. He found her seated in a black vinyl booth against the wall, her laptop on the table. Typing furiously.

His gut told him he wouldn't be happy with her latest article. He caught the title beneath the blinking Budweiser sign: BURGERS, FRIES, AND A SIDE OF JESSE BELLISARO. Which set his teeth on edge.

Scooting in beside her, he tried to read what she had written. He caught *A woman could starve to death waiting for a Rogue to join her for dinner* before she hit SAVE and closed the laptop on his fingers.

"Thought you were forecasting the upcoming season." He tried to pry the laptop open.

She leaned her elbow on the lid, squished his fingers. "That's for the Sunday edition. Sports has space for another piece this week. Something for women. Something fun."

He winced. "You're going to make fun of me?"

"You've got entertainment value." She cracked the top of the laptop and he pulled his fingers free. Her gaze next lit on his mouth. "You're pretty, Romeo, but red lipstick's not your color. You might try dusty rose or champagne pink."

Romeo snagged a napkin, grimacing when he scrubbed his split lip. "Better?"

She nodded. "Now how about some space. Would you mind sitting across from me? I feel crowded."

Crowded? His dates always snuggled close. Some hand-fed him the entire meal. Emerson, however, tapped her fingers, waiting for him to move. He begrudgingly did so.

Emerson Kent breathed a sigh of relief when Romeo got to his feet and slid into the other side of the booth. If truth be told, she couldn't bear his sitting so close. He was simply too good-looking. She didn't want to stare.

A male in his prime, he bore the all-American blond hair of his mother, the brown eyes and charm of his Italian father. He was built for play, both on and off the field. His gaze hit her like a surprise kiss. Quick, intense, and oh-so-very hot.

His scent had her inhaling deeply. The man

was all citrus and sunshine. Clean and masculine.

Memories of spring training kept Emerson focused. Women came easy to Romeo. Way too easy. She'd never seen so many phone numbers, photographs, and pairs of panties land at his feet. A bat boy had been assigned to keep the third base line clear. A job that lasted a full nine innings.

She understood his appeal. The man was a sexual force. One look at Romeo, and she'd stopped breathing. Her body had gone all soft and achy when she'd seen him in his blue Viper. Her nipples had puckered; her panties became damp beneath his stare.

A most unnatural reaction from a woman known for her brains and cool observations. Her journalism degree had landed her at the *Banner*. First in Society, then in Sports. She'd covered hundreds of social events, dealt with athletes on a daily basis.

But the most elaborate social event didn't come close to dinner with Romeo Bellisaro. His family was known for restaurant franchises. His father had started Bellisaro Italiano in Chicago. Built on traditional recipes and the warm hospitality of his Italian heritage, the restaurant was known for its pasta and deep-dish pizza and had become a national chain.

Investing in his father's footsteps, Romeo had come up with Bellisaro Americano. Surrounded by sports memorabilia, customers enjoyed grilled hamburgers and steaks. Packed booths and tables and a long waiting line attested to the restaurant's popularity and success.

This dinner with Romeo would provide Emerson with material for several columns. Juicy columns. She had the inside scoop on the sexiest man in Major League Baseball. A title he'd held for three straight years.

Since their arrival, Romeo had been in constant demand. Autographs. Kisses. Craned necks and sideways glances from both customers and employees. To stay in control, she'd gone all-business on him. She'd purposely stopped for gasoline. Purposely shopped for groceries. Purposely started writing her column under his nose.

The man looked uneasy.

Better he than she.

The scent of Chloe arrived seconds before their waitress. Tall, thin Tina dropped a menu before her, then placed one directly into Romeo's hand. As she laid out the place mats and silverware, Romeo's expression hardened.

Emerson understood his look. The Rogues' schedule glared back at him from the place mat, printed out in neat block lettering. A reminder he'd be sitting on the bench for thirteen games.

"Nice of you to make an appearance," Tina said happily to Romeo. "When you're here, tips triple."

"How's the house fund?" he asked.

She broke into a smile. "I'm almost there. An additional two thousand and I've got the down payment." Tina cast a quick glance at Emerson, then looked back at Romeo. "What can I bring you to drink?"

"The lady will have a ginger ale; I'll have a National Bohemian beer," Romeo replied.

Tina nodded, went for their drinks. She cast two looks over her shoulder at Romeo before she reached the bar. She was openly taken with the man.

Emerson unfolded her napkin, smoothed it across her lap. "How did you know I like ginger ale?" she asked.

"You drank one on the sidelines during Media Day."

The man had an eye for detail. She tried not to smile. Failed. Once again she found him staring at her mouth. She didn't understand the fascination. Her lips were too full. Her dimple cut too deep. Her front teeth weren't quite straight.

He continued to stare until his gaze darkened and his eyelids half closed. Which caused her heart to stutter. In need of a distraction, she picked up her menu. She took several minutes to scan the entries while Romeo studied her.

She didn't look up until Tina returned with their drinks. "Ready to order?" the waitress asked.

This time Emerson took the initiative. "Two Angus burgers, one rare, one medium, both with extra onion, and two sides of sweet potato fries."

Romeo's lips twitched. "Extra onion?"

"So thick and raw your eyes will water."

"I've never had a date eat onions."

"I'm not your date, onion breath."

He threw back his head and laughed. The sound was deep and rich. Contagious. She felt her body relax. Grow expectant. She kicked herself for responding to a man known to have the word *Legendary* tattooed at his groin. All the Rogues bore tattoos. The tats were a part of their rookie initiation onto the team.

"Will that be all?" Tina waited for Romeo's approval.

He nodded. "Onions are good."

Her gaze still on Romeo, Tina collected the menus and backed away from their booth, straight into a table across the aisle. Glasses and plates tipped. She mumbled an apology to the annoyed patrons.

Emerson rolled her eyes. "Your effect on women is staggering."

He crossed his arms over his chest, his big body curving low on the vinyl seat. "Do I stagger you?"

"You have every woman in the restaurant trying to catch your eye. Why would I matter?"

"For the simple reason that you're not trying to impress me. I like that."

His compliment made her shiver. She could sit and stare at him, enjoying his company and smile, or break the spell and work. She flipped open her laptop. "What else do you like, Jesse Bellisaro?"

"The way a woman smiles, the softness of her skin, the throaty sounds she makes during sex."

Her hands froze over the keyboard. "Out of the bedroom and back to the park. Talk baseball."

"Does baseball turn you on?"

"It holds my interest."

He pulled himself forward, rested his elbows on the table. "I like the sound of the sweet spot, when the bat connects with the ball for a home run. Sliding into a base a split second before being tagged out. Hearing the crowd chant my name. The ultimate rush of taking the division title." He paused. "No words can describe winning the World Series."

She typed, then looked up. "You'll hear more boos than cheers with the Bat Pack warming the bench on Opening Day."

"Thirteen games will pass quickly."

"Maybe not. My money's on the Ottawa Raptors."

He blinked. "Ontario? You have a pro-Canadian bias?"

"They've switched to a traditional pitching-and-defense approach. The Raptors are uniquely positioned to take advantage of the Yankees', Braves', and Rogues' vulnerabilities."

"The Raptors are a close-but-no-cigar team."

She flattened her palms on either side of her laptop and leaned forward. "They have an all-star-caliber bat at second and exceptional glove work at short."

He rolled his shoulders, met her nose to nose across the table. "Their shortstop couldn't scoop a ball if it stopped at his feet."

"He was named Rookie of the Year after a long line of jaw-dropping plays at third last season."

44

His nostrils flared. "The Raptors are a young team. Their rotation is dubious or disconcertingly raw. They won't win a hundred games."

"They'll take the National League title."

"Which would take us out of the race." He shook his head. "Not going to happen."

"Don't be so sure."

"Care to make a wager?"

Why not? She knew the stats of every team going into Opening Day. She'd take his bet and make sure he paid up when he lost. Her winnings would go to charity. "One thousand dollars for every Raptor win over a hundred games."

"I can live with that." His sexy mouth slowly pulled to one side in amusement. "What can you live with, Em? What do I win if the Raptors don't hit a hundred."

The mood shifted significantly. A heightened awareness and expectation settled between them at the table. She licked her lips. "What would you want?"

His gaze lit on her moistened mouth. "An opportunity to discover if you're as passionate in bed as you are about baseball."

Sex with Jesse Bellisaro. Her throat went dry. Her palms were now sweaty. She reached for her ginger ale, pressed the ice-cold glass to her overheated cheek. "I'd prefer to keep our bet monetary," she finally managed.

"I guess you don't really believe in the Raptors," he said around a deceptively lazy grin. "You were gung ho on Ontario five minutes ago.

Don't you believe in them enough to lay bed and breakfast on the line?"

She couldn't fight the look in his eye, all-male and daring her to accept the bet. A sexual heat wound low in her belly. A pulsing heat that made her breathing faster. More irregular.

Their bet set her up to win big bucks if the Raptors scored a hundred wins. If they didn't, she'd be heating the sheets with a legendary lover.

"Backpedaling?" he baited.

She gripped the edge of the table. Her fingertips were sweaty. "You're on." The words came out as barely a whisper.

"I'm always *on*." His self-assurance forced her to take notice. "I scanned the disabled list before I left the park. A list not yet released to the press. Opening Day, the Raptors starting left fielder is out with a groin injury. A sprained wrist sidelines their lead-off batter. Their starting pitcher has a sore toe, which will keep him out of the opener. The Raptors are playing as handicapped at the Rogues."

He wrapped up his rundown with a suggestive wink. "Your place or mine, Emerson, at season's end we'll enjoy breakfast in bed."

THREE

"Hello, Legs." Chase "Chaser" Tallan pushed through the gate at the Grand Slam concession stand and crossed to the athletically trim woman perched on a ladder, stacking paper cups on a tiered shelf.

Jen Reid turned slightly, and the wooden ladder shook. Chaser reached out, curved his hand over her hip, not wanting her to fall. Time and again he'd asked Jen to get rid of the rickety old ladder. Each time she'd refused. The ladder had belonged to her father. And his father before him. Generations of Reids had climbed the rungs. Jen held on to all things that were family. No matter their condition.

His hand steadied her as she climbed down. Standing before him, she gently drew his Killer Loops down his nose and whistled. "Nice shiner."

"You heard about the fight?"

"And your suspension."

47

His hand flexed before stroking upward and resting at her waist. A bare waist with an amber stud at her navel. He tugged down the hem on her blue tank top. "Big John would want you covered."

"I'm thirty-two," she reminded him.

"Your dad always saw you as twelve."

He pulled her close, and she went willingly. She wrapped her arms about his neck, rested her head against his chest. An unspoken bond held them in silence. She knew he needed her. And she was there for him.

Her calmness was an antidote to his chaotic life, providing a comfort he'd yet to find with another woman. But along with her comfort, he knew he'd have to face her honesty. Jen always told it to him straight.

He'd known her forever, as neighbors and childhood friends. Each was an only child. Each was born to older parents who had been told they'd never have kids. Jen and he had attended the same schools, been in many of the same classes. Each knew what made the other person tick.

He tightened his arms around her, rested his chin on the top of her head. She was a tall woman at five nine, with her long black hair and longer legs. In between ballet lessons, she'd played volleyball and basketball. Following high school graduation, she'd studied dance at Julliard. She'd performed with the New York City Ballet until her father's untimely death. Two years earlier.

She'd left New York and returned to Richmond.

Her inheritance lay in six concession stands at James River Stadium. Not in performing *Swan Lake*. She'd never once complained about the turn of events that had brought her home.

Jen adapted to whatever life dealt her.

Although Chaser missed Big John as much as Jen, he was damn glad she was home. She kept him sane.

"Who punched you?"

He felt her breath against his gray T-shirt. Right over his heart.

"Dane Maxin." A rookie catcher who would slip into the rotation following Chaser's suspension.

"Why did you fight?"

"I had Psycho's back."

"Maxin had Chris Colliers's." Tilting her head back, she met his gaze. Her amber eyes were as sympathetic as her tone. "The Rogues are off to a rough start. Thirteen games is a long time to warm the bench."

"I'll pack my iPod and the latest issue of *Sports Illustrated*."

She pulled a face. "Heard from Isabella?"

Isabella Mancini, a *Sports Illustrated* swimsuit model and a very possessive woman. After six dates and two breakfasts in bed, she'd announced their engagement to the press. Their breakup had lasted three months. Months of her stalking, whining, and criminal behavior. "She's gone for good."

"She was scary."

Scary *and destructive*. From the beginning of

49

their relationship, Bella had known he and Jen were close. So close, Bella accused them of being lovers. Which Chaser denied. And Bella continued to hold against him.

The woman carried jealousy to the extreme.

He'd filed a police report when she'd slashed every piece of clothing in his closet. Broken every dish in his kitchen. Smashed the screen on his computer and plasma television.

The night Isabella taunted Chaser by trashing two of Jen's concession stands was the night he'd taken out a restraining order. The model wasn't allowed near him, Jen, or the stadium.

"Your track record with women—"

"Sucks," he finished for her.

"The ladies fall in love faster than you care to commit."

"I'm thirty-three and enjoy playing the field."

"No baseball, no woman . . . Mercury must be in retrograde."

Chaser grinned. Jen followed astrology. She read her horoscope, charted the planets. She now blamed Mercury for his suspension and lack of sex. His grin widened.

"Want a snow cone?" When times were tough, Jen believed snow cones made life bearable.

Squeezing her waist, he slowly released her. "Make mine lemon."

Turning toward the shelf, she grabbed two paper cones, then headed for the freezer. She scooped shaved ice, returned, and added syrup. Lemon for him. Blueberry for her.

He planted his hands on the concession stand countertop, pushed up. "The Bat Pack gets to practice and travel with the team," he said as he accepted his snow cone, inhaling its tart scent.

Jen stood between his splayed legs. "It won't be the same as playing and you know it."

He knew it, all right. Eleven years, and he hadn't missed a game. Sitting on the bench would kill him. "Guy Powers could have gone easier—"

"*No*, he couldn't have," she said, and he blinked. "Outside the park, the Bat Pack runs wild. Powers has overlooked your reputations and indiscretions. Today you fought your own teammates. Inexcusable, my friend."

He took a bite of his snow cone, let the ice and lemon dissolve on his tongue. The taste was as bitter as his suspension. "Thought you'd take my side."

"Not when you're wrong."

That's what he loved about her. She kept things real. Forced him to face his faults and fix them.

He ran a palm down his blue-jeaned thigh. Blew out a breath. "Powers acquired a bunch of assholes in the off-season overhaul. No one gets along. No unity—"

"No love of the game."

Chaser cut her a look. "I love baseball."

"Not the way you used to." She eased back a step, beckoned with her finger. "Follow me, big guy."

Snow cone in hand, he hopped off the counter

and trailed behind her. He loved to watch her move. A woman of sleek beauty and Ivory soap skin. Ballet posture and a lightness to her step. A floating grace left over from the stage.

They were the only two on the mezzanine level. Yet the walls pulsed with the expectancy and excitement of Opening Day. On Sunday afternoon, the heart of the park would beat baseball.

Stealing Home, another of Jen's concession stands, came into view. This one sold soda, cotton candy, Cracker-Jacks, and shelled peanuts. Pennants, baseball cards, bobble-heads, and enormous foam fingers flashed behind the grilled gates at Strike Zone, the third of her concessions, which was located right before the tunnel.

At the tunnel's entrance, she took his hand. "We were seven years old, Chaser. We'd only watched baseball on television. It was Thursday noon, and Big John called us in sick at school so we could attend the game. A day that gave meaning and purpose to your life."

Chaser studied her face, her expression soft and dreamy as her memories returned him to his youth. Tugging him along, she led him through the tunnel's shadows and into the electrifying sunshine.

Even though the stadium was his second home, its sheer size hit him hard. He'd spent countless hours crouched behind home plate, in the dugout and the locker room, but not once since he'd contracted with the Rogues had he climbed into the stands and viewed the game as a fan.

He dropped onto a seat and motioned Jen to join him. A low chuckle escaped him. "I remember Big John holding us to the promise that we wouldn't move from the seats he'd found vacant. Yet throughout the game, we snuck closer and closer to home plate."

"You were a fan of Lou Wood. The best catcher of his time. He made the final out against the Yankees that took the Rogues to the 1981 World Series."

Chaser focused on home plate. "Ninth inning, one out, Yankees were down by two with a man on second. Top of the order, and the Yankee left fielder broke his bat on a pop-up. A mile-high pop-up. Woods made an over-the-shoulder catch, then fired the ball to second. The runner had taken off for third and was tagged out. An amazing double play."

Jen patted his thigh. "You're better than Woods."

"Woods never got suspended for fighting."

They sat in silence, eating their snow cones, comfortable in each other's company. Finishing up, Chaser slipped off his sunglasses and stared at the field. He took in the white brilliance of the baseline and bases, the newly designed on-deck circle, the diagonally mowed outfield. The ivy that covered the outfield wall. The eighty thousand seats soon to be filled with screaming fans.

Emotion welled in his chest. The game was his, and he'd lost it in a brawl. He pressed his palms to his eyes. Kicked his own ass hard.

"Stop feeling sorry for yourself." Jen knew him well.

"I have nothing better to do."

There was a moment's hesitation before she said, "Tell me about Dane Maxin."

He cut her a glance. "Beyond the fact the man punched me?" Maxin had thrown an unsportsmanlike punch, hitting Chaser from the side and not face-on.

"Just curious." She dipped her head, pink tinting her cheeks. "He asked me out."

Chaser ran his hand through his short, spiked hair. "He's not your type."

She punched his arm. "I think he's nice. The battery in my El Camino died yesterday, and he gave me a jump."

If Dane had done a good deed, he wanted to jump more than her car; he wanted to jump her bones. Of that Chaser was certain. "Your father gave you his El Camino when he traded up fifteen years ago. Big John didn't expect you to keep it forever."

"The car holds his memory."

"You could have called me," he said. "I carry jumper cables. I would have helped you out."

"You'd already left the park. I didn't want to call you back." Finished with her snow cone, she tore the paper into thin strips. "Aside from giving you a black eye Dane's not a bad guy."

Chaser had nothing good to say about the man. Dane Maxin was twenty-six and insolent. He had a major chip on his shoulder. He grunted answers to questions. When he did talk, he bragged about sex and threesomes.

Chaser clenched his teeth, seeking an objectivity he didn't feel. "Maxin was traded from Minnesota for two solid hitters. He's not happy being in Richmond." Dane had swaggered into the locker room snarling. The scowl still hadn't left his face. "The man's got attitude—"

"So does Psycho."

"Dane dates a lot of women."

"So does Romeo."

"He owns a souped-up red Corvette. Drives like a bat out of hell."

"You haul ass in a '68 GTO. Major muscle car. You're always over the speed limit."

She was right. Fortunately for him, law enforcement preferred his autograph over writing out a ticket.

"I like Dane's look." Jen crumpled the torn paper into the palm of her hand. "He's a sharp dresser."

Chaser snorted. "The man's in love with himself."

During spring training, Maxin had spent an inordinately long time changing from his Rogues uniform into street clothes. He wore imported silk shirts and tailored slacks. Italian leather shoes. He'd held up the team bus a dozen times, until Psycho stole his blow-dryer and styling gel, breaking Dane's affair with the mirror.

Beside him, Jen looked out over the ball field. She'd gone all quiet and thoughtful as the late afternoon sun crept toward them. The lower seats were now cast in shadow.

"Dane and I made plans to jog today," she told Chaser. "Six o'clock at Battery Park."

His heart squeezed unexpectedly. It shouldn't bother him that Jen showed interest in another man. Hell, they were friends, nothing more. But the thought of her with Dane undid him. He tamped down his initial impulse to warn her off the man.

"I'm coming with you," he stated.

She shook her head. "There's no need for a chaperone."

Chaser wasn't so sure. "I'll hang for a while, then split. I want to make sure Maxin behaves himself."

"You're worse than my father." Resigned, she linked her arm through his, rested her head on his shoulder. A light breeze caught her hair, stirred the scent of her orange-mango shampoo. Strands flirted with her cheek and flicked onto his chest. All clean and shiny. Dark and wavy.

"I'm being insensitive to the fact Dane hit you," she said on a sigh. "If you'd rather we didn't meet up, I'll pass. It's not that big a deal."

He felt like hell. Throughout the years, Jen had rolled her eyes over a few of his dates, but she'd never warned him off. When other women got petty or possessive, Jen never teased or said she'd told him so. She'd allowed him his mistakes, and he'd made quite a few.

He shifted on the seat, slid his hand beneath the turned-up collar on his blue-striped shirt. Blowing out a breath, he caved. "Meet Dane. I'll drive you to the park, and he can take you home."

"You're such a good friend!" She threw her arms around his neck.

He turned his smile on her.

She started to kiss his cheek.

Just as he bent to kiss her brow.

Their lips met.

Time slowed with the exchange of their breath. He inhaled. She exhaled.

The sweet heat of her slightly parted lips blew across his mouth.

The soft skin of her chin brushed his unshaven jaw.

The clench of her fingers dug into his shoulder.

Her breast pressed his forearm, soft and full.

Neither drew back.

The moment was magnified as each memorized the impact of the moment.

It was startling. Unsettling. And totally unforgettable.

As the afternoon shadows crept over his knee and up his thigh, awareness crossed the invisible line that separated friends from lovers.

The urge to slant his mouth over hers and deepen the kiss hit him soundly. It took all his restraint to pull back. Once they'd separated, he ran his tongue over his lower lip. She'd tasted of blueberries. Wild, ripe berries, warmed by the sun.

Beside him, Jen touched her lips with her fingers. Fingers that trembled. Wide-eyed, she swallowed hard.

Neither spoke. Neither looked away.

Each stared as if seeing the other person for the very first time. Arousal struck hard.

Clearing his throat, he said the first thing that came into his head. "Let's go home," he suggested. "A quick change and back to Battery Park."

She rose, looking down on him with soft eyes and a softer smile. "Thanks, Chaser. I owe you one."

After that kiss, he planned to collect. Sooner or later, he'd take her mouth a second time.

It was all in the timing.

The jogging path was thick with runners. Some slow, some fast, all exercise nuts, staying in shape. Jen Reid kept pace with Chaser. A hint of Dune drifted her way. The mandarin and cedarwood scent was as understated as the man. Chaser had worn the same cologne since high school. It was as constant as his presence in her life.

She cast a glance his way, took in his profile. Spiked dark hair and sharp features. A diamond stud in his left ear. Even with darkness descending, he wore his Killer Loops. Sunglasses that hid his ice-blue eyes, so startlingly clear that when he had his game face on, he froze opposing players at home plate.

Sweat now gleamed on his brow, darkened the neck of his navy blue T-shirt, arrowed down his belly toward the waistband of his gym shorts. He'd set their pace, sprinting fast, as if chased by demons.

Back at the stadium, she'd sensed his dislike of Dane Maxin. She understood. Dane hadn't fought fair. Chaser now sported a black eye. As her best friend, he had her back. He'd always looked out for her best interests. He'd agreed to keep her company until she located Maxin among dozens of runners.

"Where the hell is Dane?" Chaser muttered.

"He said to meet him by the water fountain."

"There are twenty fountains at the park. He could have been more specific." Tugging at the front of his T-shirt, he pulled it free of his gym shorts. In the gap between elastic waistband and skin, Jen caught a flash of his *Slidin' Home* tattoo right before he said, "I hadn't planned to break a sweat. I'll need a shower before I head out for the evening."

A shower . . . Her heart beat a little faster, and it wasn't from the run. She'd always admired Chaser's body. Wide chest and thick thighs. The man had muscle.

She snuck a second look, and lost her rhythm. He looked incredibly sexy. More than one female jogger did a double take. Even after he'd beaten the path for three miles, his breath came evenly, his gaze straight ahead.

Her stolen glance caused a collision at the next curve in the path. She'd been so busy staring at Chaser, she hadn't seen Dane Maxin approach.

They caught shoulders with enough impact that he knocked her into Chaser and she started to go down.

Chaser's reflexes saved her from a scraped knee. One strong arm looped around her waist until she was steady on her feet.

He pulled her against his chest and hissed in her ear, "Damn, Legs, no need to fall at the man's feet."

She jerked free, about to tell him she'd been staring at *him*, not Dane, but caught herself just in time. Such a statement would prove embarrassing. Especially following their brief, yet incredible, kiss. She hadn't expected that kiss, but it had left her wondering how he'd taste if she'd slipped her tongue into his mouth. Curiosity stroked her like a slow hand.

Before her now, Dane Maxin jogged in place. She took in his tawny hair and copper eyes. His lean body beneath the Nike sweats.

Dane ran his gaze over her, looking intimate and expectant, before nodding toward the big man at her side. His lip curled. "You know Chaser?"

"We're old friends," Jen told him.

Dane and Chaser exchanged a look, the kind of look in which a man either marked his territory or backed away.

Chaser marginally shifted his stance and Dane stopped jogging. "Glad you could make it to the park, I was hoping for some company," Dane said.

Jen wiped her terry cloth wristband across her

forehead. "Chaser's going to jog with us as far as the turn off to the parking lot."

"Lucky us." Dane took off ahead of them, only to be brought up short by twin blondes with large, bouncy, barely contained breasts. Black spandex outlined nipple rings.

Jen looked down at her B-cups. If Dane was a breast man, this would be their first and last date. She wasn't into piercing.

"Implants can't compare to what's natural," Chaser said at her side. He nudged her forward. "Let's catch up to Maxin."

Their approach caught Dane memorizing the blondes' phone numbers. Unabashed, he smiled at her. Jen smiled back. Chaser frowned darkly.

They jogged one mile, then walked the second. She and Dane were two abreast, with Chaser breathing down her neck. Her friend was an ominous presence and hard to ignore.

Dane was a touchy-feely kind of guy. He casually brushed her shoulder as they walked and talked. Bumped her hip more than once. Flattened his hand on her lower back. Then took her hand.

That was when Chaser crowded her further. His low growl forced Dane to let her go. Jen spun about, smacked her palm on Chaser's chest, and held him back. His muscles bunched and rippled and he gave less than an inch. The man was an unmovable force.

Dane looked over his shoulder more than once. He walked a little faster when Chaser replied to questions Dane directed to Jen. It was obvious

Dane wanted to shake Chaser. But Chaser wasn't a man to be shaken.

Another half mile and Dane pointed to a sign. "There's the parking lot path. Get lost."

Chaser didn't turn off. He slowed his pace and allowed them to draw ahead, but never let them out of his sight.

"How do you like Richmond?" Jen asked Dane.

His gaze slid over her. "I'm liking it better by the moment. Maybe you could show me the city."

"Maybe you could buy a road map and drive yourself," Chaser muttered, closing in on them once again. "Tourist attractions are marked red on most maps."

"Nightlife." Dane pressed closer to Jen as they continued down the path. "What's your favorite club? I've heard Jimmy Mack's draws a crowd."

"Mack's promotes hard rock." Chaser knew the clubs. "Jen prefers jazz. Billie Holiday. Eva Taylor."

"Chinese, Mexican, Thai? How about dinner tonight?" Dane inquired.

"The lady's a vegetarian."

A muscle jumped in Dane's jaw. "Damn, is there anything Chaser doesn't know about you, Jen?"

Chaser didn't know her body. He'd never seen her naked. Jen chose not to share that fact with Dane. She, however, had seen Chaser's bare backside. She'd snuck a peek one afternoon when he'd stepped from the outdoor Jacuzzi. She'd been in his pool, swimming laps. He hadn't expected her to break her stroke and track his ass. The tightest ass in Major League Baseball. Wrangler had him signed to advertise their line of jeans. No one showcased low-slung denim like Chaser.

"We grew up together," Jen was quick to explain. "Chaser's my friend and—"

"Freakin' watchdog," Dane finished. "Get lost, Barky."

Chaser's snarl was lost in the commotion of a group of female joggers. All of them became giggly once they'd spotted him.

"Can we get your autograph?" All four women stood wide-eyed and adoring. "Can't wait for Opening Day."

Dane was too new to the team to be recognized. Snagging Jen's hand, he drew her outside the circle, leaving Chaser to fend for himself.

While Jen felt guilty, Dane didn't give a damn. Free of Chaser, he came on strong. Jogging became foreplay. Their bodies moved with a rhythm he planned to duplicate in bed.

Within fifteen minutes they'd retraced their steps, reaching the parking lot. She spotted his red Corvette, slanted diagonally across two spaces. He opened the door, then looked at her. His gaze was scrutinizing, sexual. "Your eyes are bright and your body's flushed and languid. You've the look of a satisfied woman."

"Exercise pleases me."

"I could please you."

"I'd prefer a towel and a bottle of water."

"I can give you both." Pulling his car door wide, he ducked inside and retrieved an iced Fiji

63

and a white hand towel. Rounding the sleek hood, he came to stand before her. He topped her by only an inch. She'd never be able to wear high heels with this man. She was a fan of thick cork wedgies and peep-toe pumps.

All around them, deep shadows pushed dusk to darkness. The guard gate stood deserted. Chaser's GTO was no more than a black shadow in the corner of the lot. Set on timers, the streetlights flickered on. In their fluorescence, Dane's gaze glinted cougar gold.

With a disturbing slowness, he blotted perspiration from her brow, from beneath her eyes and upper lip. He then drew the towel along her neck, dabbed the V of her sports tank. His fingers tucked into her cleavage. His right palm curved to cup her breast.

His touch made Jen's skin crawl. A most startling discovery, since she'd looked forward to meeting this man. Yet each stroke evoked only a need for space. She eased back a step.

Her move surprised him. Tossing the towel over his shoulder, he leaned against the passenger door. His gaze was now hooded. "We have heat, Jen. I knew the second you ran into me we'd have sex."

The only thing she'd known was the strength of Chaser's arm, solid and secure about her waist, supporting her against a fall.

Dane ran his finger from her shoulder to her wrist. His voice was as smooth and practiced as his touch. "Take me home tonight."

"Tomorrow's Opening Day. Shouldn't you get some rest?"

"I sleep three hours a night."

"I need six."

"I want you, Jen."

She wanted Chaser. Where was the man? How long did it take to sign four autographs? "I enjoyed our run, but I'm going to pass on the sleepover."

She began to step around him, only to find her path blocked. Displeasure scored Dane's features. He turned ugly. She had no time to fight him. His strength trapped her between fiberglass and the force of his body. "No one passes on me."

His mouth clamped down on hers.

She clenched her jaw, refusing his tongue.

He jammed his thumb into her cheek, unrelenting in his determination to part her lips.

She pushed at his chest, shifted her hips, drew up her knee—

And was freed when Chaser's fist missed her nose by a tenth of an inch and connected with Dane's jaw. Dane's head snapped back, and he staggered sideways.

The heated scent of Dune and raw-edged anger struck her as Chaser grabbed Dane by the front of his sweatshirt. "Get the hell off her."

Dane's head bobbed in a semblance of a nod. Tossing him aside, Chaser stepped back, allowing the younger man his escape. Jerking open his car door, Dane slid onto the bucket seat and pressed the locks. Cracking his window, he rubbed his jaw, got in the final word. "Jen's a damn tease.

She came onto me, then wouldn't put out. I should have gone with the twins."

He keyed the ignition and the Vette rumbled to life. Floored, the car fishtailed across the parking lot, the taillights dots of disdain.

In the ensuing silence, Jen slapped her palms against her thighs, stalling for time until she was forced to admit, "You were right. I was wrong. Dane Maxin's a jerk."

"Did he hurt you? You're bruised." Chaser's tone was one of concern as he smoothed Dane's thumbprint from her cheek.

"Mostly scared me." She reached for his hand, ran her fingers over his skinned knuckles. "Major punch." She'd never seen him so mad.

"I'd always protect you."

"I'm glad you arrived when you did."

"Me too." He flexed his ink-stained fingers. "I signed autographs for the group of women, then got cornered by a Little League Team near the water fountains. I broke someone's pen in my hurry to find you."

"My choice of men is as poor as your choice in women."

"Dane wasn't the right man for you." He turned thoughtful. "From now on, if you want to go out, I'll line you up. We can double-date. I know a few decent guys."

"As decent as you?"

"I'm as horny as the next guy, Legs. I don't, however, force sex. It's always mutual."

Mutual. To be taken by a man who wanted her

as badly as she wanted him. "I'll leave the choice to you."

"My sports agent's one hell of a nice guy."

She'd met Cal Winger. Balding, nervous eye twitch, winged eyebrows. His dealings with the Bat Pack had him working a sixty-hour week. Jen doubted he could fit her into his schedule. "A possibility," she agreed.

"Maybe Dan Carpenter from the sports clinic."

The physical therapist had worked on Chaser's knee when he'd injured his meniscus, a minor cartilage tear between his femur and tibia. Dan was nice. Respectful. Close to her age. Yet there was no spark between them. "Someone to consider."

"You've choices, Jen. Don't sell yourself short."

As they walked toward his GTO, she silently wondered if Chaser fell within her options. An outlandish thought, yet one that was oddly appealing. Their brief kiss had left her curious. Perhaps a second taste would satisfy her. Then she could move on to dating other men.

One long, deep, moist kiss.

With enough tongue to make a memory.

FOUR

The reporter for *Jocks* magazine arrived fifteen minutes early for Psycho McMillan's interview. An interview set up by Rogues publicist Catherine Ambrose a month prior to his suspension. Running late himself, he answered the door wrapped in a navy blue bath towel. His hair was slicked back from his shower and water dripped at his feet. "You've got thirty minutes," he stated at the onset. "What you see is what you get."

"I'll take it." The redhead with the geometric haircut looked him over with hungry eyes. "Janelle Campbell." She held out her hand and he gave it a quick shake. "Thanks for inviting me to your home."

The invitation had been forced. He hadn't wanted to sit at the clubhouse and answer her questions following the Rogues' opening loss. The game had been lost by a wide margin. The hitting sucked. The fielding played like a six-pack

68

Sunday softball league. Yet their suspension stuck. The Bat Pack sat on the bench.

The fans were fickle. Many hissed and jeered, while others wore black baseball caps in mourning.

The locker room vibrated with animosity. Moods had been dark and tempers barely in check. Psycho had punched a metal locker with his fist. He'd needed to get the hell out before he said or did something that would give Guy Powers a reason to extend his suspension.

"Let's get started." He motioned her toward the living room, offered her one of the two green lawn chairs. When he was seated, the towel parted over his splayed thighs.

Janelle stared at his groin. He wasn't a modest man, yet Psycho overlapped the ends of his towel. And Janelle averted her gaze. Brushing dog hair from the vinyl chair, she slowly sat down. Sneezing, she confessed, "I'm allergic to fur."

Psycho had bought a lock for the dogs' fenced run. The pups wouldn't make an appearance unless he or Keely set them free.

Keely . . . he'd seen her when he'd first come home, but not since he'd showered. She'd been standing in the entryway with a grizzled man, as old as the Colonial, tape measure stretched between them from the doorway to the stairs. She'd nodded to him as he'd dashed by, but she'd been concentrating on the figures she was jotting in her notebook. Dust had smeared her forehead and forearms. She had ashes from the fireplace smudged over the knees of her rolled-up jeans. Her flip-flops hadn't matched. One was teal, the other one yellow.

"Questions, then a picture." Janelle twisted low and retrieved a compact tape recorder from her Coach bag. The hem of her gray suede skirt slid up her thighs as she crossed her legs, then fingered the top button of her white silk blouse.

Psycho sank deeper into his lawn chair and groaned. The day was going downhill fast. The Rogues had lost to the Raptors, and he now faced a pantie-flashing reporter giving him the green light. He wasn't interested in this woman. He needed to set her straight before she unfastened a second button. The lace on her bra was already visible with each breath.

"The article." He drew Janelle's gaze from his groin.

"The Top Ten Sexiest Men in Major League Baseball," she informed him. "America voted, and you placed fourth."

"*Fourth?*" He frowned, thought about demanding a recount. "Who beat me?"

"Romeo Bellisaro placed first."

No surprise there. Romeo had looks and charm. A mere smile and women dropped their panties.

"Risk Kincaid came in second."

Psycho understood the team captain's popularity. Risk was a fan's player. And a family man. Women found monogamy sexy. Psycho, however, equated monogamy with monotony. He bored easily.

"Chris Collier's third," Janelle told him.

Wimbledon? Had voters lost their minds? The pitcher was a prick. "Fourth sucks," he grumbled.

Her gaze lit on his towel once again before she got down to business. Flicking on the tape recorder, she said, "You've been described as raw and rude. Undisciplined and unpredictable. You're a known nudist and will do anything on a dare. Why would America find you sexy?"

He rolled his eyes. What a dumb-ass question. Nothing new. Nothing original. He could give a smart-ass answer—

Instead, he bit his tongue. A glimpse of Keely Douglas through the split in the brown bedsheets hanging at one window claimed his attention. Her dog obedience classes had begun. He found the class far more interesting than the interview.

Leaning forward in his chair, he watched as Keely walked the side lawn with Boris on a tight leash in an attempt to teach the Newfoundland to heel. Boris was a slow learner. He lunged, then tried to gnaw through the metal links. Soon he began jerking on the leash as if it were a tug toy. In a very short time he'd knocked Keely off balance and to her knees.

Kneeling, she took the big dog's face in her hands and spoke directly to him. Boris cocked his head as if listening. Psycho knew that puppy dog look. Beyond the drooling innocence, Boris

71

was conniving and played people. He was a handful.

Getting to her feet, Keely continued his training. Taking off at a rapid walk, she made a wide circle around a weeping willow. The branches swept the ground, and with each pass Boris grabbed a mouthful of leaves. Easily bored, the dog pulled harder. He flew Keely like a kite. Her feet left the ground several times as she tried to restrain his need to run.

After six laps around the tree, Keely stopped. She bent over, breathing hard. Psycho started to rise, ready to take Boris off her hands. Just then, Keely shook her head and broke out laughing. The pup repaid her patience with a sloppy lick to her cheek before she placed him in his pen.

"Psycho?" the reporter returned him to his chair and the interview. He sat down hard. "Why would America find you sexy?"

Who the hell knew why? Who the hell cared? He might have cooperated more if he'd placed first instead of fourth.

"Mr. McMillan says and does what he pleases," Keely announced as she entered the living room. She balanced a sandwich on a paper plate with one hand, clutched a Mason jar of milk and a pen with the other. "He doesn't give a damn. That fascinates people. He's got the freedom to be himself."

Psycho blinked. He couldn't have answered better. Keely had known him a week, yet she'd already seen and accepted how difficult he could be. He snagged half her sandwich as she walked by. Took a big bite. Peanut butter stuck to the roof of his mouth. "What the hell?" He chewed long, swallowed hard.

"Peanut butter, cream cheese, and sliced banana on sourdough bread," Keely told him as she took in his bare chest and parted towel, vinyl webbing on the chair. "You need better furniture," she observed. "An inexpensive couch and chairs before the antiques arrive. I'll shop tomorrow." She clicked the pen and scribbled on her hand.

Psycho noticed there was more than one reminder written over her wrist and along her thumb. She looked like a walking sticky note. Reaching out, he caught her leg just above her knee. His hand tightened over the denim. Her jeans were worn white at the seams and threadbare beneath her butt cheeks. Her yellow T-shirt had seen brighter days.

He made a mental note to give her an advance on her salary. A substantial amount to keep her afloat during the restoration.

"My thigh . . ." Keely looked down at his hand, which had stroked higher. "What do you need?"

Need . . . the word was spoken so breathlessly soft, it sounded sexual. He grew hard. "I need milk." He let her go, hoping she hadn't noticed the twitch beneath his towel.

She handed him the Mason jar. It was half-full and iced. He'd never known anyone to ice milk. Nor to sandwich peanut butter with cream cheese.

He released her leg, and she stepped away from him. Clear across the room to the double-sashed windows. She tugged at the bedsheet, releasing late afternoon sunlight into the room. The amber glow played across the warped and splintered floor.

He continued to watch as she lifted one of the windows and a soft breeze swept the stale air from the room. When tightly closed up, the house smelled a little of mold and mildew.

Her shirt fluttered and sunlight shot through the thin cotton fabric, outlining small, firm breasts, the rippling of her ribs, and a concave abdomen. Keely was damn skinny. She'd missed a few meals.

Janelle Campbell raised an eyebrow. "Your girlfriend?"

"My designer," Psycho clarified. "Next question?"

"You're both street smart and successful. Tell me about your childhood."

He'd grown up tough. A punk with a load of attitude. Reporters liked to tap into his past. His growing up poor seemed to make them feel richer. "I grew up on the wrong side of Philly's tracks. I was six when my old man went out for a job interview and never returned. My mom worked sixteen-hour days to feed our family. Two girls and three boys.

"Ketchup packets and warm water became tomato soup. We boiled macaroni noodles, but there was never any cheese."

"Peanut butter became your steak." Keely's

words drifted to him. He looked up, caught her deep in her own memories. "Your mother reused tea bags. You split a candy bar five ways to share with your brothers and sisters."

Psycho's jaw locked. Had his designer grown up equally poor? Had she known hard times as well?

Beside him, Janelle fidgeted with the tape recorder. She looked horrified by their comments. It appeared the reporter had never gone hungry, nor worried about having a roof over her head.

Clearing her throat, Janelle nodded to him to continue. He didn't try to smooth the rough edges of his childhood. "There was no Little League or organized sports in my neighborhood. We used back lots. Stole hubcaps for bases. I played with a secondhand glove, wore tennis shoes without laces. I never had an official uniform until I hit high school.

"Baseball came naturally to me. I played hard. A scout from Florida State caught a few games. He offered me a sports scholarship if I graduated. My coach crammed chemistry and calculus down my throat, and somehow I passed the classes. The rest is history."

Janelle sighed. "You've done exceptionally well for yourself."

"So well, he bought a Colonial reminiscent of his old neighborhood," Keely softly added.

Psycho shifted on the vinyl chair. Keely was far too observant. No one had ever guessed the rundown house was a daily reminder of growing up dirt poor. The fact that it stood in a gated community didn't block his childhood memories from returning.

The house was as broken as his mother's and father's marriage. He'd been resistant to making repairs until Keely Douglas came into his life and wedged herself between his past and his future. He still wasn't convinced he liked her there.

Janelle moved on. "You're a dirt bike jumper."

"I compete in Xtreme Sports during the off-season."

"All against your team owner's wishes," Janelle said. "Guy Powers says you're a daredevil with a death wish."

"Adrenaline is my drug of choice."

"You've a taste for trouble." Janelle licked her lips. "Women like bad boys."

"Not too smart on their part," Keely muttered from the window.

Psycho silently agreed.

"Some believe you're insane," Janelle put in, probably hoping to get a rise out of him.

He shrugged. "Crazy comes with the territory."

"Describe your special woman," Janelle requested. "Date night."

He finished off his sandwich and washed it down with two gulps of milk. He caught Keely's look of interest as she waited along with the reporter for his reply.

"I don't do special or long term," he finally said. "My bar for dating is low. I call at the last minute. Don't bring flowers. Most times it's a surprise to the woman if I even show. I like after-hours bars, strip clubs. I once dated a woman for six weeks steady. She cried more when her plant died than when we broke up."

"Bet it was an elephant ear," Keely said. "I'd have cried too."

"It was a philodendron," he said to set Keely straight. "She left the plant on the porch in the sun and forgot to water it."

"Wife and kids in your future?" Janelle asked.

"The Psycho gene dies with me."

"Pity."

"Not everyone feels that way."

Janelle pursed her lips and looked at Keely. "I wonder what it would be like to date this man."

Keely cocked her head contemplatively. "Dangerous," she decided. "Like the first pulse-pounding climb to the high diving board. The stomach-shifting ride of the Tilt-A-Whirl."

Janelle nodded. "I see him as a shot of whiskey. The burn that goes straight to your stomach, then to your head. The buzz strips off your clothes and lands you in his bed."

The women were talking about him as if he wasn't in the room. Psycho didn't like being invisible. "Next question," he prodded.

"Your favorite nightcap after a game?" from Janelle.

"Body shots."

"You feel sexiest when?"

"I'm hard." Psycho caught Keely roll her eyes.

Janelle glanced at his towel. "Feeling sexy now?"

"Semisexy."

77

Janelle's recorder clicked off, and she quickly replaced the tape. "If you didn't play baseball, you'd . . . ?"

"Find a way to play baseball."

"You're intense and competitive."

"I like to win."

"You're very restless," Janelle noted. "Ever try yoga?"

"My life is a sport. Can't score points in yoga."

"A quote you live by?"

"Some days it doesn't pay to gnaw through the leather restraints."

"Favorite food?"

He looked at Keely. "Peanut butter, cream cheese, and sliced banana sandwiches."

Keely blushed. A slow rise of color that was sexy as hell. He decided to tease her often.

"Favorite dessert?"

"I try to avoid sugar, but on occasion crave Rice Krispies treats. I make them myself."

"What else do you crave, Psycho?"

That my suspension was over.

That the Rogues would win the World Series.

That the restoration of the Colonial will get the Daughters off my back for good.

That this interview would end.

Before he could answer, the grizzled old man he'd seen in the entry hall entered the living room, tape measure in hand. He crossed to Keely. "Ready to work?"

The perfect opportunity to end the interview. Psycho motioned to Janelle. "We're done here."

"Not quite," Janelle pressed. "I have a few more questions. A reliable source hinted you're the silent partner behind Street Sweepers. You've invested millions to clean up your old neighborhood, providing affordable housing, free clinics, food banks—"

He set his jaw. Silent partners remained silent. "No truth to the rumor," he stated. The interview was over. He pushed himself off the lawn chair and escorted the reporter to the door. There she snapped six quick pictures of him leaning against the frame in nothing but his towel.

The door closed and he returned to the living room. He found Keely bent over, bottom in the air, as she hooked the metal tip of the tape measure to a floor board, then slowly backed up. Barefoot, he crossed to block her path. She didn't notice him. Not until her sweet ass bumped his groin.

"Move, Mr. McMillan." Her voice held a breathless catch that drew his smile.

"In this position you can call me Psycho." He curved his hands over her hips, his long fingers meeting over her belly. "I'm not moving until you explain the mystery man."

Keely straightened. Her slender shoulders pressed against his broad chest, her round little bottom snug against his thighs. Her body was soft even though she was so thin.

Blushing, she elbowed him in the gut. He released her. Looking toward the older gentleman, she said, "This is Franklin Langston, an architect

I've drawn out of retirement to restore your Colonial."

The restoration would take a decade at the speed Langston shuffled across the room. Up close, Psycho noticed the smell of whiskey on the man's breath and a slump to his shoulders. His hair was white blond, the color of Keely's faded T-shirt. His khaki shirt and slacks were as wrinkled as his face. Psycho heard the flush of money down the toilet.

"Keely's told me all about you," Franklin said. "Though we can't fix your attitude, I'm inspired to restore your Colonial to its original beauty."

Inspired, was he? Psycho hated the fact that Keely had hired an architect without consulting him. He cut her a look. "Kitchen."

She handed the tape measure to Franklin, then followed Psycho through the portal to the dining room and on into the kitchen. They faced off across the island counter. "I'd have liked to meet Langston before you hired him."

"You were at the ballpark when Franklin became available. Should I have called in the middle of the game?"

He could have taken a phone call. He was warming the bench, not playing ball. "What if I had someone else in mind?"

She rested her elbows on the countertop. "Did you? Or are you just being difficult?"

He raked one hand through his damp hair. "Is Langston qualified? Is he licensed?"

"Franklin's the best there is."

There had to be someone better. "The man drinks."

"He had a shot of whiskey with lunch. Doesn't make him an alcoholic. Franklin's son is a contractor. Quinn specializes in restorations."

Psycho grunted. "A family package."

"You won't be sorry."

Her words held a soothing promise that satisfied him. For all of ten seconds. "I want to meet the son."

"You'll meet Quinn when you sign the contracts and cut a check."

"Check?"

"Half to start the project, half at completion."

"You should have taken bids. Not settled on the first architect and contractor you interviewed."

"You hired me and I hired them. I'm satisfied."

He wasn't. His gaze narrowed. "Stop taking over my house," he said forcefully.

She took two steps back. He didn't like scaring her, but she was moving too fast. He'd lost control over his life. Guy Powers's suspension and Keely Douglas's restoration were taking everything out of his hands. He wasn't happy. He needed to regain control.

Circling the counter, he cornered Keely by the walk-in pantry. Her eyes went wide as he caged her with his body. "Don't get so far ahead of me that I lose sight of what's going on. I've got a lot on my mind. Coming home to a houseful of new people—"

"Franklin's one man."

"—makes me question hiring you."

He felt her body go stiff. Watched the blood drain from her face. Saw the deep blue of her eyes go even darker. "Am I fired?"

He'd had no such plans, but he felt guilty that she'd drawn such a conclusion. "I like my privacy. A houseful of workers gives me a headache."

She exhaled slowly. "You thought the restoration would be accomplished with the wave of a magic wand?"

He'd sure as hell hoped so.

"Once the architectural plans are drawn up, there will be workmen here constantly," she said. "Hammering and drilling—"

"Not while I'm in town," he said. "Plan the noise around my road trips. On Friday the team travels to Atlanta for a three-game series, then to Miami. I'll expect silence when I return."

"Fine, we'll work around your schedule."

"My schedule includes your moving into the house while I'm away. I need a pet sitter."

"Live here?" She didn't look all that taken by his suggestion.

"You can oversee the restoration and keep an eye on the pups." Still, she hesitated. "I'll pay you to keep Boris and Bosephus out of the cemetery and off the neighbor's lawn."

"It's not a matter of money. I'd watch the boys for free," she told him, "but the house is a lot of work—"

"Hire an assistant."

She looked so startled he grabbed her shoulder to steady her. "I'll contact my bank manager. He'll extend a line of credit for you to draw on while I'm away. Start the restoration, write yourself a paycheck, but don't empty my account in one week."

"Franklin should have the initial sketches drawn up before you leave for Atlanta."

Franklin . . . he couldn't imagine the old man moving that quickly on any project. Psycho still wasn't certain he was the best architect for the job.

He looked into Keely's face, saw certainty in her expression. He didn't understand his willingness to trust her. He'd never trusted another soul. And it made no sense to trust this blonde with the ability to lie as easily as she drew breath.

"Work until six," he told her. "Dinner's on me; then we go to your place and pick up what you need. I want you moved in before I head out of town."

"It's Sunday," she reminded him. "You don't leave until Friday."

"Doesn't matter. I'm free tonight to haul your suitcases, boxes, and any furniture you might need to make yourself comfortable."

She shook her head. "You're too impulsive. Once you return, I'm back in my apartment."

Stubbornness tightened his jaw. "Move in for the duration of the restoration."

"Live with you?"

"It's not a death sentence."

"I like my apartment."

83

"My Colonial's better."

"If size counts."

A cocky smile curved his lips. "Bigger is better. In houses, home runs, and doing the dirty."

Her face flushed. "I've a yearly lease. I have rent to pay."

"I'll pay your rent for seven months. Stay here until the restoration's completed. You'll save on gas and travel time."

Keely Douglas clenched her fists. The conversation had shifted from her moving in during his road trips to setting up house. The man didn't understand her need to keep her own place. However small, it was her home. She had her independence, could come and go as she pleased. Even if it meant a two-hour commute.

"It would put my mind at ease if you were here full-time," Psycho said.

"What about *your* privacy?"

"I'd hardly notice you. You're small and blend into the woodwork."

He saw her as paneling? Not much of a compliment. "I'd notice you," she said. "You're a nudist."

"Notice me all you want."

She bit down on her bottom lip. "How about I hang a bell around your neck so I can hear you coming?"

"The bell wouldn't hang from my neck, sweetheart." Untying the knot over his hip, he let the towel drop. "I'm going to work on my dirt bike. Avoid the dining room unless you want a second peek. See you at six."

Keely watched him walk away. All lean and buff, a man of roped muscle and hewed sinew, he was self-confident about his body. Her stomach took a free fall and her breathing hitched. She'd only seen him from the back, yet it took several minutes for her to recover. Her heart couldn't take a full frontal.

The rest of the day passed quickly. Skirting the dining area, Keely and Franklin continued to measure the rooms. They discussed lighting and plumbing and a new staircase. On the second floor, Franklin stopped to check the window casements while Keely located Psycho's bedroom.

His room was easy to find. A sleeping bag lay on the floor amid scattered dog toys. Dozens of boxes lined the walls. A garment bag hung near his closet. The closet held plenty of empty hangers, but no clothes. Restless energy pulsed through the air, as if McMillan's presence was captured in the walls.

Across the room, an enormous black-and-white framed photograph grabbed her attention. She crossed for a closer look. Man and dirt bike were captured in a bold portrait of Psycho McMillan clearing a treacherously steep hill. He rode all out. Charged and unafraid. The camera caught him airborne, suspended in time, a risk junkie flying without a net. Concentrated power arced his body. His expression was hard and honed on winning. It was obvious that for Psycho, losing was never an option.

His explosive energy unsettled Keely. A

woman with any sense would run when she saw him coming. Yet the photograph held her. She reached out, traced her fingers over his visor-covered cheek. For a split second, she connected to the bad boy most labeled a wild man.

A part of her understood his need to live on the edge. Psycho was a thrill seeker. He'd never settle down. A wife and kids would be far too tame.

She felt suddenly sorry for him. Sorry he'd never find peace and comfort in the restored Colonial.

Ten minutes before six, Keely stood in the entry hall with Franklin Langston. They'd measured, calculated, and evaluated every room in the house, including the dining room—after Psycho slipped on a pair of athletic shorts and took off to play with the Newfoundlands. A whole lot of barking had followed, including howls from Psycho himself.

Inside, Franklin had filled a notebook with figures and sketches. He'd assured Keely the house would again be a credit to Colonel William Lowell.

Relief made her sigh. The restoration had begun. She had faith in Franklin and his son Quinn to make the necessary structural changes. It was up to her to fill the Colonial with timeless antiques. She trusted and believed in herself. Research and Rebecca Reed Custis would keep her on the right track. She could do this—

"Hungry, Keely?" McMillan's deep voice startled her.

Her nose scrunched up and her eyes narrowed

as she cautiously turned, uncertain whether he would be clothed or not. She immediately breathed easier when she saw that he sported a *Play Naked* T-shirt and jeans. At least he wasn't taking her to a clothing-optional diner. His black hair curled over his ears and along his neck. His dark eyes looked a bit wild, his high slanting cheekbones and blade of a nose prominent in a face too cut and rough to ever be handsome.

Yet she was drawn to him. That attraction made her as crazy as he was. Maybe even more so.

"I'm ready to eat," she finally answered.

"I'm heading out," Franklin Langston told them both. He put his hand on Keely's shoulder. "See you tomorrow, Ms. Douglas-Lowell."

Keely saw Franklin out.

Once the door was shut, McMillan closed in on her. "Douglas-*Lowell*? You've started hyphenating your name?"

"The family name has opened a few doors."

"Reality check—you're not related to the colonel."

She planted her hands on her hips. "Lowell got us Franklin Langston."

"The man's a prize."

"He'll prove himself."

"He'd damn well better." He sounded angrier than was warranted.

Keely blinked. "You think I'm out to screw you?"

"Screw me?" He was no longer talking restoration. The sudden curl of his lip was as sensual as it was dangerous. One badass smile.

Tense and restless, he had energy to burn. Nine innings of baseball would have taken the edge off, yet he'd warmed the bench for three long days. He was feeling wild and reckless.

Neither working on his dirt bike nor playing with the dogs had given him physical release. The tension between them excited him like foreplay. Thick and tangible and very, very hot.

Keely suddenly needed air. Cool, fresh air. She made a grab for the door handle, but Psycho cut off her escape. He flattened her against the wood, his palms pressed on either side of her head. His breath fanned her lips. Warm with a suggestion of mint. His gaze focused on her mouth. His smile faded. "You're not going anywhere."

Her own breath backed up in her throat and her mouth went dry. "What about my furniture?"

"We'll move it after—"

"After *what*?"

With unsettling slowness, he slanted his mouth over hers for a single heartbeat before saying, "After you stop being afraid of me. I've had a bad week. I'm wound tight, but I'm not about to take you against the door. You're not my quick fix."

Quick fix. Raw physical intimacy. Images of naked skin and body friction had her ducking under his arm. She pulled the front door wide. "I'm not afraid of you," she lied. "Nor am I attracted to you." An even bigger lie. The light-as-air kiss had turned her on. Her palms had gone as damp as her panties. "I just think you'd better conserve your energy. My daybed weighs a ton. It took three deliverymen to shove it through the door."

"I'll manage, Keely," he assured her as he followed her out the door.

No matter how fast she walked toward his black Dodge Ram, the man's heat stole up behind her like stroking hands. Big, strong, callused hands that knew where to touch and to pleasure her.

Such thoughts brought heat to her cheeks.

Her blush brought Psycho's knowing smile.

FIVE

Jacy's Java made the best turkey and cranberry wraps Keely Douglas had ever tasted. She moaned low in her throat with each bite, drawing Psycho's gaze more than once.

Psycho had explained Jacy's Java originated in Frostproof, Florida. Once Jacy and Risk Kincaid married, Jacy franchised the coffee shop, opening a branch in Richmond.

Avante-garde, and amazingly bright, the eclectic shop allowed coffee drinkers to sip their gourmet drinks amid a kaleidoscope of color. The walls were vividly decorated with splashes of paint; beneath Tiffany lighting, wicker blended with chrome, Retro with wrought iron, in a diverse pattern of tables and chairs.

Carnations floated in egg cups. Freshly baked gourmet cookies scented the air. A news stand set up with free magazines and newspapers invited customers to linger over their coffee.

Keely savored every aspect of the place as she

sipped her raspberry mocha latte from an English Rose teacup. She wished she could stop at Jacy's Java every day of the week. Unfortunately, her budget wouldn't allow the extravagance. One fancy latte here cost as much as a generic grocery store can of coffee that would make twenty cups. But instant coffee didn't have the flavor of a latte topped with whipped cream and chocolate shavings.

They'd been fortunate to score a table without a lengthy wait. Avoiding the line that wrapped the restored historical landmark, Psycho had flagged down a slender woman with emerald-green hair that matched her off-the-shoulder blouse. A purple and orange gauze skirt brushed the tops of red cowboy boots stitched with pink roses. A most original look.

Psycho had kissed the woman on the cheek, then introduced her as Jacy, team captain Risk Kincaid's wife.

Keely liked Jacy immediately. Warm and outgoing, the coffee shop owner greeted and seated every coffee or tea drinker who walked through the door. She'd located a table with a wide window view of the busy street and the shoppers passing on the sidewalk.

"Pistachio tea cookie or coconut lemon square?" Jacy now stood beside their table, offering dessert.

Keely took one of each.

Psycho passed on both. "No Rice Krispies treats?"

"You haven't been around to make them," Jacy

reminded him. "Feel free to stir up a batch anytime."

Keely's eyes went wide. "You trust Psycho in your kitchen?"

Jacy smiled. "Several years ago, I broke my ankle at a charity softball game in Frostproof, Florida. The Bat Pack ran my coffee shop during my recovery."

"I was manager," Psycho boasted.

"You managed to drive everyone crazy," Jacy corrected him.

"A good crazy," he returned. "No fights broke out. Customers remained happy."

"Speaking of happy"—Jacy looked toward the door—"wonder who put that smile on Romeo's face."

Keely turned to look as well. The sexiest man she'd ever seen entered the coffee shop, all tall and blond and advertising sin. Spotting Jacy, he crossed to their table.

"Hello, darlin'." He kissed Jacy full on the mouth.

Jacy flattened her palm on his chest, pushed him back a step. "Pretty daring, Romeo."

"Risk isn't in the building. I checked," Romeo told her. "I wouldn't want the old man to come down on me for stealing his wife."

"Squeeze play," Jacy explained to Keely. "Romeo had a hand in Risk proposing. He prides himself on matchmaking."

Romeo feigned disappointment. "Sadly, Kincaid makes her happy."

"Who's making you happy?" queried Jacy. "Why the smile?"

Keely caught Romeo's surprise. "I was smiling?"

"Like a fool," Psycho noted.

"How many women are you meeting?" Jacy asked. "Last week you entertained four for an hour."

"Those four have come and gone," Romeo informed her. "I'm only seeing one tonight."

Psycho raised a brow. "The reporter?"

Romeo nodded. "Another interview."

"Considering you once ran from the press, you're surprisingly available to Emerson Kent."

Ignoring Psycho, Romeo turned his smile and full attention on Keely. "Romeo Bellisaro," he introduced himself.

"Keely Douglas." She shook his hand, then caught him checking her out, as much interest as curiosity in his eyes. Romeo was polished and perfect and amazingly hot. Yet a part of her found Psycho's dark, rawboned edginess more appealing than Romeo's All American good looks.

"You're the designer." He looked from Keely to Psycho, then back at her again. "Once you've wrapped up Psycho's Colonial, perhaps you'd consider decorating my town house. I could use—"

"Someone besides Keely," Psycho said, cutting Romeo off. "She's with me for seven months, maybe longer, depending on her progress."

The two men exchanged a look that excluded Keely and Jacy. Psycho's hard stare drew

Romeo's shrug and slow grin. "I'll scan the Yellow Pages," Romeo said.

"Let your fingers do the walking." Psycho stretched his long legs beneath the table, shifted low on his spine in a chrome chair with a high curved back. "Another cookie, Keely?" he asked.

Keely swallowed hard. Psycho had caught her eyeing the cookie tray. Sweets were scratched from her grocery list. Staples like bread, peanut butter, and toilet paper always came first. The coconut lemon square she'd sampled had melted in her mouth. She would love a second.

Still, she hesitated. "Maybe one more . . ."

"Box up those left on the tray, and include a dozen from the display counter," Psycho said to Jacy. "Don't forget a few black-and-white cookies and several banana cream éclairs."

Jacy's surprise was evident. "You don't eat sweets. You fast twice a week. You—"

Psycho's narrowed eyes stopped Jacy's chatter. "Cookies coming up," she announced, turning on her cowboy-booted heel and heading toward the front counter.

Romeo escaped behind Jacy. Catching sight of a pretty brunette sporting red glasses and a tailored gray suit, he retraced his steps to the door, greeting the woman with a most charming smile.

When the woman returned his smile, Romeo's gaze lit on her mouth. He bent close to whisper in her ear. The brunette blushed becomingly. Keely was fascinated by the exchange.

"Take our table," Psycho called to Romeo.

Romeo returned with the brunette. His hand was pressed possessively to the woman's back as he guided her between tables. "Emerson Kent, meet Psycho McMillan and Keely Douglas."

Keely smiled and Psycho stared. "You finding Romeo late-breaking news?" he asked the reporter.

Emerson stared right back. "Romeo is my go-to guy for the season. Guy Powers approved weekly articles from the players' perspective."

Psycho scratched his stubbled jaw. "Warming the bench and counting losses sells papers?"

His sarcasm drew Emerson's smile. "I'd be happy to include you in the series, Psycho. Any time you want print space, call the *Banner*."

"I'll let Romeo have the print space." Psycho got to his feet just as Jacy arrived with the boxed cookies. He pulled several large bills from his money clip. "Tips all around."

Jacy nodded. "The coffee servers love you. I wait on you and they split your tip. All the girls buy groceries for a week."

Psycho hooked his arm around Jacy's shoulders and squeezed. "Catch you after Miami."

Keely noted the concern in Jacy's eyes. "Stay sane, Psycho. I know the suspension is hard on you."

Psycho looked at Romeo. "I've been on my best behavior."

"The stadium's still standing," Romeo returned.

Psycho nudged Romeo on his way out. "Don't spill all the Rogues' secrets to Emerson. No need to let her know Chris Collier wears women's underwear or that Ryker Black pats on baby powder after his shower. Or the fact Dane Maxin paints his toenails red."

"Can I quote you?" asked an amused Emerson.

"Be sure you get my name right." Psycho paused. "It's *Kincaid*, Risk Kincaid."

Jacy groaned, Emerson grinned, and Romeo shook his head.

"Time to fly." Psycho snagged Keely's hand and tugged her up beside him. Skirting the tables, he drew her to the front door. Holding his hand felt natural. Hers fit perfectly inside his grasp. His calluses pressed against her soft, sensitive palm.

Once on the sidewalk, he stopped and looked down on their hands. Surprise darkened his eyes that he'd initiated the contact. Before he could apologize or make an excuse, she pulled free and moved to the passenger side of his Dodge Ram.

Seated inside the truck, he set the cookie box between them. "Happy birthday, Keely."

She bit down on her bottom lip. "It's not my birthday."

He curved his big hands over the steering wheel. "Birthdays should come every day. Especially when you missed so many as a kid."

She sat up a little straighter. "How did you know I missed birthdays?"

"I think we're a lot alike. You grew up as poor as me. I hit with baseball; you're still struggling."

Pride stiffened her shoulders. "I'm not struggling."

"I've seen the rusty beater of a station wagon

you drive. The way you feast out of my refrigerator at lunch. I know you pack half a sandwich to take home with you for dinner. That's not spelling success."

Her throat worked. "Gloss Interiors—"

"Started with me, Keely. I'm not stupid."

"I'm good at what I do."

"You'll have to actually restore my Colonial to advertise your greatness." He started the engine. "I'm interested in seeing your apartment. It should reflect your talent for decorating."

"You live in a flea market," Psycho announced as he took in her tiny basement apartment. "Look at all this junk. You're a pack rat."

Her deep blue eyes went soft, her tone softer. "Not junk, Psycho, *treasures*."

Definitely treasures. Circling the room, he stopped before a sculpture designed from rusted bicycle parts and machine gears. It was odd, yet definitely eye-catching. A swooping swan-neck lamp curved over a low red vinyl sofa. Visible tears scored the cushions. Old seascape paint-by-number pictures hung behind the couch, some of the numbers unpainted.

A glass-front curio cabinet held antique army buttons, tin soldiers, and two leather-bound books, along with yellow-edged rolled maps. Behind a panel of broken glass he spotted fake corsages sprayed with glitter dust. Old brooches and gaudy theatrical jewelry. And an angel cookie cutter.

He shook his head. If her apartment reflected her ability to decorate, his restoration was in deep trouble.

"A glass of water, Psycho?" Keely called from the tiniest kitchen he'd ever seen. She could barely turn around without knocking an elbow or a hip. "Your lips are pursed. You're looking parched."

Not so much parched as sucking air. "Water's good."

He crossed to where she stood, behind salvaged tennis court netting that divided the living room from the kitchen. An assortment of chipped china cups and saucers decorated glass shelves above the sink.

"Nothing matches," he said.

She smiled, pleased he'd noticed. "The divorced teacups are remarried to unmatched saucers," she told him as she ran tap water until it turned cold, then filled a jelly glass. "Secondhand pieces have the most soul."

The most soul. Psycho downed the water in one gulp and set the glass down. Two wobbly bar stools and an antique high chair flanked the counter. He raked his hand through his hair. He'd given his promise to trust Keely, yet he wasn't feeling the faith. They had to talk. "We need to—"

"Get the daybed?" She jumped ahead of him. "Down the hall, first door on the right. I'll help you."

She walked ahead of him.

He followed more slowly.

Along the short length of the hallway, clothes-pins hooked to an old washing line displayed a collection of silhouettes and black-and-white photographs. Psycho paused before a photo of a gray-haired man with thick jowls and a hawk nose seated beside a prune-faced woman in a high-collared dress. The couple looked unhappy with each other and the world at large. "Who are these people?" he asked.

Keely shrugged. "I haven't a clue, but I've adopted them. My relatives didn't amount to much, so I bought old family albums at garage sales and claimed the photographs as my ancestors."

"Do these people have names?"

She looked at the photograph he'd been study-ing. "Wilbur and Imogene Grant from Norfolk. He was a banker; she, a homemaker."

Psycho pointed to a redheaded boy on a pony. "What about him?"

"Sammy Mason. The picture was taken when he was six." She tilted her head, calculating. "He's eighteen now. Enlisted in the army."

He leaned against the opposite wall. "You have a vivid imagination, Keely."

She looked at him then, straight on and serious. "My mother was sixteen when I was born. Her parents disowned her. The boy she expected to marry claimed he wasn't the father. Single parent-ing proved tough. My mother handed me off to her older sister to raise. After a year, that sister gave me to a great-aunt, who died when I turned six. Passed like a saltshaker, I lived with nine relatives before I hit legal age. Then I was on my own."

She sighed. "Don't put me down, Psycho, for creating the family I wish I'd had."

"I'm not putting you down," he assured her. "You've branched out from Marshal Lowell to scrapbook people. Interesting family tree."

Curiosity drew him to her bedroom. The woman had a fascination with feathers. Peacock eyes, white ostrich, golden pheasant, dyed orange and pink turkey quills. They filled decorated vases, jars, antique flour sifters, and wicker baskets. He'd never seen so many feathers in his life. Then came the boas, bright red and neon green, draped across the foot of her bed.

He cocked a brow. "You have a feather fetish?"

Her blush did not surprise him. Plucking a peacock feather from a basket, she stroked the plume. "Have you ever felt anything so soft?" she asked. "Like satin."

The woman with a hard childhood needed softness in her life. He gently ran a finger along its edge. It fanned out, closed. "Soft as a woman's inner thigh."

Keely's blush deepened. She quickly returned the feather to the basket while he took in her bedroom. All in one glance. The room was the size of a walk-in closet. A single bed with a headboard built out of an old garden gate lay to his left. A small garden bench served as a bedside table. Beneath a patchwork of wallpaper samples stood an old gym locker.

"My chandelier," Keely said proudly, drawing his attention to the colorful glass drops, beads, and ribbons dangling from a metal frame with a very dull bulb.

"You're quite . . ." He searched for the right word, not wanting to hurt her feelings. ". . . creative."

"Wait until you see how I fix up your Colonial. You'll be amazed."

"Yeah, definitely amazed."

"Now about the daybed—"

He slapped his palms against his thighs, made a quick decision. "I want to buy you a new bedroom set."

Her smile faltered. "Why? I've a perfectly good bed."

"It's covered with a wool rug."

"Rugs are warm in winter. This one was a steal. Saved on buying blankets."

The need to lay Keely down on a queen-size bed with silk sheets and down comforters blindsided Psycho. To make her feel warm and safe—

Her soft hand touched his arm. "You bought me cookies, Psycho. Enough birthday gifts for one day."

He wanted to do more. Much, much more. "We'll load the daybed, collect a few feathers, but that's all we're taking. I need a few pieces of furniture until the antiques arrive. You can help me pick them out. Tonight."

"The Bargain Barn is right down the street. They have the best used—"

"No bargains, no sales." His tone was emphatic. "New, never-sat-on-before furniture is what we're after."

She stood silently, looking at him with those deep blue eyes; a small smile curved her lips. "You deserve birthday gifts as well," she finally said. "Let's celebrate."

Psycho shook his head. "It's not my birthday, Keely."

"Neither is it mine," she reminded him, "but I got cookies. You, at least, deserve a comfortable couch."

It took Psycho a very short time to load her daybed and headboard into his pickup. While she packed up her clothes, he bundled up feathers. Keely wanted to take them all. They tickled his nose. He sneezed more than once.

Psycho had an image of her naked body being teased by a peacock eye. One that stroked her as lightly as warm breath and made her entire body blush.

His jeans grew uncomfortably tight as he visualized her puckered nipples, the trembling of her belly, the dampness between her thighs. His hard-on became downright painful. And not easy to hide.

When Keely requested he *hurry up*, he told her he'd lock up and meet her outside. He took several glasses of cold water and a dozen deep breaths before returning to his truck.

Shopping at Architetto Arrendatore was by appointment only. Romeo had programmed the number of the Italian leather gallery into Psycho's cell phone after playing poker in his home. The Bat Pack and two other Rogues had sat on the floor. Romeo complained a dozen times that his ass had gone numb.

A quick call, the mention of Romeo's name, and the owner scheduled time with Psycho and Keely.

"Welcome, Mr. McMillan," Saviano Annaldo greeted Psycho at the door. He was a tall, thin man in a lavender sport coat and dark gray dress slacks. "Might I interest either you or your lady in a glass of wine while you tour the gallery?"

Psycho didn't bother to correct the man's assumption that Keely was his lady. He didn't do explanations. Nor did he do wine. A shot of whiskey might have worked, or a National Bohemian beer. He looked at Keely. "Glass of white wine?"

She looked unsure. "That would be nice."

"Trebbiano or verdicchio?" asked Annaldo.

Keely's cheeks heated. Psycho sensed she didn't know one wine from another. He'd spent enough time in bars to know the difference. His dates often chose wine over hard liquor. "Trebbiano can be sweet, verdicchio a bit lemony."

She decided on the trebbiano.

"Excuse me, please." Annaldo went to pour the wine. He quickly returned. In a most gentlemanly fashion, he handed Keely her glass of trebbiano.

She took a small sip, smiled up at Psycho. "Excellent choice."

His chest warmed. The sensation felt strange to a man known for his hardened heart. Turning to Annaldo, he told the merchant what they needed in the way of furniture. He caught Keely's jaw dropping. She hadn't expected him to choose so many pieces. Pieces she'd inherit once the antiques arrived.

"It's my birthday," he whispered in her ear as they entered the intimately lighted showroom. "Let's do happy."

He kept a constant eye on Keely as she gently touched and sat on every couch and chair on display. A navy blue leather recliner drew a sigh. Eyes closed, she swore the chair molded to her body, the leather as soft as butter.

Apparently she was drawn to softness, whether in Italian leather or peacock feathers. Psycho nodded to Annaldo. The recliner now belonged to Keely. Psycho's taste ran to black leather. He dropped onto a curved sectional couch and crooked his finger for Keely to join him.

"Sit closer," he urged her when three cushions separated them. "I want to see if this is a good date couch."

She scooted two cushions closer.

He lunged, grabbed her, and hauled her across his lap.

Annaldo discreetly set off for a second glass of wine. Which left Psycho holding a squirming Keely. Her shoulder jabbed his chest. Her wiggling bottom ground into his groin.

His dick sprang to life.

And Keely went instantly still.

Cheeks heated, she punched his arm. "Let me go."

"A man needs to know if a couch is comfortable for getting it on."

"I don't do test drives."

"Bet you do birthday kisses."

"It's not your birthday."

"I've officially changed the date."

He kissed her then, a light, teasing kiss just to see her blush deepen. Keely's cheeks flamed. As did his groin. Her hand curled into the front of his T-shirt. He couldn't tell if she was pushing him away or pulling him toward her. A restless heat filled his body, leaving him fully aroused. Any woman other than Keely and he'd have taken her on the black leather, showroom model or not. He was wired for sex.

It had been two weeks since he'd had a woman claw his back, tear at his hair, and ride his thighs. He was days overdue. And itching to make up for lost time.

Nicki Carter was always good for a quickie. Suzie Jacobs had a mouth meant for sucking more than beer. But one glance at Keely made him realize she was the one he wanted. Wanted, but couldn't have. She was his designer. Not a one-night stand. Son of a biscuit.

Saviano Annaldo made his appearance shortly after Keely scrambled off his lap and Psycho again took to his feet. He shifted his stance more than once, trying to adjust a hard-on that wouldn't go soft. Only when his mind hit on his suspension did his body go lax. The prohibition against playing ball was a total mood killer.

Without further deliberation, Psycho chose the sectional sofa and two matching armchairs for his living room. A tinted blue-glass coffee table reminded him of an aquarium. He added that to his purchases as well.

"A bedroom suite, Mr. McMillan?" Annaldo inquired.

Enjoying her second glass of wine, Keely leaned into his side, her voice low. "Time to pack up your sleeping bag."

He looked down at her. Her cheeks now glowed, no longer from embarrassment but from the wine. "I see you've found my bedroom."

"Strictly to take measurements."

"There's nothing in that room under eight inches."

She nearly spewed her wine.

"This way, sir." Annaldo motioned them into the next showroom.

Psycho reached for Keely's hand, catching himself before their fingers laced. What was it about Keely Douglas that made him want to keep her close? He had no interest in a skinny blonde with fabricated family photos on the wall. She did, however, have feathers going for her. He might keep her around long enough to see if her skin was as soft as marabou. He'd like to see her wrapped in nothing but her boas.

"What style of bed are you interested in, Mr. McMillan?" inquired Annaldo.

Psycho scanned the highly polished Italian bed frames, his focus on the mattresses and the turned-down sheets. A man could score a lot of action in this room.

A dark wood platform bed drew his attention. He dropped onto the mattress, which cuddled his body like a woman. Nice. Very, very nice.

He patted the space beside him. "Keely, come roll around—"

"Not on your life."

Her comment drew Annaldo's chuckle. "It is a wonderfully soft bed."

And Psycho was an inordinately hard man. "You're no fun," he said to Keely as he jackknifed to his feet.

"You're fun enough for two."

"Chest of drawers." Annaldo directed them to several intricately designed pieces. "Baroque or perhaps something inspired by Louis the Sixteenth?"

Psycho wasn't taken by either dresser. What caught his eye was a contemporary double dresser with a mirror. He nodded to Annaldo. "This one works."

"Most certainly, sir." The gallery owner gave Psycho a knowing look. "Six deep drawers, a commodity to be shared. Handsome craftsmanship for a man, yet sleek, sophisticated lines for a woman. It will take up less space than two separate pieces."

Shared? Psycho hadn't planned on Keely's bras and panties lying in a drawer next to his socks and T-shirts. On the flip side, sharing a dresser would bring her to his bedroom. He wasn't going to touch her. And there was no law against looking.

"Bamboo, eucalyptus, or oyster-colored silk sheets?" asked Annaldo. "The platform bed comes with a comforter and two pillows."

Psycho stuck his tongue in his cheek and looked to Keely. Let her pick out his sheets.

She set her empty wineglass on a cork coaster atop a high-boy dresser. "Bamboo."

"Very well," approved a pleased Annaldo.

Psycho and Keely left the gallery with Annaldo's promise that the furniture would be delivered the next morning.

Back at the Colonial, Psycho followed Keely into the formal living room. She clutched the cookie box to her chest as she turned in a full circle. "How would you like the couch and chairs placed? Angled east to catch the morning sun? Or west for the sunset?"

Psycho took a moment to answer. "Unload the furniture in the family room behind the stairs. If you decorate that room last, I can set up my television and have a place to hide during the restoration."

"Works for me." She smiled then, a very relaxed and pink-cheeked woman after only two glasses of wine.

He stepped toward her, tipping up her chin with his finger. "How often do you drink wine?"

"Not often enough."

That's what he'd thought. She was a lightweight. She'd gotten a buzz from the trebbiano. "I'll unload your bed, get you set up for the night."

"I don't have bamboo sheets."

"You can have mine when they arrive tomorrow."

"First cookies, now sheets. I do love gifts."

On impulse, Psycho bent and kissed her on the forehead.

As spontaneous as he, Keely rose on tiptoe and kissed his cheek. "Happy birthday to us." Her smile was as bright as a cake topped with candles.

Psycho decided then and there, as long as Keely Douglas worked for him, every day would bring a celebration. He would make up for all the birthdays she had missed. He liked seeing her happy.

SIX

Romeo Bellisaro was taking great pleasure in Emerson Kent's smile. A pleasure that faded when she wouldn't let him touch her. He'd tried all the *accidental* moves he could think of. Romeo had excellent hand-eye coordination, yet Emerson outmaneuvered him every time. The lady was fast.

She'd reached for a sugar packet, quickly withdrawing her hand before he could stroke her fingers. Jarred by her retreat, he'd knocked over the sugar caddy. Decorative pansy sugar cubes and Sweet N Low had spilled onto the floor.

"Smooth move." Coffee shop owner Jacy Grayson had shot him an amused look. "Keep swinging, Romeo, you're bound to hit something."

Curveball. Swing and a miss. Emerson elbowed him back when he tried to scoot closer. His third out came quickly. In an attempt to squeeze Emerson's knee, he inadvertently bumped the cherry-wood table leg. The cups and saucers shook, and Em's mocha latte splashed onto her suit jacket sleeve. Fortunately, a touch of club soda took care of the stain.

All in all, it was a very frustrating coffee date. The continuous tapping of the keys on her laptop didn't help one bit. He was totally ticked that Emerson paid more attention to her article than to him.

Feeling his eyes on her, Em looked up and met his stare. "You're sulking, Romeo."

He took a sip of his black coffee. "Just watching you work."

"I thought you were upset I wasn't focused on you."

She was psychic. "After your last article, *Burgers, Fries, and a Side of Jesse Belissaro,* I'd appreciate your focusing less on me and more on baseball."

"Ribbing in the clubhouse?"

"No man wants to be likened to a pickle."

"A *Vlasic* pickle. I meant it in the most complimentary way."

"I took a lot of hits."

"Poor baby." She went back to her typing.

Romeo's jaw worked. "Any questions for me?"

"Does your butt fall asleep on the bench?"

"Not nice, Emerson."

She pursed her lips. "The Raptors beat the Rogues by how many runs last night? Seven or was it eight?"

"Rubbing my nose in our loss?"

"I'm winning our bet. You're down three games."

111

Romeo circled the rim of his coffee cup with one finger. A gold china cup with red, white, and blue stars. "Down by three means little. It's early in the season."

"Down by thirteen will hit home. I predict the Rogues won't win a game until the Bat Pack is back in the lineup."

Romeo slouched on the chrome chair, crossed his arms over his chest. Emerson seemed way too sure of herself. He didn't like cocky reporters, even when they had thick chestnut hair, startling green eyes, and a turn-on smile.

Yet there was something about her that put him in the mood to hang out with her. He'd had casual relationships. Had juggled a lot of women. He'd never, however, put enough energy into one woman to see if the relationship could last beyond bed and breakfast.

Tonight was his fifth with Emerson Kent. Though her interviews centered on him, he'd learned a little about her as well. Her parents lived outside Washington, D.C. Her mother was an English professor at Georgetown University; her father a renowned cardiologist at Johns Hopkins. She was well read, held up her end of a conversation, didn't giggle. She finished the *New York Times* crossword puzzle. Collected baseball cards. Had mastered chopsticks. And, most importantly, took control of her destiny.

Emerson never planned to depend on a man for her happiness. She was one self-sufficient woman. She owned a hammer, a set of screwdrivers, and a cordless drill. Could change pipes beneath the kitchen sink. Could hang pictures without knocking out plaster.

He'd caught a glimpse of black lace when she'd bent down to grab her laptop. The lady got frilly beneath her business suits. Romeo liked frilly.

He tapped his fingers on the table and asked, "Care to place a wager on the next ten games?"

"We've already bet on the pennant race."

"Let's make the season even more interesting."

She stopped typing, saved her material. "I'm listening."

"The next ten games: for every Rogue win, I collect a kiss."

"Is everything about puckering up?"

"I enjoy making out."

"It's one quick kiss, Romeo, *if* the Rogues pull off a win."

"Never quick, Em."

He caught the slight tremble in her hands as she clutched her ivory china cup and took a sip of her latte. Should the Rogues manage to pull off a win, he wanted her sitting on a hot rock anticipating his kiss.

She exhaled, then slowly countered," "For every loss you remain celibate."

Celibate? He lived and breathed sex. Considered sex the eighth wonder of the world. Suffering blue balls was for teenagers. Not grown men.

He hated the idea that Emerson had written off their first thirteen games. Romeo would never get more than coffee and conversation from this woman. That bothered him, more than he cared to admit.

"Deal?" she prodded.

"You're pretty damn sure you'll win."

"The Atlanta Braves look strong," she told him. "The team's healthy. Their lead off batters have some serious pop. Warren Cabe, their starting pitcher, takes the sting out of a player's bat. Batters look flat when Cabe's on the mound. As far as the Florida Marlins go, their defense is on fire. They're playing like superheroes."

She flicked her tongue to one corner of her mouth, taunting Romeo with a slow, moist sweep of her bottom lip. Her expression was thoughtful. "Then there's the Rogues; you've more injuries than an emergency room. Left fielder Ryker Black strained his right hamstring and is listed day to day. Pitcher Chris Collier is still seeing double. Rookie Quade Davis collided with Risk Kincaid in the outfield and is suffering from a concussion. Pitcher John Gabriel was optioned to Triple-A Norfolk following a rough start and loss in the Raptor series. The Rogues will hit Turner Field with rookies and backups."

Romeo wished Emerson didn't have the inside info on injuries and trades. Despite her belief that the Rogues faced a losing streak, he agreed to her bet. Blue balls and all. "You're on."

Her smile came slow and easy.

His arousal swift and hard.

Shifting on his chair, he asked, "Will you be in Atlanta?"

She nodded. "The *Banner* is sending me to Atlanta and Miami."

"Staying at the Marriott?"

"Same hotel as the Rogues."

"Maybe you'll be on my floor."

"Press is one floor below."

"I like you beneath me."

Her green eyes narrowed behind her red glasses. "The elevator may go down, but not your zipper."

"I'm worth the ride, sweetheart."

She squirmed ever so slightly on her chair.

He grinned when she crossed her legs and squeezed her thighs tight, the flex of muscle visible beneath her linen slacks.

"Dessert?" Jacy Grayson arrived at their table with a silver tray of confections. "Almond crescents, Mexican melt-aways, or a butterscotch-marshmallow brownie?"

Romeo slid his arm about Jacy's waist, snugged her close. "No sweets before a shoot."

Jacy understood. "An Easy Ryder night."

Romeo caught Emerson's look of interest. "I'm spokesman for Easy Ryder Condoms," he told her. "They're shooting an ad campaign tonight. *Sex Happens. Ryde Easy.*"

Interest sharpened Em's gaze. "Can I attend the shoot?"

"For a price."

Jacy Grayson patted Romeo's shoulder. "Play nice, lover boy."

"I play to win."

"I'm not a game, Romeo," Emerson stated as soon as Jacy moved to another table. "You can't *win* me."

He rested his elbows on the table, steepled his fingers near his nose, and stared at her. Her expression was guarded, the set of her shoulders stiff and straight.

Emerson was damn puzzling. He'd never met a woman who didn't want him. Most came on to him with clingy hands and hot lips. Many he had to pry off with a promise of tickets to a game or an autographed picture. A few he took to bed.

Emerson Kent wanted nothing from him.

He couldn't give away a kiss.

The silence stretched so long, it made his palms itch. He finished his coffee and requested a refill before he concluded, "My price is your cell phone number."

Surprise flickered across her face. "You can reach me at the *Banner*. We always set up our meetings before I leave the paper."

"I might want to call you after five."

"I wouldn't be available."

She drew a wide line between writing her newspaper articles and meeting him for pleasure. She wasn't listed in the phone book. He'd already looked. If he'd located her address, he would have driven by her place, once or twice, to see if she was home. A bit juvenile, but he was curious as to where she lived. He'd chased a dozen red Beemers through traffic, hoping to catch her with the top down and the wind in her hair, the sun on her face.

Pained by her lack of interest, he shrugged. "Guess I'm no more than a sports story to you."

"You make good copy."

Apparently Emerson saw him as a feature article, nothing more. She didn't take him seriously. She believed him to be a man who loved women. Lots of women. A man who could never settle for just one.

He could do one woman. Given the right female and half a chance. He blew out a breath. "You're not into me?"

"Sorry, no."

No hesitation whatsoever. Her honesty kicked him in the groin. He looked around, wondering where he'd lost his charm.

Emerson Kent caught his lost look. She hadn't meant to hurt his feelings; had only meant to save herself. She'd nearly come undone at his proximity. His unmistakable interest, unrelenting attention, warm breath on her cheek, his need to touch her, had taxed every nerve in her body.

His body heat and male scent had made her squirm. She'd found it difficult to think straight.

The man was a turn-on.

Emerson had turned him down.

She wanted more in a relationship than a man with a *Legendary* tattoo, who scored as much off the field as he did on game day.

She slowly closed her laptop. Sighed. Romeo

Bellisaro was about to promote safe sex. Given his experience with women, he'd make the ideal spokesman. No one would doubt his sincerity when he advised slipping on a condom before getting it on.

The shoot would have made a good article.

She pushed back her chair and stood. "Thanks for the latte. See you in Atlanta."

"Not before?"

"We have no reason to meet."

"We can always find a reason, Em."

"It would need to be work related."

"Don't you ever play?"

"You play enough for two, Romeo."

"I'd like to play with you."

"Not going to happen." Glancing around the coffee shop, she caught a dozen women checking him out. Pretty, perky-breasted, oh-so-interested women. The man would never hurt for company.

One last look in his direction made her pause. His brow was drawn, the corners of his superhot mouth creased. "You don't like me much, do you?" he asked. "Should I win our end-of-the-season bet, it's going to kill you to sleep with me, isn't it, Emerson?"

Kill her, most certainly. She refused to think of rug burn as a great way to die. She didn't indulge in casual sex. She liked order and logic in her life. Business kept her on the right track where Romeo was concerned. Yet when she'd agreed to their wager she'd thrown caution to the wind. She'd felt daring, sexy, and a little light-headed when she'd agreed to their bet. Fortunately for her, all the statistics pointed to the Rogues dying a slow and painful death on the road. The team's losses would keep her out of his bed.

"It's not the end of the season," she calmly pointed out. "If I won our wager and we never slept together, I'd still live a long and happy life. Can you survive not making the play-offs?"

Her words wiped the frown from his face. His cockiness flashed. "We'll take the pennant. When we do . . ." He let his words trail off, leaving her to imagine what he'd left unsaid.

He rose then, tucking a finger beneath her chin and forcing her to meet his gaze. "Six blocks west, then turn right at the Richmond Museum. Steps are between the brick buildings. My shoot is on the second floor."

"This will cost me?"

"Objectivity," he said. "You've already likened me to a pickle. With your next article, I'd prefer no references to being ribbed and lubricated."

Romeo's photo shoot was an eye-opening experience. Taking a seat in a darkened corner of the room, Em found herself unable to type. She could only stare.

Stare at a blue-jeaned, open-shirted Romeo. The man was magnificent, all broad shoulders, lean torso and hips. A smattering of sandy hair fanned his chest and tracked low.

Romeo Bellisaro embodied sex.

Easy Ryder was his condom of choice.

He stood alone before a light blue canvas, no props needed. No bed, no motorcycle, no woman draped over his shoulder. He opted for a casual stance, his weight balanced on one leg, the other slightly bent. His thumbs hooked into the front belt loops of his jeans. Tucked into his waistband, a silver-foiled roll of condoms unfolded over his jutting hip, running the length of his zipper. The man conjured up long, hot nights of sweaty sheets and amazing, yet safe sex.

"Picture this." Carmel, the tall, willowy female photographer talked to Romeo through the shoot. "You've won the World Series. You're charged with superhero urges. The Rogues are at an after-hours bar, partying. Sexy women rub and press against you. From the corner of your eye, you catch a new arrival. She's the hottest woman you've ever seen. Lock eyes with her, Romeo, tell her you want her. *Really, really* want her. Let her know you're good, so good your memory will last a lifetime."

The curve of Romeo's sexy mouth seduced every woman in the room. Even though Emerson knew he couldn't see her sitting there in the darkness, he seemed to seek her out. His gaze promised a good time. His slightly flared nostrils seemed to take in her scent. Her mating scent. With the slightest tilt of his head, he promised kisses to curl her toes. The flex of his hands suggested touching. Knowledgeable touching. A man familiar with a woman's body.

His gaze smoldered and his body burned in invitation. Whether in a dark corner or against a wall, if the woman was willing, Romeo would take her where she stood.

Emerson's body responded. Her nipples poked her lavender silk blouse. Her panties were sinfully damp. Romeo and his Easy Ryders would leave a woman sated, yet soon wanting again. One time with this man would never be enough. He would prove addictive.

"Give me *more*, Romeo," Carmel encouraged as she took shot after shot. "The woman of your wet dreams starts walking toward you. Her lips are glossy, plump, and parted. A slinky black dress hugs her body, her stilettos showcase mile-long legs. She wants you. Bring her to orgasm with one hot look."

His *look* made Emerson tremble. And moan. She heard the sighs of the other women in the room, and knew Romeo had also affected them.

A full minute passed before Carmel came out from behind her camera; sweat beaded her brow. She drew a cigarette from her purse and lit it. Dragging deeply, she winked at Romeo. "Damn good, Rogue. I'm satisfied."

Romeo laughed, a deep, resounding sound that drew more than one blush from those looking on. "My pleasure."

He buttoned his cobalt-blue shirt, slipped the condoms from his waistband, and tossed them to Carmel.

"Easy Ryder appreciates your time and donation to their safe sex campaign. The company will send you several complimentary cases of condoms," the photographer told him. "Same as before? Magnum XL, mutual stimulation?"

Romeo nodded. "Great product." He signed several autographs, then sought out Em. His loose-hipped gait said he was feeling sure of himself. "Did you enjoy the shoot?" he asked.

She could barely form words. Romeo was worth every penny paid to advertise safe sex. "I'm going to buy stock in Easy Ryder tomorrow."

"I could show you the value of the condom tonight."

Emerson rolled her eyes. "Don't you ever give up?"

"I'll die with an erection."

"I'm sure you will."

He took her by the arm, drawing her from her chair. He stood so close, his warmth, strength, and appeal stroked her like a touch. She cleared her throat. "You did the shoot for free?"

Romeo nodded. "One of my high school girlfriends had a pregnancy scare. While I liked variety, Melinda had marriage on the brain. The night she lied, said she was on the pill, we had unprotected sex. I sweated bullets for six weeks until she tested negative."

"Would you have married her?"

He didn't miss a beat. "Melinda picked out a wedding dress and a chapel, while I filled out applications for college. Had she been pregnant, I would have filed for married student housing."

Relief sifted through her. The man had integrity. He would have taken care of his child. "I'd better go." She sidestepped left.

He walked her to the door. "See you in Atlanta."

A white-hot sky baked Atlanta. It was the worst heat wave in fifteen years. Emerson Kent had roasted in the press box along with the other sportswriters. She'd thought the Braves-Rogues doubleheader would never end.

Following the Rogues' second loss of the day, she flagged a cab and dragged herself back to the hotel. The lobby was packed with die-hard Rogues fans and tight-bloused, short-skirted, stiletto-heeled groupies. Her eye on the bank of elevators, Emerson inched her way around pot-ted plants and clutches of couches and chairs.

Once in her room, she tore off her skirt suit and moved to stand in her bra and panties before the air-conditioning vents.

She'd never been so hot. Nor so uncomfortable.

The one o'clock game-time temperature had hit a sweltering ninety-seven degrees; the on-field temperature was 106. Both teams had cut batting practice short. Action in the bullpen was nonexistent.

Cool mist fans had blown from each corner of the dugout and the team trainers had ammonia towels at the ready. Hydration was always a ma-jor concern in such heat. The players had drunk plenty of fluids with electrolytes.

Seated at the far end of the visitors' bench, Psy-cho, Chaser, and Romeo had gazed out onto the field, their expressions tight, enigmatic. Pitcher Chris Collier sat several feet to their right, alone and ignored.

Affected early by the heat, Psycho had tipped back his head and poured a cup of water over his face. He'd then shaken his head like a wet dog. Romeo and Chaser had shifted farther down the bench.

The concession stands had run out of bottled water by the bottom of the sixth. Paramedics were stationed in the stands by the top of the seventh.

Many of the fans had dispersed before the evening game, sunburned, sweaty, and too irritable to sit any longer.

Emerson had remained in the press box throughout the doubleheader. Her wrist was sore from fanning herself with the game program. The stadium air-conditioning had heaved, choked, and proved less than effective.

She'd worn her new outfit to the park, the one chosen by Romeo Bellisaro. The champagne linen suit now lay in a heap at her feet. The matching pumps were buried beneath the hem of her skirt.

The memory of shopping with Romeo remained fresh on her mind. He'd taken her to Lord and Taylor, to the designer salon. Every personal shopper in the store had merged on him, offering assistance and grasping for his attention.

Emerson never grasped. She didn't believe in falling over any man for any reason. She'd shaken her head over all the flirting and fawning.

And while she tried on clothes, she'd listened

to Romeo's comments on her selections. In the end, she'd made the final decision on her outfit. An outfit he'd called "stunning."

Emerson agreed. The double-breasted jacket fit as if made for her. The lapels parted to reveal an ivory silk blouse. The short pleat at the hemline flirted with her calves. Kicky, yet stylish.

Romeo had personally delivered a pair of champagne pumps to her dressing room. "You decent, Em?" he'd called from the hallway.

Not quite decent. Unbuttoned, her ivory silk blouse revealed both cups of her satin bra, along with her bare belly. Her short silk slip hit an inch above her thigh-high stockings.

Glancing up, she'd found his reflection in her mirror.

Open interest darkened his eyes as he rested his arms along the top edge of the latticed swinging doors, a shoe box in hand. She'd stood frozen as they both stared into the glass. Frozen until his gaze left her face and traveled over her body. A slow, sensual sweep that left her flushed and tingly, and threw off her breathing.

With no more than a look, he'd stripped off her blouse and slip, unhooked her bra, unrolled her nylons, and pulled down her panties. Her lips parted and her heart pounded. She'd never felt more naked.

Grabbing a plum-colored crinkle skirt off a hanger, she'd covered herself. She'd jabbed a finger toward the sign in the hallway. "Ladies' Dressing Room."

"I can read, Em."

"Then *why*?"

"I promised you a new pair of shoes."

"One of the personal shoppers could have brought them."

"I preferred to deliver them myself." He'd handed her the shoe box, then scratched his jaw. "Thought you'd be more business cotton than Playboy lace." His gaze flitted to her thighs. "You've got the legs for garters."

A slow wink, and Romeo departed. When her heartbeat slowed, Emerson lifted the lid on the shoe box. Size 7 designer pumps. Outrageously expensive.

How had the man guessed her size? A warmth spread in her chest. Romeo's effort to match her shoes to her suit pleased her greatly.

She'd developed a soft spot for the third baseman.

Sighing heavily, she removed her red-framed glasses and faced the air-conditioning vent. The cold air tossed her bangs and chased the heat from her cheeks. A shower was in order. She wanted to wash away the memory of the Rogues' loss.

The day had been long and tiring. And very depressing. She'd felt the Rogues' defeat more strongly than she'd anticipated. A dull ache was centered in her chest. She hurt for Romeo. A most unexpected feeling, and one she couldn't shake.

After showering and shampooing, she slipped into brown silk lounging pajamas. Her stomach growled. She wondered if room service would deliver a sandwich this late. She scanned the menu on her bedside table, noted it was already past the cutoff time for deliveries.

She'd eat a big breakfast.

Tossing back the bedcovers, she caught the blinking red light on her bedside telephone. Someone had tried to call while she was in the shower. It was the far side of midnight. Who would call at this hour?

A knock on the door turned her from the phone message. "Room service," a male voice called.

Em crossed to the door and cracked it slightly. "I'm sorry, I haven't placed an order."

The man rechecked the room slip. "Emerson Kent. Six fifty-seven."

"You're sure?"

"I've followed directions to the letter."

She edged back a step, allowed him entrance. The man was all smiles and politeness as he settled the cart before the dresser. "An assortment of sandwiches," he informed her before departing.

Emerson scanned the silver cart. Covered dishes, place settings for two, and a souvenir bobble-head of Romeo Bellisaro made it obvious she wouldn't be dining alone.

She picked up the bobble-head, which had been sold at numerous concession stands at Turner Field. From his brown eyes to the sexy curve of his mouth, the souvenir bore a striking resemblance to the third baseman.

"Mind if I join you?"

Em looked up and found Romeo leaning

against the door frame. He was dressed casually in a dark gray Polo and worn jeans. Leather flip-flops were all he had on his feet. He hadn't shaved.

She hesitated. "It's late."

"But too early for bed." He pushed off the jamb, took one step toward her, then a second. His gaze was narrowed, shaded, his lips turned into a half smile. "I'm better company than the bobble-head. I pack more lumber than that little piece of wood."

Heat sketched her cheeks. "Perhaps you've mistaken me for someone with glossed lips in a little black dress. I'm not a groupie looking for sex. And I'm too tired to keep up my end of a conversation. I'm not good company."

"Neither am I." He ran one hand down his face. "I've run out of charm. I promise no lines or come-ons. No further mention of sex. It's been a rough day, Em. The dugout steamed like a sauna. Let me eat, unwind, and I'm gone."

"How did you get room service?" she asked. "The kitchen closed an hour ago."

"The hotel caters to visiting teams. The promise of an autographed Rogues cap and jersey prompted the prep cook to fix some sandwiches."

Emerson pursed her lips, debating. "Where's Psycho and Chaser?"

"Chaser's already crashed. Psycho's wound tight. He prowled the hotel, had drinks with two female flight attendants."

"Psycho's flying the friendly skies?"

Romeo shook his head. "Two beers and he

split. Psycho returned to his room and called his designer."

"Talk of restoration calmed him down?"

"I heard Psycho wish Keely a happy birthday. He asked if she'd received a pink feather duster. Not sure what Psycho's into, but it's not dusting."

"Maybe he's into Keely Douglas."

Romeo shrugged. "Keely's definitely claimed his interest. Yet Psycho bores easily. At least discussing ceiling fixtures and wall lighting took his mind off the Rogues' loss."

"An ugly loss."

He crossed to a comfortable chair and dropped into it. He looked like a sun god, all blond and tanned, seated on the bronze and burnt-orange paisley fabric. "The Rogues played Triple-A ball today."

"Definitely minor league," she agreed. "Did Risk Kincaid kill Dave Walker in the locker room?"

Romeo rolled his eyes. "That rookie had a base-running brain-freeze."

"I mentioned Walker's freeze in my column," she said. "How Kincaid's solid ground double sent him to second only to have Walker misinterpret the third base coach's signal. The kid froze between second and third, then spun around. When he saw that Kincaid claimed the bag, he turned as white as the infield lines. The relay from right field took Walker out. What should have been a home run closed the inning.

"We all sat in disbelief until Psycho punched

the dugout wall. Chaser kept Psycho from going after the rookie."

Emerson curled up on the chair next to Romeo. "How's Dean DeAngelo?"

Romeo closed his eyes against the bad memory. "Right fielder should never have called Risk Kincaid off the pop-up. Blinded by the sun, DeAngelo misjudged the catch."

Em grimaced. "He took that fly ball on the chin."

Blood had splattered like a pink mist. Davis had hit his knees and covered his face with his glove. Kincaid had retrieved the ball and fired it home. Close, but no cigar. Two additional runs padded the Braves' lead.

The team trainer had assisted DeAngelo off the field. His replacement a veteran with a strained bicep and little run in his legs.

"DeAngelo fractured his jaw, lost three teeth." Romeo slouched deeper into the chair. "There's major dental work in his future."

A compatible silence settled between them.

Romeo crossed one ankle over the other knee. Stretched his arms over his head.

Emerson clutched her knees tightly to her chest.

There were no words necessary until Emerson's stomach growled. "Can I bring you a plate?" Romeo offered.

Emerson nodded, unable to speak as he stood up and crossed to the cart. Suddenly food didn't appeal to her half as much as his backside. Muscles strained against his Polo, his jeans emphasizing the tightness of his butt and the long lines of his legs. The man looked good enough to eat.

Instead she settled for a club sandwich.

Romeo had roast beef on rye.

They ate and digested in silence, aware of each other yet feeling no need to converse. Taking her last bite, Em wiped her mouth and inquired, "Curfew?"

He glanced at his Tag Heuer. "I've never made one yet. Tonight will be my first."

He rose, held out a hand, and pulled her to her feet. They stacked their dishes on the cart, then faced each other at the door.

"Thanks for joining me for dinner."

"Thanks for bribing the prep cook. It's always nice to have dinner with a friend."

He looked down at her, amusement and heat in his all-knowing gaze. "Buddies now, lovers later. When the Rogues win a game and I kiss you, you'll want to be more than friends."

SEVEN

Lovers. It was a very real possibility now.

The Rogues lost three games to Atlanta, then fought their way back to win one game against Miami. Because of that 2–1 win, Emerson now owed Romeo a kiss. The very thought left her pulse pounding. When, where, how would it happen? The question remained foremost on her mind.

Following their win, Romeo had pushed off the dugout bench and looked toward the press box. Even through the tinted glass, she'd felt his heat and anticipation. The man would soon come and collect his kiss.

Emerson hadn't drawn a steady breath since.

Back in Richmond, she faced a day off. She'd submitted her sports stories along with an article titled "Do-over," a column in which she'd speculated on how the baseball season might have started if the Bat Pack had not brawled on Media Day.

At seven-fifteen, with coffee mug in hand, she

was perched on the cushioned seat in the big bay window overlooking the city park. She loved mornings. Loved the never-ending shuffle of life as dog walkers jogged to keep up with their pets, new mothers pushed baby strollers, and bench sitters sipped coffee and read the paper while waiting for their bus.

The daily occurrences were soothing to her. Emerson liked routine. She hated surprises.

The surprise of her life hit three sips into her second cup of coffee as a blue Viper parallel-parked before her condo. Her breath backed up in her throat. She nearly hyperventilated.

How had Romeo found her? She'd refused to give out her home phone number or address. Yet there he was, walking up her brick sidewalk. His hair was brushed back, revealing the sharpness of his features, handsome, lean, and hungry. A pale blue button-down shirt and stone-washed jeans showcased his athletic body. The man made her world stop. And tilt on its axis.

Checking the number on her front door, Romeo rang the bell. Emerson set down her coffee cup and slowly slid off the window seat. She dragged her feet all the way to the foyer.

With the security chain in place, she cracked the door. She could see half his face and one broad shoulder.

"Morning, Em." His greeting was far too enthusiastic for so early in the day.

She narrowed her eyes at him. "Who sold me out?"

Her bluntness made him smile. "The receptionist at the *Banner*. Your address cost me two tickets to the next Rogues home game."

Another bribe. First the prep cook at the hotel. Now the curvy redhead at the front desk of the newspaper. The latest hire shouldn't have released her address.

Romeo had invaded her privacy.

He wedged his fingers between the door and its frame. "You're here. I'm here. Invite me in, Em."

"I'm not awake yet," she lied. In reality she was wired and uneasy about his forthcoming kiss.

"Coffee, breakfast, I'll stick around until you feel human."

She refused to let him in. "Don't you have practice? Team films? A workout?"

"Not until tomorrow. Today's free."

Great, just great. "My day is jammed. I'm cleaning house, running errands—"

"Reviewing a list of upcoming Rogue activities?" He fished a palm-size calendar from his shirt pocket. Waved it before her eyes. "Thought you might like dates for all team social functions, charity events, and fan appreciation days. This stuff would make good articles."

"Thanks, I'll take a look." She slid her fingers beneath the security chain, hoping he'd hand the calendar over and leave.

Instead, Romeo pulled back. "You can take a look once you invite me in."

He was crafty. From what she could glimpse, all the Rogues' activities were mapped out on the calendar: black tie dinners, social events, charity auctions.

She'd give her right arm for that calendar. It carried the inside scoop. She'd have the advantage covering events not publicized.

"Five minutes," she told him as she unhooked the chain and allowed him entrance.

Romeo's self-assured grin faltered with his first step inside. His gaze narrowed on her Florida Marlins jersey, his expression none too happy.

"You into fish?" he asked.

She looked down at the aqua and white jersey. "I liked the colors."

"I prefer red, white, and blue."

"You're all Rogue."

"It's called team loyalty, Em."

"I'm a sportswriter. Objective and fair. I won't show partiality."

"Take off the jersey."

She took a step back. "You're joking, right?"

The look on his face told her his humor had died at the door. "You can't wear it out with me."

"Out with you? We've made no plans."

He pointed to the calendar. "Today the players fly beneath the public's radar. Check the handwritten notation. Hollywood Harts. Here's your chance for an exclusive. The Bat Pack supports a sanctuary for retired animal film stars."

Emerson blinked. "You mean Fancy and Sky Dog?"

Romeo nodded. "Animals with attitude. Most were replaced in movies and on television sitcoms once they passed their prime. Some of the animals are arthritic, others half blind. Sophie Hart, an old college—"

"Flame?" she innocently inserted.

"Yeah, we flamed," he openly admitted. "For about three months. I moved on to baseball and she became a studio trainer. She hated to see the animals abused or put down once their careers ended. She asked for my help and we joined forces. Twice a month Sophie opens the sanctuary to hospitals and foster homes. The animals perform. The kids go nuts. The children attending today are all cancer survivors. We're not Disneyworld, but it's a real fun day."

"Will Psycho and Chaser make an appearance?"

He placed his hand over his heart, looked hurt. "I'm not enough for you, Em?"

The man was larger than life. A sexy baseball superhero. Who was going to collect a kiss sometime today. "Merely curious."

"The Bat Pack will show, as well as a few other players. Anyone who's free today. We sign autographs. Talk a little baseball. Throw a few Frisbees, which Sky Dog retrieves, then delivers to the kids."

Emerson smelled a great human interest story. "I'm game."

"Change clothes and we'll hit the road."

She licked very dry lips. What should she do with Romeo while she switched outfits? Should she leave him in the entrance hall? Or invite him in? "You can wait in the living room if you like," she finally decided.

"I like." He followed her down the hall.

She could feel him behind her. So close that he'd run her over if she should stop. She walked a little faster.

The end of the hallway opened into an octagonal floor plan. Em viewed her home through Romeo's eyes as he took in the three split levels all connected by short, open stairwells. Without walls or doors, the open levels gave the space a feeling of freedom. The floor-to-ceiling windows to the east and west provided maximum sun exposure.

"Sweet damn," he said as he took six steps down into the sunken living room.

The room had been furnished with chunky, comfortable wood furniture. The earth tones were accented by sage and lavender throw pillows, and oriental rugs were scattered across the floor.

Four steps up was another level where bookshelves rimmed the entire southern wall. Here, leather-bound classics, poetry, and paperback best sellers mixed freely. Many pages had yellowed, the corners dog-eared. A few had broken spines. Emerson cherished both the old and the new. She'd read all the books once, some twice. Several three times. She took comfort in books. There was no better escape in life.

Gazing up, Romeo turned full circle. "You can see the entire condo in one sweep," he said admiringly.

"The kitchen and dining room are up the stairs and to the right. Breakfast and sunrise get me going in the morning. My office is on the left. Sunsets and moonlight help me to unwind."

"Bedrooms?" he asked. "Bath?"

"Two bedrooms, a guest and the master on the third level. Two full baths."

He rolled his tongue inside his cheek. "It's your design, isn't it?"

Romeo was the first visitor to feel her heartbeat in the walls.

"The architectural plans came from my amateur sketches."

"I like your place, Emerson Kent. It's not all girly-girl with sherbet hues. Your condo could be shared with a man. He'd feel at home here."

Shared with a man . . . not one of her immediate goals. Maybe someday, but not now. Although she might waver a little if Romeo continued to look at her with those warm brown eyes.

Leaving him to her collection of books, she shot up the stairs to her bedroom. It was set back from the landing, with connecting bamboo screens that could be opened or closed for privacy. She closed them now.

Tugging the Marlins jersey over her head, she hung it back in the closet, alongside her Yankees, Orioles, and Tampa Bay jerseys. A row of Atlanta Braves tomahawks chopped the waistband on her bikini panties. Romeo would not be pleased with her support of other ball clubs.

A slate-blue blouse, navy blue cropped pants, and peach Sketchers seemed appropriate for a casual day out-of-doors. Grabbing her hobo shoulder bag, she returned to Romeo.

The scent of burnt toast led her to the kitchen. She found him scraping the blackened edges on a slice of cinnamon bread into the sink.

"I wanted to make you breakfast." He glared at the toaster. "Your dark setting turns bread to charcoal."

She popped two new slices of cinnamon bread into the toaster and adjusted the dial. "Let's try again."

She poured Romeo a cup of coffee, buttered the toast, and grabbed a basket of fruit off the counter. She then motioned him to the kitchen table. A table piled with glossy magazines and displaying a small television at one end. She often read when she dined alone. When she cooked, she liked to have the TV on.

She took a seat across the table from him. Kept her chair pulled back so their knees wouldn't bump. She caught him hiding a smile. Romeo knew he made her nervous. He liked watching her twitch.

"This is a first," he stated. "My having breakfast with a woman without having spent the night."

"If your toast-making skills match your seduction—"

"I have a way of making things burn, Em," he returned with a slow smile. So slow and knowing, her nipples puckered.

He finished two slices of toast, then surprised her by flipping the calendar to December. "Do you decorate for the holidays?" he asked. "Between your sunken living room and high ceilings, I'm envisioning an enormous tree."

She loved talking about Christmas in April. "Last year I bought a twenty-foot evergreen. It took five men to secure it in my living room and four to take it down. I spent a fortune on ornaments and tinsel. I hung wreaths on the bookcase, bought a gingerbread house, placed a singing Santa in the entrance hall. My condo looked like the North Pole."

"All for you?" He finished off his coffee.

"All for me, Romeo. I don't need a man in my life to enjoy the holiday."

He leaned his elbows on the table. "You're a competent woman, Emerson Kent."

Too competent sometimes. The men she'd dated declared her independent. Oftentimes unresponsive, because she preferred her own company to theirs.

Though she was comfortable in her own skin, the heat in Romeo's eyes, the lazy curve of his smile, made her eager to spend time with him.

"Ready to go?" she nudged.

He rose, scooped up his dishes, and placed them in her sink. "Your call, Em—ride with me or take your own car."

The Viper was hot, the interior tight. What if he leaned over to kiss her? There'd be no escape.

Her BMW would allow her time alone; she

could listen to her favorite radio station, not have to worry about making conversation. She'd be safe. Sane. Secure.

"I'll ride with you." Her response surprised them both.

"Thought you'd prefer to drive yourself."

"Whatever gave you that idea?"

"You're a mass of nerves, sweetheart." His gaze lit on her arms, swinging at her sides, then hit the pulse at her throat. "You're all flitty and twitchy, with a wild heartbeat."

I'm waiting for you to kiss me. She was on pins and needles and not herself. "I'm excited about Hollywood Harts," she fibbed. "The sanctuary will make great copy."

"Anticipation." He had the nerve to wink. "The thought of a dancing pig, a miniature horse, and an acrobatic monkey turns me inside out."

Pig grunts, the sound of a dog barking, and a soft meow announced Romeo's arrival at Hollywood Harts. Exiting his Viper, he scanned the fifty-acre reserve where the retired animal stars ran free.

Emerson held back, her expression one of interest as she jotted down notes on a yellow pad.

The first animal to approach them was Fancy, the square-dancing pig from an eight-season run on *Tanglefoot Creek*. Known for her yellow ruffled petticoat and cherry-red dance skirt, she could do-si-do and allemande left with the best of them. All at two hundred pounds.

141

Romeo patted her pink head. "You're looking thin, Fancy. Sophie have you on a diet?"

"You have a way with words, Romeo. All females love being told they've lost weight. Even my sweet pig."

Romeo looked up to find Sophie Hart walking his way. She had crimped blond hair, soft curves, and a deep love for animals. She welcomed him with a hug.

A silver German shepherd with the golden eyes of a wolf came next. Outfitted in a red, white, and blue cape and silver boots, Sky Dog had six superhero movies to his name. He'd played the sidekick to Captain Venture and Dash Danger. A mighty crime-fighting canine.

Sky Dog wagged his tail in greeting, then wandered toward the Viper to sniff Emerson.

A limping American curl followed more slowly. ZZ Paws, the short-haired tiger cat with ears that curled back from her face, soon wound between his legs. She was ready to perform in her black vest and matching kitty leggings. She'd played on *Clawed Mystery Theater*. The feline who chased cat burglars.

"Arthritis?" Romeo asked Sophie when ZZ didn't jump into his arms. He bent instead and scooped her up to his chest. The American curl purred against his shoulder.

"Animals age like people," Sophie reminded him. "They have similar aches and pains as they grow older."

Romeo glanced toward the enormous white-washed barn with the bright blue doors. Silver maples framed the corners. Ivy twined over its shaded contours. The sounds of the city and screaming ballpark fans were forgotten in the stillness of the land. He liked the quiet, which would be broken as soon as the children arrived.

"Who showed up?" he asked Sophie.

"Psycho, Chaser, and Chris Collier."

Romeo spiked a brow. "Collier?"

"Psycho's none too happy, but he's promised not to act out in front of the kids."

"I'll keep an eye on him."

"Who, then, will keep an eye on the lady?" Sophie nodded toward his Viper.

A Viper with its door swung wide. With ZZ Paws still clutched to his chest, Romeo crossed to Emerson's side. "This is Emerson Kent from the *Virginia Banner*. Emerson, meet Sophie Hart," he said.

Sophie looked surprised. "You didn't tell me there'd be press."

"It was a spur-of-the-moment invitation," Romeo informed her. Bending slightly, he held ZZ with one hand as he assisted Emerson from his low-slung car with the other.

Sophie took in his solicitous manner, then turned and shot Romeo an amused grin.

He shrugged. "First time for everything."

Sophie's grin widened. "Welcome, Emerson." She gently dislodged a purring ZZ from Romeo's arms, then passed the cat to Emerson. "Meet ZZ Paws."

143

Em held the cat as if the creature were porcelain and breakable. Aside from Sophie, Romeo had never seen anyone handle an animal with so much care. The American curl responded with loud purring and a slow kneading of her paws against Emerson's right arm.

Emerson looked up and smiled at Romeo.

The urge to kiss her hit him so intensely, he could barely breathe. She owed him a kiss and he didn't care who saw him take it. Sophie, the animals, or the busload of children pulling into the parking lot.

"Romeo?" Sophie elbowed him hard.

He blinked. Came to his senses. There would be no quick kiss. When he claimed Emerson, the kiss would be special. In private. And dragged out until their lips went numb.

"What?" He turned to Sophie.

Her eyes laughed at him, as if she found him incredibly amusing. There was nothing funny about his situation. All he'd done was stare at Emerson. The woman's smile tied his insides in knots.

"Help me prepare the animals for their performances," Sophie requested. "It's time to get them into their costumes."

Romeo motioned Em to join them. "Behind-the-scenes action. Good notes for your article."

They crossed the yard and entered the barn through a set of sliding glass doors. The animals followed at their own pace. Sophie's home was airy and splashed with sunlight. The animals' nails and hooves clicked on the blond hardwood floors. A big-screen television was positioned on one wall. An enormous ballroom mirror, the kind found in ballet studios, hung near a ramp slanted toward the loft where Sophie slept.

Three wooden tables bordered the kitchen. All of different heights. Bowls of kibble were scattered around the floor. Buckets of water stood damp at their bases. Testimony that slurping was allowed.

Animals were as welcome in Sophie's home as any man or woman. The barn was set up to accommodate their needs as well as her own.

Romeo watched as Emerson nuzzled ZZ Paws, then slowly released her. Turning slightly, she touched his arm. Her eyes were wide and bright, her expression appreciative. "Thanks for inviting me."

Her touch to his forearm shot straight to his groin. Inappropriate and unwanted images sprang into his mind. Images of her nails raking his back and her hand working him to hardness. Images that taunted his body and had him shifting his stance. Clearing his throat, he managed, "The sanctuary's a great place to spend your day off."

Before he could add anything further, Psycho came through the main door. Dressed all in black, including his baseball cap, he informed them, "The kids have filled the bleachers."

"They've started to chant 'Sky Dog,' " Chaser added from the doorway.

"Where's Chris Collier?" Sophie asked Psycho.

Psycho shrugged. "Around."

"*Where* around?" Sophie pressed.

"Wimbledon's keeping company with Hogan."

Sophie shot Psycho an exasperated look. "I left *you* in charge of the African gray."

"Life craps enough on me," Psycho returned, unrepentant. "I don't need a bird on my shoulder."

Worry scored Sophie's brow. "Hogan gets nervous around people he doesn't know well. His bill is as sharp as a can opener. If he's not properly positioned, he could take off a lip—"

"If told to kiss," Psycho said innocently.

"You didn't?" Sophie glared at Psycho.

"He did." Chris Collier joined them in the barn. Hogan was now perched on his right wrist. The parrot's feathers were as ruffled as Collier's expression. One corner of the man's mouth dripped blood onto his starched white dress shirt.

"Hogan, *fly*," Sophie commanded. The parrot flew across the barn and landed on her shoulder. There, he flapped his wings and shrieked. "Kiss, Wim-ble, kiss Wim-ble-don." The bird hiccupped on the third syllable. Hogan mimicked Psycho's voice so perfectly, everyone knew who had encouraged the bird to take off Collier's lip.

"Tattletale," Psycho muttered.

Sophie stroked Hogan's gray back. White patches surrounded his eyes. Red tail feathers gave him color. "African grays are smart and vocal," Sophie told Chris. "Hogan has a two-hundred-fifty-word vocabulary. On top of that, he's a mimic."

Romeo glanced at his watch. "Twenty minutes until showtime, Sophie. You doctor Chris's lip and the rest of us will get the animals into costume."

Sophie scanned the barn. "Sky Dog and ZZ are dressed to perform. That leaves Fancy, Tobias, and Gigolo."

"We've got it covered," Romeo assured her.

Sophie blew him a kiss of gratitude.

"What can I do?" Emerson was first to ask.

"You're here to observe. There's no need for you to participate," Romeo returned.

"I'll make this a hands-on article."

Romeo took over the group. "Chaser can dress Tobias, the miniature packhorse from the *Gold Rush* miniseries on CBS. Tobias needs saddlebags and that white cowboy hat with the holes cut for his ears."

Chaser nodded, then went to retrieve Tobias's costume from hooks by the door. "Off to the horse pen," he shot back over his shoulder.

"I'll deal with Gigolo, the spider monkey who played Pat Morrison's sidekick in *Palm Beach Streets*," Romeo continued. "Gigolo sometimes fights getting into his tux."

"That leaves Fancy," Emerson noted.

"You and Psycho can tackle her together."

"Hello, Reporter," Romeo heard Psycho say as Emerson crossed to where he now stood.

"Hello, Benchwarmer."

Romeo watched as one of his best buddies and the woman he wanted to bed made eye contact

147

until Psycho nodded and accepted her participation. "We're stuck dressing Fannie."

"*Fancy*," Em corrected.

"The pig gets my humor. I grate on Sophie's nerves."

Emerson Kent knew Psycho could be a royal pain in the ass. He was dark and dangerous and disrespectful. She found him more amusing than annoying.

A glance toward Romeo fitting the spider monkey in a tux drew her smile. The monkey squirmed and chattered, and withdrew his arms before Romeo could fasten the tiny front buttons on his little black jacket.

Romeo was a patient man. His tone was soothing as he gentled the monkey into his costume. Once dressed, Gigolo showed off with a series of back flips. Which Romeo applauded.

Heartwarming, Emerson thought. Catching the Rogues out of their element was well worth the trip.

The men were more than bat-swinging superstars. They cared about life outside the ballpark. Even Psycho couldn't hide his affection for the big pink pig.

"I could use a little help here," Psycho said.

He and Fancy now stood before the ballroom mirror. The pig's snout was pressed to the glass as she appeared to admire herself. "Take one end of the petticoat and wrap it under her belly," Psycho instructed. Em did as she was told.

"Fancy's put on a few pounds," Psycho grunted

as he struggled with the top snap. As if irritated by his weight-gain comment, the pig shifted sideways, nearly knocking him over. "I can't help it if the petticoat makes your butt look big."

"Sanctuary rules, Psycho," Sophie called from the kitchen, where she was working on Chris Collier's lip.

Psycho rolled his eyes and recited, "Never shout, curse, belittle, or harm any of the animals." He then lowered his voice for Em's ears alone. "You should see how pissed Sophie gets when I ask the price of bacon."

Emerson couldn't contain her laughter. Psycho was sinfully bad, his humor out of control, yet she found she liked him.

"You get me." One corner of his lip curled in a half smile. He then nodded toward Romeo. "Smile and wave at the man so he doesn't think I'm rack-jacking."

Emerson turned to find Romeo staring at her. His slitted gaze shifted from her to Psycho. "Trying to steal my reporter?" he asked his teammate.

"If I was?"

"I'd have to hurt you."

"I'm not into pain today."

Romeo's face relaxed. "Put on Fancy's square-dancing skirt and she can lead the parade."

It took all Emerson's strength and a little help from Psycho to tug the red custom-made skirt over the yellow crinoline.

"Cut back on the sweet corn," Psycho whispered in the pig's ear, "and I'll buy you a boar."

"Animals aren't brought here to breed." Sophie had overheard Psycho's comment.

Psycho patted Fancy's head. "We'll work her down."

Sophie shot Psycho a my-word-is-law look. "Are we ready?" she asked.

He looked down at Fancy. "Ready to rock 'n,' roll?"

"It's barn dancing," Sophie reminded him. "Don't confuse her." The trainer crossed to her pig. "She looks pretty."

"A real silk purse out of a sow's ear."

"*Psycho!*" Her tone threatened bodily harm.

Psycho moved beyond her reach. "Let's get this show on the road."

Emerson watched as Sophie and Fancy led the parade. Chaser came next with Tobias, the miniature horse. Psycho trotted beside Sky Dog. Romeo followed with the acrobatic Gigolo. Chris Collier, sporting a fat lip, had taken Hogan back on his shoulder. In Em's eyes, the man was a team player.

When she heard an insistent meow, Emerson scooped up ZZ Paws. They got in line behind Collier.

The children sat on bleachers beneath an enormous tent, bags of popcorn and soft drinks in hand. They ranged in age from three to thirteen. Many of the cancer survivors were bald, pale, and weak. Yet all had indomitable spirit. Their excitement topped that of the crowds at any ballpark.

The animals' performances did not disappoint.

Each one showed off as if being filmed for prime-time television or for the silver screen.

Hogan's *dive bombing* left everyone breathless as the African gray spread his wings and took flight. He swept skyward, steadily climbing, then suddenly spiraled back to earth, his wings flat against his body, a streak of gray and red tail feathers.

With split-second timing, the parrot leveled out and made a smooth landing on Sophie's outstretched arm. Hogan earned a standing ovation.

When it came time for Fancy's barn dance, Emerson stood to the side and watched Sophie select two children from the audience, a boy and a girl. She then asked for one of the Rogues to volunteer as well.

Sophie's gaze lit on Psycho, but he shook his head. "I've two left feet."

Before Sophie could call on Chaser, Romeo stepped forward. "It's my day to dance."

Fancy squealed as loudly as the crowd. The pink pig in the yellow ruffled petticoat and red overskirt was as taken by the third baseman as Emerson herself.

Forming a square, Sophie showed the children the steps. Romeo was opposite a little girl with peach fuzz hair. The young boy partnered with Fancy.

Inserting a tape into a recorder, Sophie called the steps to the tune of "Turkey in the Straw." She slowed down the call so the kids could keep up. The audience clapped throughout the do-si-dos and allemande lefts.

Once the music ended, Romeo stepped aside, insisting the children take a bow alongside Fancy. Emotion hit Emerson so hard, her breath stuck in her lungs.

Warmth and kindness radiated from this man with the reputation of bringing women to orgasm with just a look. While Psycho, Chaser, and Chris Collier gently threw Frisbees for Sky Dog to retrieve, Romeo worked the bleachers, his smile steady as he shook hands and hugged every child in attendance.

Every visitor left the sanctuary with a heart full of memories. Beyond the memories, Emerson took away a new respect for Romeo Bellisaro. He might be sexy on the outside, but he also had a giving, caring spirit. A man to be admired.

When the bus pulled out, Emerson looked at Sophie, "What's next? Removing costumes? Cleanup?"

"There's no reason for you to stay," Sophie said. "Chris has offered to help with the animals, so go enjoy the rest of your day."

Emerson noted that the Bat Pack stood their ground. "We don't mind helping," Psycho said. "We back the sanctuary—"

"As does Chris." A hint of color pinkened Sophie's cheeks. "He made a generous donation when he arrived."

Psycho pulled out his wallet. "I'll double his donation—"

"Knock it off, Psycho. This isn't a contest." Sophie stopped him from shelling out cash. "The three of you are major contributors, but smaller donations support the sanctuary as well."

The softening of Sophie's expression when Chris approached told of her interest in the pitcher. The attraction appeared mutual. Chris's gaze remained on the trainer even when Psycho moaned, "Ah, hell, Sophie, not Wimbledon."

Romeo proved more sympathetic. "I'm gone. Catch you in two weeks, Sophie. Larger crowd next time. We'll need three buses for the kids coming from foster care."

Sophie waved them off.

"No speeding tickets." Romeo's shouted reminder was lost on Psycho. The wild man gunned the engine of his Dodge Ram as he peeled out.

Moments later, Chaser's GTO rumbled to life. The muscle car looked as good as it had in 1968. "That man treats his car as well as any woman," Romeo told Em.

Once seated in the Viper, Emerson decided it had been a spectacular morning. Hollywood Harts would make a great article. She sighed contentedly.

Romeo reached for her hand and squeezed it lightly. "Good day?" he asked.

She nodded. "I never thought—"

"You'd enjoy spending time with me?"

"This was work related."

"This . . . isn't."

Unexpectedly, Romeo leaned across the console and kissed her. Not a you-owe-me kiss, but one born of warmth and promised pleasure. She gasped at the suddenness of it.

Tilting his head left, then right, he took her mouth from both angles. A prolonged, open-mouthed kiss, both intimate and impassioned.

Emerson leaned into him.

Still, he didn't touch her.

No stroking, caressing. No need for hands.

It was all in his kiss.

The soft press of his lips. The penetration of his tongue. Slow, then fast. Raking the roof of her mouth, then thrusting deep. A building mating rhythm that left her heart pounding at an orgasmic rate.

The single kiss went on and on, showing no signs of ending. He tasted of moist hunger and profound need.

Emerson Kent came undone.

Her scalp tingled.

Her heartbeat sounded in her ears.

Her breasts swelled beneath her slate-blue blouse. Her nipples were now pebble-hard.

Her skin was super sensitive.

Heat pooled in her belly, shot lower. She wiggled on the car seat. Wanted his hands on her.

He made no move to feel her up.

His kiss grew hotter, more demanding. More sinful as he flicked his tongue over her upper lip, then nipped her bottom one. Then sucked both hard.

Her hands curled and her nails scored her palms.

Her breath came in hot, short pants. Had that

deep moan risen from her throat? She'd gone mindless as the pleasure became a taunting tease.

The tease of a man skilled in kissing.

So skilled, she climaxed.

She was a boneless mass of spasms and satisfaction as her ragged sigh broke against his mouth.

One final flick of his tongue and Romeo eased back.

Shaky, Emerson forced herself to look at him. Look at him through steamed-up glasses. She'd expected smug dominance. He granted her mercy. Not a word was spoken as he started the Viper.

His kiss had said it all.

EIGHT

Fatigue and the challenge of a busy day rode with Jen Reid from James River Stadium to her family home on Hamilton Street. A street she could locate with her eyes closed.

Her heart warmed at the sight of the wood-and-brick two-story house. She'd grown up on this quiet street edged with Virginia pines. Pink and red hollyhocks defined the property lines, thick as a fence and far more fragrant.

Generations of families lived side by side, the children returning to the neighborhood as Jen had done when her father had died. Although she'd had her own apartment in New York City, she'd chosen to live with her mother on her return. She and Katherine needed each other. They both missed Big John. Though her mother was a strong person and actively involved in the community, both Katherine and Jen found evenings the hardest. It was hard not to remember the nights when Big John's hearty laugh and daily stories had held them in the kitchen long after dessert.

She climbed out of her El Camino, noting the rows of clay and peat pots across the front of the house. The seeds had been planted, and now they were waiting for gold dwarf marigolds to make a summer appearance.

She glanced next door, toward Chase Tallan's house. He'd purchased it from his parents when they'd retired to Arizona. An outside porch light burned, but there was no shadowed silhouette or visible activity.

Nor any sign of his GTO. Chaser had the night free from baseball, so he probably had a hot date. She wrinkled her nose at the thought.

The scent of sugar and cinnamon met her at the side door. She closed her eyes and breathed deeply, instantly soothed.

Just beyond the pantry, voices rose from the kitchen.

One light with laughter.

Her mother.

The second, deep and masculine. Teasing.

Chaser.

Her heart jumped. He wasn't out on a date. Instead he was camped at her kitchen table, eating ovenwarm Snickerdoodles as fast as her mother could slide them from the cookie sheet and onto a plate.

Katherine doted on Will and Jacqueline's boy. Her mother still saw Chaser as ten and growing.

Jen saw him as a man.

A big, broad-shouldered man who'd glanced over his shoulder and was now checking her out. His clear blue gaze skimmed her pale pink T-shirt and skinny black jeans. He'd never looked at her so long or so intently. Nor with so much heat.

His stare made her nervous. Her hands fluttered at her sides and her stomach gave an unexpected twist.

"Cookie?" he offered, holding up the plate.

She snatched one, broke it in half. It was moist and delicious. "I thought we'd decided on peanut butter." She sent a look toward her mother. Peanut butter was her favorite.

Katherine pulled the last cookie sheet from the oven and set it on an iron trivet to cool. "Chaser showed up and requested Snickerdoodles. He always liked them as a kid."

"No one bakes like your mother," Chaser stated.

"He's requested a German chocolate cake on Saturday," Katherine informed Jen.

"I asked for angel food." Her mother baked cookies on Mondays and Thursdays. A cake on Saturday. Jen loved cake.

"Come on, Legs," Chaser implored. "I'm a guest in your home."

Guest, her ass. "You *lived* here as a kid," Jen reminded him. "Big John had to toss you over the hollyhocks at bedtime."

"The man could throw."

Katherine untied her apron, hung it on a hook. "You two battle it out." She tapped the cover of her cookbook with one finger. "Leave me a note as to your decision." Glancing at her watch, she finished with "I'm off to church. The spring bazaar is on Saturday and I'm helping to price donations. Chaser gave a team-signed baseball and two Rogues jerseys. Wasn't that sweet?"

Sweet enough to give him cake advantage on Saturday. German chocolate was her second favorite, but Jen had been tasting angel food.

Jen watched her slim, petite mother hurry from the room. She had a lot of energy for a woman in her sixties. Jen had gotten her height from her father. Her black hair and green eyes from her mother.

"Are we going to battle over cake?" Chaser rose from the table and came to stand before her.

Feeling overpowered by his maleness, she pressed her back against the counter. She flattened her palms against his chest. Held him off. "Size and intimidation won't work, big guy."

"Who's intimidating?" His sugary warm breath fanned her cheek as he planted both hands on the counter on either side of her hips, rocking forward until their bodies touched.

With the counter at her back and Chaser at her front, Jen felt flustered. They'd been in this same position a hundred times before. Him cornering her to get his way. He would tease and tower until she gave in. Before, she'd always felt safe and protected by his closeness. Today she felt aroused.

The sudden punch of his heartbeat echoed her

own. Like filings to a magnet, the pull between them was inescapable. Their bodies touched more intimately. Her nipples poked the hard wall of his chest; her belly was flush with his groin.

A groin that stirred.

The stirring drove Chaser back a step. He turned away from her, color working up his neck. Embarrassment struck him as hard as his erection. His breath hissed through his teeth as he threw back his head and stared at the ceiling.

Seconds stretched into minutes before he managed, "I came by to set you up on a date. The man's name is Josh Burke, an old friend and a nice guy. He's in real estate. Financially secure."

"I'm not sure—" she said to the back of his head.

He spun around. "Don't let Dane Maxin put you off men. We can double if you like. You'll be safe with me, Jen."

Safe with him? A part of her wanted to throw herself in his arms and see how unsafe she could be. Her saner self asked, "What kind of date?"

"Something simple. A late afternoon outing, light and easy. It doesn't have to run into the evening. Josh suggested a Parade of Homes."

Jen blinked. "A tour of model homes?"

Chaser nodded. "Josh is the realtor for a new residential development north of town. For tax purposes, he suggested I invest in a couple of the homes as rental property. I thought I'd check them out tomorrow afternoon following the game."

She looked around her mother's kitchen. Their

home had been built in 1935. The room was small, but homey. "Might be fun to see the new construction."

"You can collect ideas on how to redecorate your kitchen."

Her heart slowed. She shook her head. "Redecorating? No one's planning any changes."

He looked suddenly pained. "An oversight on your mother's part. She's been contemplating new cabinets and countertops and a fresh coat of paint for some time. She's so busy, she may have forgotten to tell you."

"Yet she found time to discuss it with you." A dull ache settled in her chest. The kitchen was done in yellow and gold; filled with warmth and laughter. There was no need for change. The room still held the love and vitality of her father. She wanted things left the way they were.

"Nothing's going to happen overnight, Legs," he reassured her. "When you're ready, I'll strap on my tool belt, haul over my paintbrushes and roller, and go to work."

A distinct image of a shirtless Chaser in low-riding jeans hit Jen square between the eyes. Whether catching a baseball or wielding a hammer, the man had large capable hands. She shivered with the thought of how those hands would feel on her body.

"Guess change is inevitable," she finally managed.

"You'll get used to the idea."

"What makes you so sure?"

Kate Angell

"You're the most resilient person I know. No matter the circumstance, you bounce back. If new cabinets and paint make your mother happy, you'll go along with it."

She crossed her arms over her chest. "I'll agree to the redecorating in exchange for angel food cake on Saturday."

"No deal."

She stuck out her tongue.

And Chaser's mouth parted.

French-kissing came to mind. She wanted to slip her tongue between his lips. Engage in lots of tangling and teasing and penetrating thrusts. An oral preliminary to hot, sweaty sex.

Her breathing hitched and her knees gave out. She sought a kitchen chair. "How was the road trip?" she asked.

"Humiliating as hell." Chaser moved to the refrigerator.

"The Rogues took a game against the Marlins."

"The win didn't alter the standings. We should be leading the league; instead we're sitting in last place."

"Four more games and you're back on the field. You've been working out, staying in shape."

He patted his flat stomach, grinning. "I *was* in shape until I ate a tray of your mother's cookies."

The tray of cookies wouldn't run to fat. The man had a solid six-pack. And buns of steel, Jen noted as he poured himself a second glass of milk and returned to the table.

"Meet anyone on the road?" She'd asked the

162

question countless times, yet tonight her heart slowed in anticipation. She found herself afraid to hear his answer.

Out-of-town games and one-night stands were as much a part of baseball as the game itself. Groupies gathered at the hotel, available and willing. How could any single man resist glossy red lips ready to lick more than a lollypop?

A part of Jen wanted Chaser to resist.

She wanted him to come home to her.

Chaser took his sweet time answering. He slid lower on his chair, stretched out his legs, and studied her with those unreadable ice-blue eyes. For the first time ever, he made her nervous. So nervous, she reached for a cookie, broke it in half, then tried to fit it together again.

The cookie crumbled.

She then toyed with the edge on a red woven place mat, ran her tongue over her teeth, and crossed her legs. Her right foot pumped to the beat of her heart. She avoided his gaze for as long as she could. Eventually she looked up.

She found his eyes narrowed, his expression thoughtful. He ran his hand down his face, then leaned forward on his chair. "Do you want to hear about the sheet-burning sex in Atlanta or about the headboard-banging in Miami?"

Jen swore her heart stopped. She felt the color drain from her face. In times past, she would have been able to listen and laugh over the women who shared his bed.

Tonight, however, something had shifted.

She didn't want to hear his stories.

She wanted . . . wanted—

"Listen to me, Jen." Chaser's voice reached across the table, deep, yet soft, as if he was about to tell her a secret. "Atlanta was hot, the dugout pure hell. Returning from the park, I bought a bag of peanut M&M's from the gift shop at the hotel and called it dinner. I watched an hour of television, zoned out long before midnight.

"In Miami," he continued, "I had a beer with Romeo and Psycho in celebration of our win. All three of us called it an early night."

"You're over the hill."

"I'd call it becoming selective. Screwing around gets old. I, uh—" He hesitated. "Want sleeping with a woman to be more than a hit-and-run. A good-bye kiss in a hotel lobby leaves a lot to be desired."

Jen absorbed the change in Chaser. He was no longer interested in road-trip sex. She wondered how many women he'd date before he finally settled down.

"Who's your date for the Parade of Homes?" she asked. Her heart squeezed at the thought of seeing Chaser with another woman.

"Amber Parrish. You met her at Romeo's Christmas open house last December."

Jen remembered the woman. The former Miss Virginia had a tumble of dark hair, a beauty mark at one corner of her mouth, and a body that made men hard in a heartbeat.

Jen had never seen the woman without her

GET UP TO 4 FREE BOOKS!

You can have the best romance delivered to your door for less than what you'd pay in a bookstore or online. Sign up for one of our book clubs today, and we'll send you **FREE* BOOKS** just for trying it out...**with no obligation to buy, ever!**

HISTORICAL ROMANCE BOOK CLUB

Travel from the Scottish Highlands to the American West, the decadent ballrooms of Regency England to Viking ships. Your shipments will include authors such as CONNIE MASON, CASSIE EDWARDS, LYNSAY SANDS, LEIGH GREENWOOD, and many, many more.

LOVE SPELL BOOK CLUB

Bring a little magic into your life with the romances of Love Spell—fun contemporaries, paranormals, time-travels, futuristics, and more. Your shipments will include authors such as KATIE MacALISTER, SUSAN GRANT, NINA BANGS, SANDRA HILL, and more.

As a book club member you also receive the following special benefits:

- **30% OFF all orders through our website & telecenter!**
  (Plus, you still get 1 book FREE for every 5 books you buy!)
- **Exclusive access to special discounts!**
- **Convenient home delivery and 10 days to return any books you don't want to keep.**

There is no minimum number of books to buy, and you may cancel membership at any time. See back to sign up!

*Please include $2.00 for shipping and handling.

YES! ☐

Sign me up for the **Historical Romance Book Club** and send my TWO FREE BOOKS! If I choose to stay in the club, I will pay only $8.50* each month, a savings of $5.48!

YES! ☐

Sign me up for the **Love Spell Book Club** and send my TWO FREE BOOKS! If I choose to stay in the club, I will pay only $8.50* each month, a savings of $5.48!

NAME: _____

ADDRESS: _____

_____

TELEPHONE: _____

E-MAIL: _____

☐ **I WANT TO PAY BY CREDIT CARD.**

☐ VISA   ☐ MasterCard.   ☐ DISCOVER

ACCOUNT #: _____

EXPIRATION DATE: _____

SIGNATURE: _____

Send this card along with $2.00 shipping & handling for each club you wish to join, to:

Romance Book Clubs
1 Mechanic Street
Norwalk, CT 06850-3431

Or fax (must include credit card information!) to: 610.995.9274. You can also sign up online at www.dorchesterpub.com.

*Plus $2.00 for shipping. Offer open to residents of the U.S. and Canada only. Canadian residents please call 1.800.481.9191 for pricing information.

If under 18, a parent or guardian must sign. Terms, prices and conditions subject to change. Subscription subject to acceptance. Dorchester Publishing reserves the right to reject any order or cancel any subscription.

JOIN NOW!

rhinestone headband, which at first glance looked strikingly like a tiara. Amber lived life on fast-forward. Self-absorbed, she liked conversation to be centered on her.

"I look forward to seeing her again," Jen lied.

The corners of Chaser's mouth twitched, but he didn't fully smile. Straightening, he got off his chair. Once standing, he stretched his hands toward the ceiling until his back cracked. "Catch you tomorrow after the game."

"See you then," Jen called to him as he ducked through the side door.

Chaser pulled into Jen's driveway at five o'clock. He flicked off the radio without having heard a single song. Thirty minutes had passed in which Amber Parrish had chatted endlessly about her day while Chaser half listened. Amber was so into herself, she didn't expect him to respond, so he only gave an occasional nod.

Why had he chosen Amber for this date? Because she was the total opposite of Jen, and he wanted to keep things light. He knew Amber well enough not to be tempted by her. Amber understood he wasn't offering more than an afternoon trip to view model homes. They'd wrapped up any attempt at intimacy long ago. She'd wanted Chaser to give while she took. Once the woman was satisfied, she'd left him hanging. He'd gotten tired of walking out her door with a hard-on.

Jen was now the woman who held his attention. She had for the past week. He couldn't get her off his mind. Ever since their unexpected kiss at the ballpark, she'd looked at him differently. He stared as well, fully aware the girl next door was an amazing woman.

He just wasn't sure how to take their relationship to the next level. Or whether it was even wise to try.

He swung his car door open, just as Jen came through the front door. Her steps were as flowing as her calf-length dress in pale yellow with sprigs of blue flowers. She looked fresh and wholesome with her long black hair hanging free.

"Hi, Jenny," Amber greeted Jen, who hated to be called Jenny.

Chaser shot Jen an apologetic look as he rounded the hood of his car. "Three in front?" he offered.

Jen hesitated. "I'll ride in back."

Chaser pulled open the passenger door and she climbed in. Once he returned to the driver's side and settled himself, she caught his eye in the rearview mirror. He slid his dark Killer Loops down his nose and met her gaze.

His best friend blushed. "Sorry about your loss," Jen managed.

"*Loss?* Who died? Anyone I know?" Amber asked. "When's the funeral?"

"We're talking baseball," Chaser told his date. "Rogues fell to the Red Sox, 5–1."

"Oh." The game didn't hold as much interest for her as someone dying. Amber patted her hair, fiddled with her headband. "Win some, lose some."

"Some get rained out," Chaser and Jen said simultaneously.

He held Jen's gaze for a dozen seconds before she looked away. An odd response from someone who'd once beat him at staring contests when they were kids. He'd always blinked first.

Repositioning his sunglasses, he focused on driving. It took fifty minutes to reach the model homes. Time passed slowly with Amber's one-sided telling of her new position as spokesperson for Size-down, a weight loss program that promoted protein shakes and granola bars.

"The shakes taste like raw eggs and the bars like tree bark," Amber confessed. "But put me in an infomercial and I'd chew nails."

Jen coughed from the backseat. Glancing in the rearview mirror, Chaser spotted her hands covering her mouth as she contained her laughter. He suddenly wanted to park the car, climb over the seat, and join her in the back.

He wanted them to laugh and tease and enjoy each other. He didn't want her to overthink their heat.

"Look at those houses," Amber gasped as they passed an empty guardhouse and followed flapping orange flags to a nicely wooded cul-de-sac. Here, three-story traditional brick homes were displayed on double lots. "Impressive, wouldn't you say?"

"Could make for a good investment," Chaser agreed.

"Maybe it's time for you to move?" Amber suggested. "Your neighborhood is so *Leave It to Beaver.*"

Chaser restrained himself from giving his reasons for staying. They all centered on his friend, Jen. With his bank accountant, he had money enough to buy an entire suburb. Yet he liked living next to the Reids.

When Jen had moved to New York, her parents were just a jump over the hollyhocks. They'd kept him informed of her ballet performances. When Jen moved home after Big John's death, he liked the fact that only a driveway separated them.

It had taken an unexpected kiss at the ballpark for him to see her as more than a friend. He wasn't about to turn back now. He wanted to see where a second kiss might lead.

Before him, people swarmed the sidewalks. Cars jammed both sides of the roadway. Chaser circled the model homes twice before he found a place to park. Beside him, Amber fluttered with excitement. She'd jerked the door handle and left the car before he'd cut the engine. She gave him her beauty queen wave. "I'll follow the signs and catch you inside." She was soon lost in the stream of visitors.

Apparently model homes excited her more than having Chaser as her escort. He let Amber go.

Glancing back at Jen, he found her gazing out the window, her hair shadowing her face. Only the arc of one brow, the tip of her nose, and the point of her chin were visible to him.

Even in profile, she looked soft, desirable. He

had the urge to reach across the seat, brush her hair off her cheek, skim his fingers—

She turned to him suddenly, caught him staring.

Her eyes went wide, her lips parted softly.

His heart slammed against his ribs.

She hesitated a moment before saying, "Stop staring at me."

"I'm not staring."

"Yes, you were. I caught you looking in the rearview mirror. At least twenty times."

It was probably more like thirty. "I was checking traffic."

"I felt your eyes."

He turned sideways, draped his arm over the seat. One corner of his mouth curved. "You were watching me watching you?"

She sucked in a breath. "Just . . . stop."

He didn't want to stop. She was easy on the eyes. He'd watched her all his life. They'd shared rattles and playpens. At age five, his G.I. Joe had declared war on her Barbie Dream House. Barbie had kicked Joe's ass. He'd sat through her ballet lessons and volleyball practices and had taught her to drive.

Right after she'd moved to New York, he'd traveled to the city on several occasions. Her performances in *A Midsummer Night's Dream* and *Sleeping Beauty* would live always in his memory. Jen was liquid grace.

Following the applause and backstage congratulations, he and Jen had snuck off for a late-night dinner at 21, New York's most famous speakeasy.

The beautiful ballerina had more requests for autographs than the Rogue at her side.

Chaser had watched and admired the time Jen took with each fan. The thought of watching her for the rest of his life made sense. He wasn't, however, sure Jen was ready for him.

Last evening in her kitchen, he'd cringed, embarrassed at his physical response to her closeness. This was a first for both of them. It would not be the last time electricity sparked between them. They'd be thrown together often during these double dates.

He nodded toward the model home. "Ready to go inside and meet Josh Burke?"

"More than ready." Her relief was evident.

They walked up the sidewalk together. Lifted on the breeze, her gauzy skirt fanned out and flirted with his thigh. Jen jerked her skirt down, flattening the material against her own long legs.

A man jarred her shoulder at the crush near the front door of the first model home. Jen swayed sideways, and Chaser caught her shoulder. He was slow to release her.

She looked up at him.

He looked down at her.

Suddenly, every person pushing to get inside faded away. "You're always there to catch me," she said.

"I'd never let you fall."

She bit down on her bottom lip. "I know."

The ornate oak door with its arched beveled window stood ajar. Jen preceded him into the foyer. Voices drew them into the living room. Stark white and mirrored, the richly furnished room invited people to stand, not sit. Visitors skirted the white leather couch, gave a wide berth to the ivory baby grand piano.

Chaser found Josh Burke quoting preconstruction prices to a young couple. Spotting Chaser, Josh waved, wrapped up his conversation, then crossed to where he and Jen stood.

"Great to see you, Chaser." Josh slapped him on the shoulder. "This must be Jen."

Chaser watched as the two shook hands. He tried to see Josh through Jen's eyes. A man of almost six feet, with curly brown hair and a lot of business hustle.

"Can I show you around?" Josh asked Jen.

"Go with him." Chaser nudged her forward. "I need to find Amber."

"Amber . . ." Josh pursed his lips.

"Miss Virginia 2003," Jen supplied.

Josh nodded. "The lady with the tiara?"

"It's actually a headband," Jen corrected.

"I saw her. She snatched a brochure, then shot through the house like her shoes were on fire," Josh remembered. "I think she left for the Stratton model next door."

Chaser blew out a breath. Tracking his date could take a while. When he noticed Josh pressing his palm to Jen's back and steering her toward the kitchen, he held back, wanting to keep an eye on the two of them.

Touching was allowed only in moderation.

He'd catch up with Amber when she came full circle.

Chaser wandered the first model, then the second, falling back among the visitors so as not to appear more interested in Jen than in the Parade of Homes. She seemed to be enjoying herself. Smiling, conversing, showing interest in the designs and furnishings. She took a long time in each kitchen, studying the granite countertops, the raised panel cupboards and double ovens.

Chaser moved closer in the third model, eavesdropping as Josh exposed floor plans, price ranges, and the occasional comment on how attractive Jen was.

"Have dinner with me," Josh requested.

As if sensing that Chaser was near, Jen scanned the game room. She found him by the billiard table. "Dinner?" she mouthed.

Chaser wound around the table and joined them. "Team meeting tonight. I'm tied up."

"I'll see you home," Josh told Jen.

Jen looked at Chaser, then back at Josh. "I'd like that."

Chaser wasn't the least bit happy. Although he'd lined them up, he hadn't expected them to go off alone. He clenched his teeth to prevent himself from insisting that Jen return with him. Josh was a decent guy. Chaser had promised Jen an opportunity to date. He backed off.

"Chaser, there you are!" Amber Parrish flew across the game room to his side. "I've seen all the homes and am ready to go."

"Not before Chaser and I have time to talk business," Josh said. "He needs to invest before the prices skyrocket."

Chaser slid his wallet from his back pocket and pulled out a business card. "Fax the specs to my financial adviser. We'll meet with you in a week or two."

Amber gave Jen and Josh a beauty queen wave, then took Chaser's arm and tugged him to the car. Chaser turned up the radio a little higher on the drive home, but Amber only raised her voice to be heard over the music.

He dropped Amber off at her condo, without a promise to see her again. He then headed to James River Stadium for the team meeting.

The meeting ran late. Team captain Risk Kincaid had delivered a long and hard-hitting speech about sportsmanship and the need to pull together. The Bat Pack would soon be returning to the lineup, and he wanted everyone to get their heads out of their asses and play World Series ball.

Despite Risk's speech tension filled the locker room. Shouting, name-calling, and clenched fists followed. Chaser had grabbed Psycho by the shoulder and blocked a second confrontation with Chris Collier.

Psycho's backstreet attitude didn't mix with Collier's country club views. The men came from two different worlds.

In Chaser's mind, it was time to play ball. Serious ball. He'd told Psycho to take his temper out on the opposing team once they hit the field again.

Psycho had settled, for the moment. Chaser understood his friend's restlessness and need for physical release. Every nerve-ending in Chaser's body longed to be behind home plate.

After the meeting, he grabbed a beer with Psycho and Romeo, then headed home. He pulled into his driveway the exact moment Josh delivered Jen home.

Chaser took his time getting out of the GTO. Removing his sunglasses, he stared in the side-view mirror, trying to catch their good-night kiss.

In the yellow glow of the porch light, their heads came together and their lips locked. For longer than he liked. He took several deep breaths.

A good ten minutes passed before Jen exited Josh's car. The man must be doing well to be driving a Bentley, Chaser thought. Jen waved Josh off, then walked straight to his GTO.

Poking her head inside the driver's window, she raised a brow. "Spying on me?"

"I was listening to the end of a song on the radio."

"Your radio's off."

"It was on a moment ago."

Her expression showed she didn't believe him. "How was the meeting?"

"Long, productive. How was Burke's good-night kiss?"

"Short. He banged his knee on the steering wheel. The romance was lost."

"Plans for a second date?"

"Not enough chemistry."

Chaser patted the seat beside him. "Sit with me, Legs."

He caught her hesitation before she rounded the hood and climbed in beside him. She hugged the passenger door.

They both sat quietly, until Chaser snagged her wrist, tugging her across the front seat until their hips bumped. "You've never been afraid to sit by me before."

"I'm not afraid now."

She damn sure was. She'd crossed her legs so their thighs wouldn't touch. He didn't want her afraid of him, so he took her back in time. "How often have we sat in my car and shot the breeze?"

Her smile broke in memory. "Too many times to count. In high school, Big John used to tap on the car windshield. He wanted to make sure we weren't fooling around."

"Maybe he saw something we didn't."

"Dad caught our 'practice kiss,' when we were sixteen and inexperienced," she reminded him. "We bumped heads, laughed it off, remember?"

He remembered, all right. He'd found humor in their fumbling until Big John slammed his palm against the car window and called Chaser out. He'd nearly wet his pants. Her father's glare had sent him hurtling over the hollyhocks, scared shitless.

While his forehead had merely bruised, Jen had sported a bump just above her right eye for an entire week. He'd felt she was off limits ever since.

"I'm better at kissing now," he told her.

Her lashes swept down, hiding her eyes. "I bet you are."

Silence, heavy and thick as foreplay, settled between them. Jen wet her lips, then slowly slid her hand from Chaser's hold. He hadn't realized his fingers were still wrapped around her wrist. Nor was he aware he was drawing small, smooth circles over her pulse-point with his thumb.

It had all felt natural. As if he'd done it a thousand times. A lover's touch. Gentle, yet possessive.

Turning slightly, Chaser found his lips a mere half inch from her mouth. Her breath tickled his chin. The scent of her perfume wafted to him, fresh and floral, and utterly feminine.

Anticipation spiked.

And pleasure slammed his chest.

His body hummed, and his hands itched to touch her.

Yet he held back. Endless seconds passed as he debated kissing her. This was Jen, his very best friend.

She swallowed, her lashes lifted, and trust darkened her eyes. She trusted him, yet he didn't trust himself. Their unexpected kiss at the ballpark had turned him inside out and he wanted to taste her again. Really taste her, when they had all the time in the world. He wanted more than steamed-up windows and fumbling with their clothes on the front seat of his GTO.

He fell back against the seat, pinched the bridge of his nose, and took a deep breath. Got his body under control. "I've planned a second double date," he finally managed.

"Thanks for consulting me," Jen muttered as she slid across the seat and pulled on the car door handle, ready to leave.

"Mike Sutton owns a Cadillac dealership," Chaser said to her back. "I've got tickets for Saturday's Jazz on the Green."

"I love jazz."

That was why he'd gotten the tickets.

She turned slightly. "Your date?"

"Cashmere DuMont."

"The exotic dancer from Peek-A-Boobs?"

"She looks as good in clothes as she does without."

Jen rolled her eyes. "I thought you were looking for someone special."

Chaser chose his words carefully. "I'm on the lookout. When I find my special woman, I'll focus fully on her."

"Until then?"

"I need a date when we double," he explained. "Otherwise I'm a third wheel."

She nodded. "Saturday night, we'll celebrate your return to baseball."

"Come Sunday, the Bat Pack's going to kick some Yankee ass."

NINE

Seated on a blanket in Centennial Park, Jen looked at Mike Sutton, who was sprawled out beside her fast asleep. His soft snores rose with the smooth jazz that electified the night air. How could anyone sleep through such phenomenal sound?

She cut a glance to the blanket next to hers. Less than five feet away, Chaser reclined against a tree in his burgundy-and-blue-striped shirt and jeans, looking relaxed and as attentive to his date as he was to the music.

Unexpected jealousy sliced through Jen as the exotic dancer snuggled against her best friend. Cashmere's clingy little red dress outlined every attribute. And there were many. Full breasts, tiny waist, stilettos to show off her tight calves.

The exotic dancer touched Chaser with the intimacy of a woman who knew his body. Cashmere's whispers annoyed Jen as much as his responsive smiles. Her neighbor was enjoying himself. Too damn much.

Jen looked at the sky. Dusk cast fiery pinks and fuschias around the setting sun. She sighed. Whatever had possessed her to go on another double date when all she wanted was to be alone with Chaser? Watching him and his double-D date stole all her enjoyment from the open-air festival.

She straightened her black Moroccan skirt. The sequins, seed beads, and tiny mirrors reflected the onset of night. Her heart charm ankle bracelet had been a high school graduation present from Chaser. Her strappy black sandals a gift to herself just last week.

She rolled her shoulders beneath her silk blouse in Tuscan gold. She toyed with the black opal pendant that hung between her breasts. Feeling Chaser's eyes on her, she looked up. Found his gaze locked on her cleavage.

She lowered her hand, and his gaze lifted. He nodded toward her date. "Music put the man to sleep?"

She shrugged, forced a smile. "That, or his inability to sell me a new car."

"You *need* a new car."

"The El Camino only has two hundred thousand miles."

"It's time, Jen," he said gently. "New car, new kitchen, new man in your life."

The car and kitchen would prove hard decisions. The man she'd already chosen. She wanted Chase Tallan. The thought jarred her. So much so, her surprised expression drew his attention.

"You okay?" Chaser asked.

Words failed her. She could only nod. Returning to the music, she let the jazz play over her. Richie Cole's "There Will Never Be Another You" both soothed and inspired. She would agree to no more double dates.

Three hours of jazz, and Jen felt rejuvenated. Mike Sutton, on the other hand, was deep in his dreams. He also moaned a lot in his sleep. Some moans low, others guttural. The name "Kayla" escaped his lips more than once.

Jen poked his shoulder on the last note of the night. Sutton woke with tented khakis and a sheepish smile.

Picking up their blankets, the foursome headed toward Chaser's car. It took nearly an hour to clear the parking lot. When Chaser wanted to call it a night, Jen and Mike readily agreed. Only Cashmere pouted.

Once parked in his driveway, Chaser hinted, "I'm tasting German chocolate cake."

Jen cut him a look. "Thought you were tired."

"Never too tired for cake."

She invited him into her kitchen, where she served up thick slices of cake and poured tall glasses of milk.

"Your mother loves me." Chaser grinned between forkfuls of cake. "She baked my favorite."

"Only because I agreed," Jen retorted, wiping the grin from his face. "I could have pushed for angel food."

"You gave in?"

"Just this once."

"That means you love me too."

"Not as much as my mother," she lied.

Chaser's next big bite left frosting at one corner of his mouth. Without thinking, Jen grabbed a paper napkin and went to wipe his lip.

Unplanned, yet perfectly timed, his tongue darted out and swept two of her fingertips. She dropped the napkin, and time came to a standstill. His gaze locked on her, his debate with himself apparent.

Jen didn't press or hold back. She merely looked into his eyes, seeing that the ice blue was charged with both constraint and need.

His need won out. Their breathing slowed, shallow and intimate, as he swirled his tongue over her fingertip, then fully sucked her finger into his mouth.

Sensations fluttered in her belly, both erotic and electric. The nip and pull of his lips drew images of what his mouth could do to other parts of her body. Her nipples hardened.

She could pull her finger away at any time. Yet the heat of his mouth, the moistness of his tongue, held her motionless.

Her heart quickened when he placed a kiss on her open palm, then bit the sensitive skin at the underside of her wrist. Her pulse visibly jumped.

Jen forced herself to breathe. More slowly. More evenly. The task was nearly impossible.

"Does my daughter taste as good as my German chocolate cake?"

Katherine Reid's question startled Jen so much,

she nearly fell off her chair. She'd been so focused on Chaser, she hadn't heard her mother's approach. Katherine stood in the doorway now, a curious expression on her face. How much had she witnessed?

Chaser didn't seem the least bit fazed. He slowly released her hand, started to explain, "Chocolate on my—"

"His mouth," Jen cut in.

"—needed a napkin," from Chaser.

"My finger touched his lip—" Jen felt as if she were twelve, with her hand caught in the cookie jar. Or in this case, Chaser's mouth.

Katherine put them at ease. "You're adults. I've no need for explanations." She covered her mouth, softly yawned. "I was reading, heard Chaser's car pull up, and came down to check on Jen. How was your date?"

"Bored," Jen replied. "He slept through the jazz festival."

"Your date?" Katherine asked Chaser.

"Cashmere was more into Chaser than the jazz," Jen answered for him.

"How would you know that?" her mother asked.

"Jen can't keep her eyes off me," Chaser teased.

His words were too on target to be funny. Jen's blush made her cheeks hot. "Egotistical man. I don't watch you."

Katherine shook her head. "Children, behave. I'm off to bed." She looked at Jen. "Turn off the kitchen lights when you're done eating cake. And, Chaser, good luck tomorrow. Beat the Yankees."

"We have every intention of winning," Chaser assured Katherine.

As soon as her mother left, Jen lowered her gaze to her hand. The hand that Chaser had kissed and tongued. She could still feel his mouth on her fingers. The hot tingle in her palm might never go away.

"About our next double date." Chaser pushed his plate aside and rested his elbows on the table. "I'm thinking—"

"Don't think." She held up her hand, met his gaze squarely. "I appreciate all you've done, but no more setups."

Chaser winced. "They've been that bad?"

"I'm not looking for love," she tried to explain. "If it comes my way, that makes it twice as special."

"We can still hang out?"

"You're my best friend."

"I just sucked your fingers."

He'd definitely turned her on. "A spontaneous suck, nothing for the scrapbook."

His ice-blue eyes narrowed. "I can do scrapbook."

She was certain he could.

"I've been waiting to do scrapbook for four weeks now," he stated. "Ever since our kiss at the ballpark."

"It wasn't a *real* kiss." She needed to keep things light. "It was an accident."

"Then I need to make it real."

A kiss to make a memory.

He moved slowly, yet with purpose, tugging

183

her chair forward, and sliding his denim knee between her skirted thighs. His touch was strong, yet gentle, as he smoothed his hand into her hair. His breath blew warm against her cheek, her ear, when he bent to kiss her forehead.

The scrub of his stubble against her cheek drew attention to his maleness. Chaser shaved twice a day and still had whiskers. Fascinated by her mouth, he traced her lips with his thumb. Over and over his thumb brushed, until she parted her lips and flicked her tongue.

His pupils dilated, and his desire embraced her.

She'd never been as aware of a man as she was of Chase Tallan. Her neighbor and best friend. And a man about to kiss her. *Really* kiss her.

The kiss would have consequences, she knew. Consequences to her heart. Her anticipation escaped on a sigh as his mouth hovered over hers. It was her last chance to escape to safety. She wasn't running.

The first touch of his lips marked her forever. She wanted no other man but him. There was history in their kiss. A lifetime of friendship and compassion and . . . something deeper, not yet ready to surface.

His lips were strong, his hand firm at the back of her neck. From soft and playful nips, their kiss quickly escalated to a full-fledged mating of tongues. He tasted of chocolate and delicious man.

He pulled her closer. To the edge of her chair. The abrasive rub of his denim knee against her sensitive inner thigh sent goose bumps all over her body. She curled her fingers over his shoulders, felt heat and contoured muscle beneath his linen shirt.

With utmost intent and care, he ran his fingers down her neck, over her breast to her belly. Her heart was pounding so fast she felt light-headed. Her palms grew as damp as her panties.

The scrape of a chair leg as he hauled her across his lap reminded her that they sat in her mother's kitchen. With the lights on and the refrigerator humming. The chance that Katherine Reid might return for a glass of water was a distinct possibility.

Jen didn't want her mother to find her with her skirt hiked, riding Chaser's thighs.

"No sliding home," she breathed against his mouth.

He took a deep, calming breath and brought a halt to what could have gone on all night. "Come home with me." His dark, sexy whisper caressed her neck.

Her stomach fluttered at his words. And her heart smiled. His house was right next door. "You've never fooled around on the night before a game."

"Old rule, new woman." He raised his hips against her bottom. The full press of his erection was long and hard. "For you, I'd make an exception."

"We've waited thirty-two years. One more day won't matter."

"Matters to me."

She slipped off his lap, stood, her knees weak. "Take matters into your own hands. Cold shower, soap—"

Chaser shook his head. "Heartless woman."

He rose then, turned and adjusted himself. His expression was pained. "I'll find you after the game."

"You find me and I'm yours."

He gave her one final kiss, with enough tongue to tease her into following him through the hollyhocks and into his house.

With a ragged sigh, she resisted.

As midnight draped her bed in shadow, Jen hoped Chaser was getting more sleep than she was. She'd gone from counting sheep to naming them as she waited for the sandman.

Sleep or no sleep, Chaser was wired to play ball.

It was a home game, and as the players were introduced, he allowed the applause and roar of the crowd to claim him. He belonged to the fans who spent a big chunk of their paychecks on seats at James River Stadium. He wouldn't disappoint them again. He'd never sit out another game for fighting.

"Pitcher's so freakin' tall it appears he's releasing the ball right in front of the batter," Psycho commented as the team sat in the dugout and watched Yankees right-hander Roger Cooke pitch from the mound. "The man should be playing basketball."

At six foot nine and topping two hundred sixty

pounds, Cooke looked like a mountain on a mole-hill as he warmed up.

"Change in the lineup," batting coach Wayne Sanders shouted down the bench. The man was as old as baseball, with a weathered face and a fanatical loyalty to the sport. "Risk Kincaid's on deck, followed by Driscoll, Dunn, Black, Lawless, Bellisaro, McMillan, Tallan, Collier."

Chaser's gut cramped. The Bat Pack had led the lineup for five years. They'd scored more base hits and home runs from the leadoff positions than any players in the league. Yet their suspension had dropped them to the bottom of the order. Chaser sat one slot above the pitcher.

"Further payback for our suspension?" Psycho voiced what Chaser had been thinking.

"You've worked out, practiced, and traveled with the team, yet you haven't played for thirteen games," Sanders stated. "You want leadoff, earn it."

Psycho swore.

Romeo shook his head.

And Chaser swallowed his disappointment.

At one fifteen, following the singing of the National Anthem, the Rogues took the field against the Yankees.

Game on.

It was a volatile eight innings. Each team flexed its muscle. Offensively, Psycho took chances. He hit strong line drives. Once on first, he took long leads and stole second. He slid headfirst into third so many times, Chaser swore he must be brain-damaged.

Defensively, Psycho hit the warning track at an all-out run. He leapt and caught fly balls that should have been fan souvenirs.

Romeo played all out as well. He caught ground balls that hopped and should have shot past him. At bat, he connected for a triple, which brought two teammates home.

Behind home plate, Chaser caught a major pop-up that ended the eighth inning. With the score tied 3–3, they headed into the top of the ninth. And managed to keep the Yankees from scoring.

The crowd was on its feet. They shouted for that one run that would lift the Rogues to two wins. Batters started at the bottom of the order. James Lawless, Romeo Bellisaro, and Psycho McMillan.

Chaser sat with his head in his hands as Lawless struck out. One down. He didn't want the game to go into overtime. He wanted it to end with this inning.

"Don't go for the wall," Psycho told Romeo as Psycho switched brands of bubble gum. He chewed Dubble Bubble at bat and Bazooka in the outfield. "Get on base. Chaser and I will bring you home."

Chaser caught the aggressive determination in Psycho's eyes. That wild-ass look that won ball games.

For a heartbeat, he wondered if Jen had caught any of the game. She worked her tail off in the concession stands, but he knew she kept a small television plugged in near the snow-cone machine to track the score.

With a 3–2 count, Chaser saw Romeo glance toward the press box. Romeo and the reporter definitely had something going outside baseball. Rolling his shoulders, Romeo stepped into the batter's box and stared down Roger Cooke.

The pitcher fired a curveball. Romeo loved curveballs. He connected with the sweet spot and took pleasure in his second straight double for the day.

Chaser watched Psycho take up his bat. The man was all raw energy and competitive spirit. If anyone could hike it out of the park, Psycho could.

He was never given the chance. Psycho was feared as a home-run hitter, and the pitcher didn't take any chances with him. Cooke pitched around him, and the crowd broke into hisses and boos as Psycho took a slow walk to first.

Psycho was as ticked as the fans. He shouted a few choice words in Cooke's direction. The first-base coach met him halfway down the baseline and escorted Psycho to the bag.

Chaser heard his name announced over the loudspeaker. The Rogues' best hope of scoring sat with him now. He approached home plate with a mental vision of slamming the ball out of the park. He'd never let pressure faze him.

Jaw clenched, his shoulders hunched, he blocked out the noise from the stands and focused solely on the first pitch.

It was down and outside. He checked his swing on ball one.

An inside fastball shot by him, was called as a strike.

He punched the next ball foul.

One ball, two strikes. His entire body tensed, then released on a slider. Hit off the end of the bat, the line drive followed the right field chalk, stayed in play.

From the corner of his eye, he saw Romeo run as if his life depended on it. Psycho was on his heels.

Chaser wasn't a great sprinter. As catcher, his legs were muscled for stamina, not speed. First base seemed a mile away. His heart pounded as the Yankees first baseman stretched, keeping one foot on the bag, for the incoming throw from right field.

Chaser wasn't going to make it. The ball would be relayed to first, then fired home. Three outs, and they'd be into extra innings.

He dove, sliding headfirst into the bag. His fingers connected the exact second the ball smacked into the first baseman's glove. Shit.

Safe!

The umpire's call had him blinking dust from his eyes. Romeo and Psycho had crossed home plate.

He'd scored a victory for the Rogues.

The Bat Pack was back.

Fans screamed; the noise from the stands was deafening.

Mobbed by his teammates, Chaser was hauled to his feet and slapped on the back. Arms pumped and high fives were exchanged all around.

"Could you run any slower?" shouted a grinning Psycho as he pushed through the players to punch Chaser's shoulder. "A snail could have beaten you to first."

Romeo found them both. "We brought it home," his voice shouted over the celebration.

Following lengthy interviews, a short locker room celebration, and a very hot shower, Chaser faced fans gathered by the exit collecting autographs. He signed alongside Psycho and Romeo. Ninety minutes passed before security broke up the fan frenzy.

"Beer?" Psycho asked.

Romeo shook his head. "Interview with a reporter."

Psycho cut Romeo a look. "You still newsworthy?"

"I'm good for a few more articles."

"I'm catching up with Jen Reid," Chaser told them.

Psycho scratched his jaw. "Old neighbor drawing new interest?"

Chaser nodded. "View's decent over the hollyhocks."

Psycho didn't press. "Guess I should check on my designer."

"Guess you should," Romeo agreed.

The three men parted ways.

Without a second thought.

As Chaser went in search of Jen, he realized that this was the first time the Bat Pack had passed on a round of beer. The men had always played fast and hard. Yet each now went his own way to be with his chosen woman.

He found Jen on the mezzanine level, at her desk in her business office, enjoying a blueberry snow cone. Spreadsheets littered her desk, while her fingers punched figures on a calculator.

He removed his sunglasses, took her in. Her back was to him; she looked sleek and slender beneath a scarlet T. Her hair hung straight down her spine in a fancy braid. The roll of her hip on the seat of the chair indicated her legs were crossed. Her bottom was encased in designer jeans.

He cleared his throat, and her fingers skittered over the calculator pad. She turned to him, her amber eyes bright, her lips parted and slightly blue from the snow cone.

Her reception made him smile. Jumping off her chair, she charged him. As hard and fast as he'd run for first base. Six steps and a leap, and she was on him. Her arms wrapped his neck, her legs his waist. She squeezed so hard, he got a full-body press.

She felt good.

"You won!" Her excitement rolled over him. "I stood frozen over the ice machine until you were called safe at first." She punched his shoulder. "Run faster next time."

"I'm built for stamina, not speed."

She smiled. "Stamina is good."

"I'm good for an hour."

She eased off him then in a slow slide so that every inch of her sweet body put him on alert.

Moving to the door, Jen pulled down the shade and slid home the dead bolt. Crossing to her work area, she switched the three-way bulb on her desk light to low. The room was enveloped in shadow. As was her face. Darkness deepened the natural hollow beneath her cheekbones, along with the soft indentation between her lower lip and chin. The sweep of her neck, the dip at her throat, all hid from his eyes, waiting for him to rediscover her.

"Here, Legs? In your office?" His voice was barely audible.

She folded the spread sheets on her desk, shoved the calculator to one side. Boosting herself onto the polished oak, she leaned back on her hands and finally answered, "Doesn't matter where, Chaser, as long as I'm with you."

Frustration hissed through his teeth. "No condom."

She plucked a foil packet from beneath her desk calendar. "I've got you covered."

He went hard.

So hard, he barely managed the four feet to her desk.

She welcomed him between her splayed legs. He slid his hands along her thighs, pulled her to him. The press of denim between them was rough and arousing.

He took her mouth, kissed her, the barest touch of his tongue inside her lower lip. She bit the tip and drew his tongue fully into her mouth, where she sucked and teased and showed no mercy.

Slipping his hand beneath her T-shirt, he ran his palm over her belly, then up and under her bra. He cupped the warm underside of her breast, flicked his thumb over her nipple. Her nipples went as hard for him as his dick was hard for her.

Jen touched him with need. A lifetime of need. No part of his body escaped her fingers. Each stroke sent blood to his groin. He'd never wanted a woman so badly.

She wanted him right back. Unbuckling his belt, she pulled the leather free. Tossed it to the floor. The flick of the snap on his jeans, the lowering of his zipper, seemed life-altering sounds.

Now, as he stripped away her jeans and panties, he understood commitment. After tonight there was no going back. The thought of having sex with Jen for the rest of his life created a physical ache so strong he could barely breathe.

He prolonged their kiss. Ran his hands over every erogenous zone of her body. He wanted to satisfy her as no man before him had.

It was Jen who shoved his jeans over his hips and tugged down his jockeys. Jen who tore open the silver packet and rolled on his condom. Jen who wrapped her dancer's legs about his waist, and tilted her hips to accept him.

He gave one shallow thrust. Found resistance. Not a virgin's resistance, but the tightness of a woman who did not have regular sex.

"It's been a while." Her words, spoken against his neck, were soft, almost apologetic.

A while . . . His body grew even hotter. Withdrawing a fraction of an inch, he worked his hand between their bodies and touched her. Touched her with all the knowledge he had of a woman's body.

She grew slick, and her body loosened. He watched as her eyes closed and he took her to the edge of orgasm. He held her there, spread, flushed, and finger-stretched.

Ready for him now, she accepted him easily. They moved as one, their focus on the sound of their breathing, the rhythm of their bodies, soon bringing them to climax.

Jen shattered with Chaser's name on her lips.

A single heartbeat later, and Chaser's own satisfaction spilled deep. It took a very long time to catch his breath.

Muscles slack, he slid out, eased back, and disposed of the condom. Then he bent his head for one last kiss. A kiss that tasted of woman and lovemaking. The scent of sex surrounded them. She sat before him, her T-shirt shoved over her bra. She was naked from the waist down, looking dazed, disheveled, yet sated. The dampness from the backs of her thighs and bottom slicked the desktop.

"Great post-game sex," she murmured, smiling.

"This was a regular season game." Confidence curved his smile. "If you think I'm good now, wait until we win the World Series. You won't leave my bed for a month."

TEN

Psycho McMillan burst through the front door of his Colonial, all wired and ready to celebrate the team's victory. "Keely—" His voice echoed off the newly paneled walls in the foyer. His boots scuffed the polished hardwood floor.

"In here," she called from the formal living room.

He found her seated between Rebecca Reed Custis and architect Franklin Langston on a newly arrived blue velvet sofa with ornate carvings across the back. An antique tea caddy rested on a cherry-wood coffee table. The room smelled of apples and cinnamon.

The threesome looked too damn cozy, like a family. A rather disjointed family with Rebecca dressed in her prim gray suit, Keely in her faded T-shirt, worn jeans, and mismatched flip-flops, and Franklin in his wrinkled khakis.

Psycho didn't like this picture at all.

"Becky," he acknowledged the older woman.

196

"Mr. McMillan." The Daughter of Virginia tilted her head, looked down her nose at his white T-shirt enscripted with *First the Good News—I Made Bail*. She sniffed disapprovingly.

"We're taking tea." Keely reached for a cup and an assortment of decorative tea tins. "Would you like blackberry, cinnamon apple, or Earl Grey?"

Screw the tea. "I'll pass."

Keely sat back on the sofa. "How was the game?"

Obviously, she hadn't watched him play. Disappointment socked hard. "We won, 5–3. The Bat Pack kicked butt."

She nodded. "That's nice."

Nice? The word ripped through him. Nice was used for sweet old ladies, vanilla ice cream, two-for-one pizzas. He didn't want nice. He wanted Keely all amped up and ready to party.

"Did you catch any of the game?" He'd be happy with the last fifteen minutes.

She shook her head. "Rebecca stopped by to check on the restoration. Turns out she and Franklin are old friends. He did some work for her years ago. They both lost their spouses last September. They've been catching up on old times."

Keely had played tea party while he'd played ball. A part of him hated the fact that her interest lay in his Colonial, not in his career. She'd taken more pleasure in the over-sixty crowd than she had in his victory.

Locking his jaw, he tried to contain his anger.

Unreasonable anger that left him as mad at himself for seeking Keely's praise as he was at her for not paying him tribute.

His lips flat against his teeth, he managed a civil "Enjoy your tea" before stalking up the staircase.

He hit the second floor and made it to his bedroom without slamming his fist into a wall. Energy pounded through his body. The hot, restless need-an-outlet energy he'd wanted to expend with Keely. Now he needed another form of release.

His thoughts ran to Peek-A-Boobs. Only a twenty-minute drive. He'd be welcomed with a stiff drink and a sexy lap dance. Both would take his mind off his designer.

He drew off his T-shirt and drop-kicked it across the room. Shucked his jeans. He located a pair of workout sweats. A round or two with the speed bag would take the edge off and contain his need to race off somewhere in his track.

The Hemi on his Dodge Ram kicked ass. He'd talked his way out of several tickets over the past year. But there was always the off-chance a cop meeting his quota would write him up. He needed to pull himself together before he headed out.

Bare-fisted, he went after the bag. He punched until his arms ached and he was soaked in sweat. Gradually, the tension left his body. As he relaxed, his mind returned to Keely once again. He'd been rude to her, his usual m.o. He'd hired her to restore his Colonial. It shouldn't matter

whether or not she followed baseball. But somehow it did. A whole hell of a lot.

His disappointment had struck him in a way
he'd never expected. It slammed into his gut and
brought back the misery of his childhood. Of the
time when his mother had told him that his old
man had deserted them.

Back then, his dad hadn't cared enough about
him to stay. Today, Keely had blown off the
Rogues' game. The similarities stung. More than
he wanted to admit.

"Psycho?" Her voice turned him toward the
door. She stood, one narrow shoulder hitched
against the frame, her deep blue eyes filled with
concern, her ponytail lopsided. "Rebecca and
Franklin have left."

He wiped the sweat off his forehead with the
back of his hand. "You should have invited them
to dinner. Unpacked the fine china and broken in
that fancy new dining room table."

"The oil smell from your dismantled dirt bike
would turn everyone's stomach."

"Bike's almost ready to ride. I'll have it out of
the dining room in a week or two."

"During tea, Rebecca suggested an open house
once the Colonial's fully restored. She'd like to
invite the Historical Society and the Daughters of
Virginia for brunch."

"My house, my invite. Becky's not on my list."

"Your home would be worth showing off."

He narrowed his eyes at her. "You deliver Colonel William Lowell's oil painting as promised and I'll do brunch."

She looked at the floor, stared at her mismatched flip-flops. No comment.

He knew she didn't have the oil paining. Without it, there'd be no brunch with the Daughters. Ever. "I'm headed out—"

"You and your raw knuckles?" She'd lifted her gaze, noticed his damaged hands.

Without his gloves, the speed bag had torn up his knuckles. The skin was split over two fingers, his hands red and slightly swollen. He didn't give a damn.

"I'll get some ice," she offered.

"Don't do me any favors."

She pushed herself away from the door frame and stood a little taller. "You have a problem with me?" she demanded.

A big problem. "No."

She wouldn't let it go. "You came charging into the house, ignited like a fuse. A fuse that soon fizzled. What's got your jockeys in a bunch?"

"I'm not wearing jockeys."

She rolled her eyes. "I came upstairs to discuss the furniture I've ordered."

"Leave the invoices on the kitchen counter."

"I thought we'd go over them together. I wanted to justify the costs. I've spent a lot of your money."

He looked her over. "Money spent on furniture, but not a dime on yourself?"

Her chin shot up. "I've cashed my paychecks,

bought a few new items. I don't plan to work in my good clothes and get them dirty."

Growing up, Psycho had worn the same pair of jeans throughout elementary school. The jeans had been purchased long and got shorter with each grade. His first day of middle school, his mother stretched the family's budget and bought him a new shirt and pair of slacks. He'd hung the clothes in his closet and never removed the tags. He'd been afraid to wear them, afraid to get them dirty. In six months, he'd outgrown them.

"Psycho?" Keely's voice pulled him from the past. "About the furniture—"

He shrugged, blew her off. "I don't care what you spend. The furniture means as little to me as my game meant to you today."

She stood silent for longer than he liked, as if fitting missing pieces into a puzzle. She had no business trying to figure him out.

"Later, Keely." He nudged her toward the door.

He jerked off his sweatshirt, in need of a shower. He tugged on the drawstring of his sweatpants, realizing she hadn't budged. "Staying for the show?"

She shook her head. "It's Memorial Day weekend. I'm taking two days off. The Rogues play at home. You'll be around for the dogs. I'm going back to my apartment."

Back to her place? He'd allowed her into his life, only to have her cut him out? Son of a bitch. "Your bed's here," he reminded her.

"I'd planned to sleep on my couch."

He hoped she'd get a crick in her neck. "Deliveries," he ground out. "If furniture arrives, I won't be here to sign off on the pieces." His gaze narrowed. "Can your assistant work this weekend?"

"I never hired anyone," she returned evenly. "I wanted to save you money. I can work hard enough for two people."

Irritation pricked him. She had dark circles under her eyes and looked even skinnier than usual. "Hire someone."

"If I get behind on the restoration, I will. Besides, there won't be any deliveries this weekend," she assured him. "I've lined them up for next week."

Isn't she efficient? He sliced his hand through the air. "Fine, see you Monday."

Expecting her to leave, he dropped his sweatpants. One step toward the shower, and an unexpected slap on his bare ass spun him around.

"Congratulations on your win," Keely managed, blushing. "Isn't that what jocks do? Slap rear ends to celebrate?"

"You're not a jock." Psycho stared at her, finding it hard to believe she'd smacked him.

The sting of her slap had shot straight to his groin. His wood hardened. Nothing outside of sex was going to appease him now.

What had she done? What repercussions would she face now? Keely's mind scrambled with questions. She urged her body to move, and move fast. Her legs refused to walk away.

Psycho stood before her, tall, dark, and fully

aroused. His arms hung loosely at his sides, his legs braced. His muscles stood out, ripped and defined. His erection pointed directly at her.

Expectation rolled off him in tangible heat. His body promised sex, hard and fast, down and dirty.

Panic pounded in her ears. She saw his lips move, but didn't hear his words.

Ten minutes had passed since she'd realized his bad mood stemmed from her not cheering his win. The boy inside the man needed rah-rahs and she'd offered him tea.

She'd hurt his feelings, let him down. She'd realized she needed to make it up to him. But being spontaneous wasn't her strong suit.

When he'd dropped his sweatpants, swatting him had seemed like a good idea. But only jocks slapped asses. She should have kept her hands to herself.

"Keely, get out." The harshness in his voice drew her gaze to his face. His eyes had gone jet-black; his expression warned of sexual consequences should she stay. "Don't trust me to do what's right."

The pull between them was poignant and strong, and made her stomach go soft. She was a heartbeat from staying when he abruptly turned his back on her. "I'd be your biggest mistake," he warned over his shoulder.

The slam of the bathroom door sent her down the hall to her bedroom. She grabbed two clean pairs of jeans, tank tops, and underwear, and stuffed them in an expensive leather suitcase Psycho had given her on one of many birthdays. She escaped the house before he stepped from the shower. Her battered station wagon got her across town. Her need for coffee landed her at Jacy's Java.

"Toffee Nut Latte," Keely ordered at the counter.

"Whipped cream, cherry?" Jacy offered with a smile.

Keely nodded. "And an apricot scone."

Once served, Keely found a table near the newspaper stand. A copy of *Jocks* magazine caught her eye. She flipped through the pages until she found Psycho's interview. The article made her smile. The photograph of him wrapped in a towel fresh from his shower gave her a hot flash. She now knew what lay under that towel. He was more man than she'd ever imagined.

"Where's my favorite wild man?" Jacy asked, joining Keely at the chrome table. Dressed in a plum-and-silver brocade jacket and zebra-printed cropped pants, Jacy was as brightly decorative as her café. Red highlighted her blond hair. Gold and silver bracelets curved around her wrists. She wore a ring on every finger.

Keely took a deep breath, sighed. "Psycho's going out to celebrate the Rogues' win."

"And you're . . . ?" inquired Jacy.

"Alone, enjoying a latte and a scone." Keely sipped her latte from a china cup rimmed with holly berries. She let the flavor play over her tongue, then confessed her sin. "I didn't watch the game."

Jacy looked surprised. "That upset Psycho?"

Keely bit her lip. "Bothered him a lot."

Jacy's grin was unexpected. "Well, it's about time."

Keely didn't understand. "Time for what?"

"Time for another scone." Jacy rose, then returned with both an apricot and a chocolate chip scone.

Keely ate hungrily. Her conversation with Psycho had delayed her dinner. The scones hit the spot. "I've decided to buy a television," she told Jacy between bites. "A small eighteen-inch screen for my apartment."

"So you can watch baseball?"

"Once the renovations are completed, I'll need my own television for next season."

"Out in right field, Psycho's a show unto himself," Jacy said fondly. "Quick and explosive, and very intense. Psycho comes across as tough, bored, and totally crazy. He looks like a fallen angel and sins on a regular basis. Most people never see his good side, but it's there."

Keely finished off her latte. "You know him well."

"Strictly through observation," Jacy admitted. "He's my second favorite Rogue."

"I damn well better be your first."

The deep male voice came from behind Keely. She tilted her head and found herself staring at a massive chest. Looking up, she admired the maturity in the man's face, the strong character lines about his eyes and mouth. The strength of his jaw.

"My husband, Risk Kincaid," Jacy said. "This is Keely Douglas, Psycho's designer."

Risk had a strong handshake. His gaze seemed to evaluate her. His words held understanding and an offhanded compliment. "Psycho's not easy to work for. You must be doing something right to have lasted a month."

"She's doing everything right," Jacy told her husband. "I hear the Colonial's coming along beautifully."

Keely wasn't so sure. One mistake, and Psycho could boot her to the curb.

"Close the coffee shop and have dinner with me," Risk invited. He moved to stand behind Jacy, who was perched on a turquoise stool. He curved his hands over her shoulders and pulled his woman back against his chest. The gesture was intimate, possessive, loving. "Rogues won. I want to celebrate with you."

"Excellent triple," Jacy said, complimenting his hit.

Risk's eyes warmed. "Connected with the sweet spot."

Keely took it all in. Jacy's easy slide off the stool, her stroll to the door, the easy flip of the OPEN sign to CLOSED. The regular customers took her hint and cleared the café within seconds.

Keely also rose. Jacy surprised her at the door with a white dessert box for the road. Kindness radiated from Jacy's smile. "Always good to have snacks on hand in case of unexpected company."

Keely had never had someone drop by unexpectedly.

Once inside her apartment, she flipped on the lights, looked around her place. It was small, cozy, and suddenly very lonely. No barking dogs, no Psycho shouting for the remote, only silence. It was the kind of silence that made her heart feel heavy.

Placing the dessert box on the counter in her kitchen, she decided a bath would soothe both body and spirit. She lit a single candle perched on the edge of the bathroom sink and poured a stream of pear-magnolia body oil into her bathwater. She stripped off her clothes and sank into the tub. Closed her eyes . . .

There was a sudden impatient pounding on her front door. Startled, Keely sloshed water over the edges of the tub. Her hair stringy and uncombed, her body slick with oil, she rose, grabbed her worn terry cloth robe, and tore to the living room.

All buttoned up, her sash tied, she cracked the door.

"I was in the neighborhood . . ." Psycho stood in the hallway, dressed all in black and looking dangerous. His baseball cap was turned backward. There was a scowl on his face.

In the neighborhood. She lived an hour from his home.

"I was just taking a bath."

"I showered earlier."

Something she already knew. He'd stood before her, naked and aroused, and pushing her out the door.

"I have treats." A silly statement, but all that came to mind.

"Sounds good."

He straightened from the wall, followed her inside. He trailed her to the tiny kitchen, leaned against the sink, his eyes jet-black, his expression unreadable.

Standing on tiptoe, she searched the cupboard for a plate without a crack. Flipping open the white box, she stared at its contents. "Rice Krispies treats."

"My favorite." Psycho reached around her, his body brushing hers as he chose the biggest one.

Keely blew out a breath. Jacy Kincaid had anticipated Psycho's late-night visit.

"Milk?" he asked.

She shook her head. "I've been living at your house. My refrigerator's empty."

"You need food." He took her in, his gaze catching on her protruding collarbone and bony knees. "You're too damn skinny."

"I ate three scones at the coffee shop."

"Eat more." He shoved a Rice Krispies treat into her hand.

Their fingers generated a quick, explosive heat that sparked up her arm and shot down to her toes. She felt flushed and tingly. She took a quick bite of the treat to steady her nerves.

"Boris and Bosephus miss you."

She'd been gone three hours. His admission made her smile. "Remember to give them each a Milk-Bone at bedtime."

"You spoil the boys."

"I'm better with dogs than I am with people," she softly admitted. "I've never owned a television. Never watched a baseball game. I don't know how to stroke your ego."

"It's not my ego in need of stroking."

She couldn't move. Couldn't think. Could barely breathe as Psycho set down his plate and moved in closer. He was twice her size, lean, strong, and unpredictable. Heat pulsed between them.

She caught the gold flecks in his dark brown eyes; the banked need in his uneven breathing. She sensed that his control was slipping fast. She should be afraid, very afraid. Strangely enough, she didn't fear him.

"I'm going to count to three." His whisper played against her ear. "Duck under my arm or be taken against the wall."

Keely shuddered, dropped her Rice Krispies treat. The man didn't play fair. His closeness confused her. She couldn't think with the rasp of his whiskers against her cheek, the tickle of his warm breath on her chin.

"One . . . two . . . you've been warned."

So much for three. Sensation burned with the touch of his lips. He caught her hair in his hands and kissed her hard. There was nothing slow or sensual in his move. Psycho McMillan was all over her, all at once.

His body stamped hers, and his hands were everywhere as he worked to get her naked. Within seconds, her robe hit the floor and he was kissing the hollow where her neck and shoulder met. He nipped the sensitive skin above her right breast, then swirled his tongue over what would surely be a bruise.

His mouth covered her nipples, first one, then the other, tugging lightly with his teeth. The sensation shot straight to her belly, then lower. Her legs trembled, barely able to keep her upright in the face of his onslaught.

Through it all, Keely's heart slammed and her body burned. She curled her fingers in the front of his T-shirt and held on tight as the floor shifted beneath her. She was aware of every aroused atom in his body. Passion pounded in her bones, her heart, and deep between her thighs.

She was never certain which was harder, the man before her or the wall at her back. Adrenaline surged through him and electrified her. His kisses grew deeper, his mouth more demanding.

There was a lot to be said for nudity. Psycho had an incredible body. His shirt and pants had been kicked aside, and now her pale hands clung to his tanned arms. The sculpted solidness of his hair-roughened chest crushed her small, round breasts. The roped muscles of his thighs spread her slender legs.

His *Stands on Command* tattoo was a testament to his readiness to take her.

She wasn't ready for him. . . .

Psycho's body spiked white-hot. His breathing was rough and rapid. It took him several minutes to realize Keely's kisses didn't have the same frantic intensity as his own. Her kisses were softer, slower; she wanted to make love, not hump off excess energy.

He growled, threw his head back, his muscles bunched and burning for sport sex. He silently swore, then figuratively kicked himself. Keely wasn't one of those women he took so fast and furiously he forgot her name.

He'd started his evening at Peek-A-Boobs. But he'd tipped the exotic dancer to get *off* his lap. He hadn't wanted just any woman's touch. He'd only wanted Keely's.

The feel of her hands on his lower back made him moan. She rubbed his spine a long time. Her fingers kneaded and massaged and slowed him down. His knotted muscles loosened and he no longer felt flaming hot.

She held him until the tension left his body. Until his male animal retreated and the wildness stilled.

He pushed himself back, bent, and pulled a condom from the pocket of his jeans. Taking her hand, he led her to the red vinyl sofa. A sofa with too many tears and very little padding. It was as hard as a wood frame.

He settled himself first, then positioned her straddling his thighs. His erection rose flat against his stomach, awaiting further command.

"Let's celebrate your win." Her whisper-soft kiss requested gentleness.

Psycho didn't have a tender bone in his body. He could, however, practice patience. Even if it killed him. He let Keely do the kissing. And the touching. Let her learn his body. All over.

Her eyes dilated.

The pulse at her throat was visible.

When she bit his jaw, he bit her back.

It took every ounce of his control not to flip her over on the vinyl and finish what she'd started.

No woman had ever tried so hard to please him. She gauged his reaction to her every touch. Which stroke made him groan. What had him sucking in air. What tightened his abdomen. What caused his dick to twitch.

Lengthy foreplay left them both breathing heavily, their bodies tight and needy. When Psycho finally sheathed himself and slid inside her, he nearly came.

He fought back his own need and pleasured her fully. From her teacup breasts to the soft, sensitive skin at her belly, his fingers grazed and tortured, bringing exquisite pleasure.

She rode him, the strength in her slender thighs setting the pace for mutual satisfaction. He cupped her bottom, as small and compact as the rest of her body.

A strange burning filled his chest. An enveloping heat that was more emotional than sexual.

"Don't hold back," Psycho pushed her. "Come hard, like we're going to die tomorrow."

She shattered in his arms, slick and sweet and

explosive. If that was the last orgasm of her life, she'd be buried with a smile on her face.

Psycho spun out with such force, he swore he'd lost his sanity. If he'd ever been sane, which was highly debatable. Satisfied to his soul, he held Keely against his chest until their breathing slowed.

He left her only to rid himself of his condom. Returning, he found her still naked and staring up at him. She looked small and vulnerable, her cheeks pink, her lips kissed red. Her deep blue eyes were as soft as her sigh. "Some celebration."

"It feels good to win." Win the game, win the girl.

Settling back on the sofa, he let her snuggle. Snuggling was new to him. With other women, he had sex, then split. With Keely Douglas, it felt right to hold her. At least for a little while.

Within a very short time, her body went slack and he knew she slept. He rested his head against the back of the couch and closed his eyes. He'd stay for a few more minutes. . . .

He awakened six hours later, disoriented by the soft light above the stove in the tiny kitchen. Keely's apartment. The memory of what had happened hit as hard as his morning erection. He'd slept sitting up, and his ass was now half numb, his shoulders cramped against the wood frame.

Keely was still pressed against his side. One of her arms was wrapped around his chest; one of her legs curved against his thigh. In the coolness of the living room, she stole his heat.

The heat he didn't mind. He was hot-blooded. Stealing his heart was another matter. He'd enjoyed Keely beyond the sex. Which had been phenomenal. He'd taken her twice more, just to be sure he hadn't imagined how good they were together. Each time only got better.

A part of him refused to get too comfortable with her. He wasn't ready for the emotion he'd seen in her eyes when they'd made love. She'd been open and honest and vulnerable. Psycho didn't do vulnerable. For any woman. Ever.

The idea of letting go and letting her into his life set his teeth on edge. Somewhere deep inside, he was certain he'd inherited his father's leave-and-never-return gene. The gene that closed the door on relationships.

Women came and went in Psycho's life. He just didn't do long-term. But he didn't want to hurt Keely.

Once his house was restored, she'd be gone.

There would be no reason for her to stay.

But somehow, the idea of her leaving didn't feel right to him.

Thoughts of the day crowded him now. He needed to return to the Colonial, see to the Newfoundlands, and get himself psyched for afternoon play.

Today, the Rogues again faced the Yankees in game two of the three-game series. When they won, he'd celebrate with Keely. This time, with birthday gifts.

He brushed her bangs off her forehead, dropped

a light kiss between her brows. He then eased off the sofa. Still asleep, she stretched out on her own. He went in search of a pillow and a blanket. Found neither. Snagging a twin sheet from the hallway closet, he went to cover her. She definitely needed new bedding.

His clothes lay atop her robe on the kitchen floor. Memories of stripping her naked, his sense of urgency, and her need to slow him down drifted over him. Only with Keely had he ever taken his time. With her, slow felt better than hit-and-run.

He dressed quietly, then jotted a note on a sheet of paper towel: *Your couch is uncomfortable—my bed tonight. I've got presents.*

He crossed the room and hit the day at dawn.

He was already contemplating Keely's gifts. And how she'd open them with smiles and enthusiasm—totally naked.

ELEVEN

"Give me the remote," Keely ordered Boris. The big dog held it between his teeth, tightening his jaw whenever she tried to pull it free.

"I promised to watch the game this afternoon," she explained to the Newfie. "I can't let Psycho down."

Not after last night. Psycho had made sure their time together was unforgettable. He'd cupped her bottom, controlled her ride. Drawn out her pleasure. They'd moved together until her climax and total satisfaction were echoed by his growl and slow smile.

She'd felt completely taken.

But even though he'd given her his body, he'd closed off his heart. She'd felt his moment of weakness, when the sex had been so good neither one could believe it. She'd allowed her feelings to show in the hope he'd respond in kind. But his emotional response was fleeting. No more than a second, and he'd shut down. He'd kept his gaze down and his jaw locked when he'd disposed of his condom.

She'd expected him to leave after sex. Surprisingly, he'd stayed. He'd allowed her to snuggle. But deep inside, she knew that Psycho McMillan would let her only so close before he pulled away.

"Sit." Keely attempted another training tactic with Boris. She'd been working the command into the dogs' daily routine, but they'd yet to master it. To her surprise, Boris did as he was told.

He sat and looked up at her, awaiting her response. "Good boy," Keely praised lavishly. She reached for a tug toy near one leg of the coffee table. "Switch," she said, offering the toy for the remote.

Boris remained undecided, until Bosephus bounded into the living room and took Keely up on her offer to play. Bosephus grabbed one end of the toy and nearly pulled her off her feet. Wanting to get in on the action, Boris dropped the remote, which Keely immediately scooped up. The Newfies continued their tug of war.

The living room stood empty except for the couch and the coffee table. After several tugs, the dogs lay down for a nap. A nap Keely wouldn't mind taking herself.

She'd expended a lot of energy last night. Three rounds with Psycho had left her sore. The man had worked muscles she'd never known she had.

She made popcorn, grabbed a soda, and headed for Psycho's domain. Settling on the black leather couch in the family room, she faced his home theater television. Remote in hand, she pressed ON. Not a flicker, not a sound. She shook the remote, tried again. Nothing. Running her hands over the buttons, she noticed deep teeth marks over the battery pack. In his playfulness, Boris had destroyed the remote.

Full-fledged panic slammed her chest.

She had to watch the game.

She charged the TV, searched for the manual ON button. She punched it hard. Still no picture, no sound. Lying on the floor, she noticed a separation of cord and plug. One of the Newfoundlands had gnawed through the wiring.

She'd scold the pups later. Right now she needed the nearest sports bar. She left the house with uncombed hair and mismatched flip-flops.

Wally's was a ten-minute drive away. When she arrived, Keely knew she was in the right place. All the cars in the parking lot had either Rogues bumper stickers or red, white, and blue pennants waving from their radio antennae.

Inside, Keely found the bar packed. Lots of smoke, lots of leather, little room to squeeze through the crowd. She searched for a place to sit or even stand. A far corner of the bar caught her eye. She avoided a dart game, a beer-chugging contest, and finally reached the empty spot.

"I'm Wally," the bartender shouted over the noise. "First beer's on the house." He nodded toward an empty keg. "Twenty bucks gets you in the pool."

It turned out that people were betting on the

number of hits by any one Rogue player. The keg
was already half filled with money. Those partici-
pating in the pool wrote down their name, along
with their favorite athlete and the number of sin-
gles, doubles, triples, and home runs the player
would score.

Keely stared at the paper for a long time. So
long, the bartender raised his brow. "Rookie," he
nicknamed her on the spot, "need some help?"

She scratched her head. "I want to bet on Psycho McMillan."

"You and half the bar." A woman in her late
twenties squeezed in beside Keely. She wore a
Rogues T-shirt, cutoff jeans, and a sassy smile.
"Psycho's my man."

"Mona, Rookie." Wally introduced the two
women.

"My man too," a redhead called from a table
behind Keely. "Love them bad boys."

"That's DeDe," Mona pointed out. "Give her a
little tequila and some home runs and her clothes
come off."

Keely's eyes widened. Should prove an interesting game.

Talk of the Rogues swirled around her. It didn't
take long for Keely to realize that it was not just
Psycho who belonged to the bar. The patrons
claimed the entire team as kin.

When she handed her paper to Wally, he cut
her a look. "Pretty damn hopeful, aren't you,
Rookie? I've seen Psycho hit two home runs in a
game, but never three." He pointed to the keg.

"Well, if he scores big, you'll be taking home a load of cash."

After the preliminary singing of the National Anthem and the introduction of the players, the game got under way. Keely stood, her back to the bar, and took in the game. She followed most of the lingo, although a few phrases flew over her head.

Her heart jumped when the camera swung to Psycho. He followed Romeo, batting sixth. Two bats in hand, he raised them over his head and took several practice swings.

"He's got his game face on!" DeDe hopped up and clapped her hands. Her breasts nearly spilled from her halter. "Check out those hips. Baby's nice and loose."

"The man's had sex." Mona smiled knowingly. "His practice swing says he screwed his brains out."

Laughter lifted from the surrounding tables.

Heat rose in Keely's cheeks as she turned to Mona. "How do you know he's had sex?" She kept her voice as low as possible.

Mona ordered two fingers of Wild Turkey and tossed the whiskey back in one swallow. "A player's hips never lie," she stated. "His swing reflects his life. If he's all tight in the shoulders, his wife's bitchy or he's between girlfriends. When there's swivel in his hips, a man's gotten lucky. Looks like Psycho got lucky more than once last night."

Three times actually—information Keely kept to herself. She stared at the screen, seeing, yet not really knowing the man who now stood in the batter's box.

Not just stood . . . but *owned* home plate.

Psycho's game face scared the hell out of Keely. His baseball helmet fit low on his brow.

His dark brown eyes looked black with purpose and intensity.

The set of his mouth was severe.

She could feel the hum of his body through the television screen as he dug in, took his first pitch.

The bar crowd bemoaned his strike.

"Come on, baby," Mona shouted. "Mama needs a double."

"A triple," another customer shouted.

All around the bar, voices rose as to what each person needed to win the pool.

"Home run." Keely crossed her fingers, then kissed the tips.

A foul ball into the lower deck drew the redhead's scream. "Straighten it out, Psycho!"

Straighten it out he did. He connected with a fastball. A ball he hit so hard, Keely swore it would be caught in Norfolk.

The bar exploded. Beers were shaken, the foam spewing like champagne. Bowls of peanuts were thrown in the air like confetti. The fans jumped up and down, hugged each other, and shrieked.

Keely watched it all from her corner of the bar. She'd never seen anything like it. The excitement and enthusiasm rolled over her, making her giddy.

"Some woman needs to take a bow," Mona yelled.

Kate Angell

"That woman needs to ride him again tonight," DeDe shouted in agreement. "Keep his hips loose."

Keely's face couldn't get any hotter.

The game progressed, with solid Rogue hits and countless Yankee errors.

"Chaser's been greased," Mona noted. "Catcher's got swivel."

More than one Rogue had had sex last night. Risk Kincaid hit two doubles and a triple; apparently his wife, Jacy, had warmed him up for to-day's game.

"Romeo's not on his game," DeDe commented. "He's usually the loosest of the Bat Pack. Today he's one tight muscle. Man can't pay for a hit."

Psycho made up for Romeo's hitless streak. He captured the day with two home runs. At the bottom of the eighth, the score was 6–4, with the Rogues holding off the Yankees. The bar went collectively silent with Psycho's last at bat. Keely held her breath, hoping for that third home run.

After two balls and one strike, Psycho delivered.

Keely was so stunned, she couldn't move.

Jostled by hugs and deaf from screams, she found herself lifted off her feet and swung around by a biker named Mad Dog. DeDe danced topless between tables. Customers patted each other on the back as if they'd been the one to score.

Keely was doused with National Bohemian. Her shirt was so damp she looked like she'd entered a wet T-shirt contest. Her hair hung limply

222

about her face. She smelled of beer. And the biker's cologne.

At the top of the ninth, the first three Yankee batters fell to a series of strikes. The Rogues had won. The celebration at Wally's turned wild.

When her name was called for winning the pool, two men lifted her up on the bar to claim her victory money. The bartender introduced her as Rookie, and the name stuck for the next hour as she bought several rounds for the house.

Time got away from Keely. Ten minutes turned into two hours. Wally lent her his leather vest to cover her wet T-shirt, then stuffed her winnings in a bank bag. After plying her with souvenirs, he escorted her safely to her station wagon.

She drove to the Colonial, flying high, her heart happy. She'd not only seen Psycho play ball, but she'd won the pool. Her little eighteen-inch TV had just been replaced by a state-of-the-art television. Next season Psycho would fill her apartment on a wide screen.

"Where the hell have you been?"

Psycho stormed down the staircase to corner her by the fireplace. His eyes were dangerously dark, his lips flattened against his teeth. Keely pressed her hands behind her back to hide her souvenirs.

"I walked in the house and you weren't here," Psycho growled. "I found Boris with his face in a popcorn bowl and Bosephus licking spilled Pepsi off the coffee table in the family room. You didn't leave a note."

She heard the concern beneath his anger. Despite his scowl, the fact he cared was very sweet. "I left in a hurry," she explained.

"Reason for the great escape?" His hard gaze lit on the man's leather vest that hung nearly to her knees. He flicked one edge with his finger, exposing the see-through cotton beneath. "A wet T-shirt contest?"

She drew one hand from behind her back and poked him in the nose. Twice. "I got caught in a Rogues celebration."

He snagged her wrist to stop her poking. "Where did you get the foam finger?"

"At Wally's."

A muscle jumped along his jaw. "*Wild* Wally's?"

She pursed her lips. "The crowd shook and sprayed beer with every Rogue hit. I met Mona and DeDe and got hugged by Mad Dog. The bartender called me Rookie. I won the pool."

He waited for her to run out of breath before he plucked peanuts from her hair. "Why Wally's when you have a home theater right here?"

"Blame Boris." She stifled a yawn as exhaustion caught up with her. "He chewed both the remote and the cord on the television."

"Which sent you to a sports bar to watch the game."

"I promised to watch you play."

"You kept your word." He drew her to him, holding her loosely. "Next game, you'll sit in reserved seating at the stadium. Chaser, Romeo, and I hold a section of baseline seats for family and friends."

Keely reminded herself she was his designer, not family. "I'm fine watching TV right here once the set's rewired."

His knuckles bumped the bank bag still held behind her back. "How much did you win?"

"Four thousand dollars." She grinned. "I bet you'd hit three home runs."

"You bet high."

"Not according to your hips."

"My *hips*?"

"The ladies in the bar said hips don't lie. Yours were loose from sex."

He rocked against her. "Nice and loose."

"I wanted to slide under the bar when they said that."

"If the customers had known you'd gotten me loose, you'd have drunk free for the remainder of the season."

"I'm not a drinker, nor do I broadcast my sex life."

"When most women do a jock, they go out and rent a billboard."

"I prefer to remain anonymous."

"Embarrassed to be having sex with me?"

"That's not why I blush."

Psycho slid the foam finger from her hand. He then ran the tip along her cheek, her collarbone, between her damp breasts, and down the zipper on her jeans. He pressed the foam finger between her thighs. "This would make a great shower mitt."

She sniffed; the scent of stale beer was heavy on her skin. "I could use a shower."

"I'm available to soap your back."

"More than my back needs soaping."

Psycho soaped Keely to two major orgasms. Later that night, she came to him wrapped only in a red boa. One of his gifts to her. Tickly feathers and a soft woman greased Psycho's hips all night long. He was hyped to play ball the next day.

The Rogues continued to play hard. As did every other team in the league. They climbed to third in the National League East standings in June, then slipped to fourth in July. By August they were holding fast at second.

Through it all, Psycho never tired of the grueling schedule. Nor did he tire of Keely Douglas. She'd refused his offer of sideline seats and had taken to watching his games at Wally's. She went to the bar strictly as a fan, not as the woman who warmed his bed.

Only the bartender knew Keely's true identity. Psycho had made an after-hours visit to the bar and pointedly spoken to Wally. He didn't want Keely to be hit on by other men or crushed in the exuberant crowd. Wally had promised to keep one eye on the designer at all times.

Today Psycho had the day off. He lay in bed and stared at the ceiling. A full day of nudity would be good. Keely had promised no workmen in the house. No deliveries. The day was his to enjoy. And he planned to enjoy it . . . and Keely.

Keely's thoughts, however, ran to travel. She

entered his room wearing a soft peach sundress and a softer smile, and threw him a curveball. "I'd like to visit Colonial Williamsburg today."

"Not my idea of a great day off."

She came closer to the bed, yet remained just beyond his reach. She was wise to the fact that he'd grab her and lay her out flat. The trip would soon be forgotten.

"The restoration on your home is progressing nicely," she said. "You have a responsibility to this house. In Williamsburg, you can experience the history of this place firsthand. Learn about Colonel William Lowell. Afterward, you'll feel his presence in your home."

He wasn't feeling responsible, nor did he need a Colonial ghost in his life. Three would be a crowd. "I want to feel you, not Lowell."

"You felt me up all night long."

"I want all day too."

"I want Williamsburg."

Crap. Psycho stretched, then rolled out of bed. He stood naked before her, fully aroused. "I always get mobbed in public places."

"The employees won't bother you," she promised, holding his gaze and not letting her eyes drop. "They're dressed in period clothing portraying colonists. Baseball won't be foremost on their minds."

She had done her research. "I hate tours." The thought of sightseeing stole his erection.

"No tours; we'll walk the grounds. We'll avoid big groups. We'll buy you a pair of sunglasses

227

with an attached nose. There's a costume shop on our way out of town."

People would laugh at him. "No fake nose."

"You can carry a cane, limp a little." She was on a roll. "No one will recognize you."

He scratched his belly. "I'm not limping."

"I'll wrap a doll in a blanket. You can carry a baby. Fans won't be looking for a Psycho Daddy."

No way in hell. "Not going to happen."

She blew out a breath. "Fine, I'll go alone. I'll gas up the station wagon—"

"Your muffler's broken and blowing black smoke. Highway patrol would pull you over before you hit the city limits."

"Can I borrow your truck?"

"No."

"I'll rent a car."

He liked that idea even less. "Convince me to take you." Sex might get him there.

"No convincing, Psycho," she said firmly. "You have to want to go. I won't drag you there."

"I could drag you in the shower."

"No sex."

Keely sounded a little cranky. "Your time of the month?"

She shook her head, hesitating. "I'm . . . sore."

Psycho couldn't help himself; he smiled. He'd worn her out. Knowing her muscles ached from bed play made him relax. A cold shower would take the edge off.

"We'll do Williamsburg today." Walking would ease her stiffness.

"And I'll do you tonight," she promised.

A solid compromise.

Thirty minutes later, they hit the highway and cruised south. Arriving in Colonial Williamsburg, Psycho parked his truck, then agreed to a carriage ride.

Keely was a history buff and knew more about Williamsburg than their guide. She pointed out homes, taverns, and Market Square, relating interesting stories about each. On her request, their driver slowed the carriage near North England Street so they could watch African-American interpreters reenact "jumping the broom," a marriage ceremony.

As soon as the ride ended, Psycho backtracked with Keely to the numerous locations that had caught her eye.

The Magazine showcased an arsenal of muskets and cannon. Visitors could watch the militia drill and listen to the fife and drums.

Psycho could only shake his head over the Colonial clothing. All along the cobblestone streets, they passed men in linen shirts, cravats, waistcoats, and breeches. They wore cocked hats on their heads. White stockings fell to black buckled shoes. The Colonial costumes looked stifling in the August heat.

The ladies had to be sweating bullets. Whether a wealthy planter's wife, corseted in taffeta, or a slave wearing coarse wool, they were all weighed down with layers of clothing. Most of them also wore wigs.

The wigs made Psycho's own head itch. He sweated for the reenactors.

On Duke of Gloucester Street, a milkmaid boldly winked at him. He didn't wink back. At the milliner's shop, the dressmaker flirted with him from behind a fan. He looked the other way.

Across the street, the sweaty blacksmith flexed his muscles, and Keely smiled.

Her smile didn't sit well with Psycho and he tightened his hold on her hand.

They crossed to Palace Green Street, explored the green, and took in the governor's palace. It was an immense structure, complete with gates, gardens, offices, walks, canal, and orchards.

The George Wythe House came next. A house inhabited by the ghost of Lady Ann Skipwith. Keely knew the woo-woo. She whispered the story to him. "Lady Ann and her husband attended a gala at the governor's palace," she began. "Because of some slight, her temper flared and she left in such a hurry, one of her slippers broke. She hobbled up the wooden staircase at the Wythe House, sounding like someone with a wooden leg."

She swallowed nervously, darted a look toward the staircase in the old Colonial. "It's said she took her own life. And that she's buried in the graveyard of nearby Bruton Parrish Church. Many have heard her ascending the stairs in her one good slipper."

Psycho rolled his eyes. "I'm not staying overnight to hear Annie limp up the stairs."

Keely poked his chest, then turned toward the door. "Respect the dead."

In Psycho's opinion, Keely needed a reality check. Following close behind her, he purposely began to limp. The scuffing sound of one boot drew Keely's shriek. And his laugh. She punched his arm so hard his muscle spasmed. Seemed she couldn't take a joke.

Keely was fascinated by the apothecary. She knew all about the antiquated methods of setting bones and extracting teeth. How to bleed patients with leeches. She knew the mystery of mixing various ingredients into potions, which herbs cured headaches and colds. Psycho was impressed.

Back on the street, a puppet show caught her eye at the Folk Art Center. Psycho drew the line at puppets. Not his thing.

Keeping one eye on her, he slipped into a building with a sign that read ENGLISH REVOLUTIONS. The room was narrow and dark, and smelled of wealth and age. Oil paintings hung on the walls in heavy frames. Colonial artifacts were displayed on floor-to-ceiling shelves. He'd entered an art gallery.

"Can I be of assistance?"

The male voice hit Psycho like a punch to the gut. *Wimbledon*. It took several seconds for Chris Collier to emerge from the shadows. Psycho stared at the Rogues' starting pitcher. Lean and blond in a coral polo shirt, charcoal slacks, and tasseled loafers, he had *country club* written all over him.

Whereas Psycho was backstreet Philly.

Dislike churned deeply. Collier wasn't earning his paycheck. Once his vision had cleared, the pitcher had started strong, only to fade midseason. The man wasn't "on" with every game. He lacked the all-out dedication that would take the Rogues to the World Series.

He'd pitched straight to Baltimore last week. Every Oriole had gotten a hit. Collier had the outfield running their asses off. He had more hits off him in five innings than the opposing pitcher had in the entire three-game series. The man sucked.

"Williamsburg, an odd place to spend your day off," Chris said dryly.

"I could say the same for you."

"My family owns the gallery," Chris returned. "I chose today to visit."

"I had my arm twisted."

"Feel free to look around," Collier said stiffly. "I'm working in the back."

Psycho glanced out the front window. A large crowd was still gathered around the puppet show. A show that still held Keely's attention. He glanced into a side room. Noted oriental carpets on the floor and a dozen large oil paintings. All of Revolutionary War subjects. Battle scenes and decorated Confederate officers.

One painting stood out. Looked damn familiar. He blinked, stared, couldn't believe his eyes. Before him, a Confederate colonel sat astride his warhorse, amid a backdrop of autumn trees.

Psycho moved in closer. The scripted brass plaque on the heavy gilded frame read COLONEL WILLIAM LOWELL. The painter was Winslow Homer.

Keely's painting. The one she'd sworn belonged to her family and that she'd promised to place on his mantel when the house was fully restored. A painting Psycho knew she'd never truly owned.

To Keely's credit, her initial claim to be William's illegitimate grandniece had won over the Daughters. The restoration had begun.

But the full preservation of the Colonial wouldn't be achieved without this painting. The painting belonged in his home.

A small discreet sign on the wall indicated that patrons must consult with the gallery owner prior to a purchase. He needed to find Wimbledon to ask the price.

The man hated Psycho, and might not consider him a legitimate buyer. For Keely, he had to try.

He went to the door and shouted down the hall, "Consultation on a painting."

He swore he heard Collier grind his teeth. "My father does all presale consultations," the man shot back. "Call him tomorrow."

"I want to discuss Colonel William Lowell."

"That painting's not for sale."

Bullshit. Psycho took off down the hallway and confronted Collier behind his desk. "Not for sale to the public or strictly to me?"

"To you."

At least the man was honest. Psycho fought back his temper. "I own the Lowell House," he informed Chris. "I'm having it restored. The colonel's painting belongs in his home."

"The painting is an original Winslow Homer," Chris stated. "My father has thought long and hard about donating it to the Museum of Fine Arts in Richmond."

"Give me a price and I'll write you a check."

"Money can't buy bloodlines."

Psycho slammed his hands on the desktop. "That painting is very important to someone in my life. I'm asking nicely a second time, how much?"

Ticked by Psycho's persistence, Chris pushed himself from his chair with a wince. Only a slight wince, but enough of a grimace that Psycho took notice. "What's wrong with your leg?"

"Not a damn thing."

Psycho came around the corner of the desk, caught the Ace bandage that held an ice pack to the pitcher's knee. Chris wasn't on the injured list. He was scheduled to pitch tomorrow.

"What the hell?" Psycho raised a brow.

Chris dropped back in his chair and swore. "I didn't want anyone to know," he finally said. "I twisted my knee two months ago. Some days are better than others."

Psycho ran the Rogues schedule through his mind. "Did the injury happen on the road against the Dodgers or at home against the Twins?"

Chris couldn't meet his gaze. "At home, at Hollywood Harts."

"The animal sanctuary?"

The pitcher's breath hissed through his teeth. "Never thought I'd be sharing my personal life with you."

"I'm only interested in the damage to your knee."

"I was injured by Fancy. I've been helping Sophie on my days off. At dinnertime, I mistakenly got between Fancy and her trough—"

"And your life flashed before your eyes."

Chris rubbed his knee. "Fancy bumped me hard. She let me know in no uncertain terms the food belonged to her."

The pig packed two hundred pounds of squealing hunger. Psycho seldom laughed appropriately. He broke out laughing now, yet was quick to sober. A right-handed pitcher needed a flexible left knee. Normally his knee took all his weight when he released the ball, but Chris's knee was damaged. "How bad is it?"

"I've seen a specialist; the tear is minor. A cortisone shot controls the pain during the game."

A bad knee was the reason for Chris's erratic pitching. "No one knows?"

"You do now."

Psycho had played with a sprained ankle and broken ribs and never consulted the team trainer. A part of him understood Chris's need not to broadcast his injury. It would leave the man vulnerable to both the opposing team and the press. He didn't need to be under a microscope.

Psycho rested his hip on the corner of the desk. "I've played beat up. It's your business. I won't say anything."

Chris looked visibly relieved. "Thanks."

"My silence comes with a price." Psycho pressed his advantage. "Sell me the painting."

Chris's nostrils flared. "Asshole."

"Asshole with a Winslow Homer."

At the end of a short but heated discussion, Psycho wrote Chris a check. A moderate check. Chris agreed to hold the painting until Psycho called for delivery.

"Psycho?" Keely's voice came from the main door.

"Give me a sec." Psycho caught Chris's look toward the gallery, followed by his smile. "My designer," he explained.

"Yeah, and Sophie Hart means no more to me than a monthly donation to her sanctuary."

"Mind your own business."

"You'd better go mind yours. The lady's checking out the paintings."

Psycho found Keely by the artifacts. "Nothing worth seeing here," he told her. "Let's hit Merchants Square for souvenirs before we leave."

Souvenirs was the magic word to get her moving. She'd brought her purse and had her own spending money. She refused to let Psycho pay her way.

At Liberty Gifts, he discovered her flipping through a copy of George Washington's version of *Rules of Civility and Decent Behavior in Company and Conversation*. "You wouldn't have lasted a day in Colonial America," she teased. "Read rule number seven."

He peered over her shoulder and read, *"Put not off your Cloths in the presence of Others, nor go out your Chamber half Drest."* So much for nudists.

He tapped rule number two with his finger. *"When in Company, put not your Hands to any Part of the Body, not usually Discovered.* No slapping my ass."

"I did that in private, not in public."

Keely bought tins of the strong Jamaican coffee that had been served in the eighteenth-century coffeehouses. They argued over knickknacks. She wanted a wooden canteen and he chose a round pewter flask. She preferred a Colonial dollhouse and he picked up a wooden toy pistol. Her quill pen and ink powder paper gave way to his board game of Goose and Dice.

They agreed on a fruitwood compass pedestal table. When Keely turned her back, Psycho paid to have the table shipped to Richmond, along with every item in the store she'd touched and admired. There were more birthdays ahead.

They ate a late lunch on the terrace of the Williamsburg Inn before heading home. Psycho was finding it more and more natural to call the Colonial his home. With Keely under his roof, he'd begun to feel grounded.

There were still times he felt unsure of their future. Times when he wanted to block furniture deliveries and pull out new electrical wiring. He'd thought about rolling up the oriental rugs and tossing them in the construction dumpster. But one small smile from Keely settled him down. It scared him to think such a small, skinny woman could have such an effect on him. But she did.

Back in Richmond, after a night of marathon sex, Psycho pushed himself up on his elbow and stared down on the sleeping woman at his side. She hadn't been sore going into their lovemaking, but he was pretty damn certain she'd be moving slow in the morning.

At the onset, he'd taken her so slowly, she'd begged him to go faster. Every muscle in his body had stretched and strained, the physical ache as satisfying as nine innings of baseball. With his second taking, his wild man had escaped. He'd taken her with an abandon she'd come to match. Keely could get it on.

She had love bites on her neck and just below her navel. A raspberry abrasion from his stubble on her inner thigh.

Marks that claimed her as his.

He'd lay claim awhile longer.

He had her until October, when the restoration would be completed. A part of him couldn't imagine the Colonial without Keely Douglas in it. She, the dogs, and Colonel William Lowell had somehow become his family.

TWELVE

"No running, Em." Romeo Bellisaro's voice stole into Emerson Kent's cubical two seconds before he stepped into view.

She should have known he was in the building. The sound of female sighs grew louder with his approach. But she'd been concentrating on her next sports story, and had tuned out all noise. She should have been more alert.

Em looked up. Romeo's smile was both sexy and disarming. After that climactic kiss at Hollywood Harts, she'd been leery of letting him close.

So leery, she'd asked the receptionist at the main entrance to buzz her cubical when he arrived unannounced so she could escape him. Somehow he'd gotten by the watchdog today.

"A signed baseball for her nephew." Romeo was both mind reader and ladies' man. He'd bribed the receptionist so he could catch Emerson unaware.

She looked at him over the red rim of her glasses. "What do you want, Romeo?"

"World peace. To win the World Series." He produced a brown bag from behind his back. "Lunch with you."

She was hungry. And Romeo had remembered how much she hated leaving her desk and battling the noon rush. He'd thoughtfully brought lunch to her. A meal that consisted of a club sandwich and a cream soda. Two of her favorites.

His consideration touched her. "Thanks."

He pulled up an extra chair and ate alongside her. He seemed to fill her cubical with sin and testosterone. He looked incredibly handsome. Recent haircut, early afternoon shave. Lavender pullover and khakis. Not many men could pull off pastels. Romeo had never looked more masculine.

Their knees bumped, and awareness shimmied up her thigh, all the way to her panties. Her cotton crotch grew damp.

Annoyed by her body's reaction, she shifted on the seat and placed six inches between them. The space wasn't enough.

Deliberately or not, he brushed her again. A faint graze of his shoulder against her arm as he leaned in to take a bite of his pastrami on rye. The big-bodied Rogue had her cornered. And he knew it.

The glint in his brown eyes told her he'd purposely sat between her and the door. She wasn't bolting on him. No matter how he overwhelmed her.

Emerson liked having control over her mind

and body. With Romeo, she lost her professional edge. She went from reporter to woman. He had all the power. The sexual power that made her mind go blank and her heartbeat quicken.

"Miss me?" he asked between sips of root beer.

She shook her head. "You've been away three days. Not long enough to be missed."

"Some women miss me the moment I walk out the door."

"Women with too much time on their hands."

He grinned and nudged her with his elbow, which created goose bumps all over her body. "Did you catch our win over San Diego?"

She'd been glued to the television. "The Rogues played hard. You deserved to sweep the series."

"You should have made the trip."

Instead, she'd decided not to travel with the team. She'd needed to distance herself from the third baseman. Romeo made her nerve-endings hum. She'd needed to quiet her thoughts and clear her head.

She sat a little straighter and drew her body away from his. Which he noticed.

He reached out and tugged the lapel on her suit, drawing her back toward him. He ran his fingers along the navy blue satin trim. "Headache, cold?" he asked. "Touch of the flu? You're not coming on to me like you usually do."

"I've never come on to you."

"There's always a first time. I know when a woman wants me."

"I want you to go."

He brushed a strand of hair behind her ears. The tip of his thumb lingered near her lobe. "I make you nervous."

So nervous her skin itched. "You're sitting too close."

"I could be sitting across the room and you'd feel the same way. Chemistry, Em. Hot and undeniable."

She pulled back slightly. "Such a big ego."

"Not as big as my—"

She held up her hand, imagining, but not needing to know the size of his package. She glanced at the Rogues calendar on her desk. "You're back on the road tomorrow. A grueling schedule: Boston, Toronto, Cincinnati."

"Grueling can wait. I need a date for Readers for Life tonight."

"A fund-raiser for the new children's library." Em was aware of the event. "Championed by Afton Patterson."

"Afton promotes any cause that lands her on the Society page," Romeo stated. "She's mentioned in About Town twice a week."

That, she was. Emerson knew the socialite well. Prior to Sports, Em had worked Features. She'd covered Afton's fund-raisers. A party girl and social piranha, the redhead lived off gossip and an obscenely large trust fund.

What Afton wanted, Afton got. She wrote fat checks, then seduced others to do the same. She'd slept with nearly every man, single or married, who supported her causes. Emerson knew that for a fact. She'd walked in on Afton and a senator having sex in a hall closet at the Horseshoe Ball prior to the Kentucky Derby. Em did not vote to reinstate him in the next election.

"Date me, Em," Romeo pressed.

"Interviews only," she said firmly. "I already have plans for the evening."

"Man plans?"

"Plans," was all she'd confirm. She closed her day planner, as if to hide a name from him. Let Romeo think she was meeting a man for dinner and drinks. Someone other than the sexiest man in Major League Baseball. She had to protect her heart.

She was no more than a novelty to him. A reporter who refused to have sex with him. Even though their bet had struck sparks between them, once the season ended he'd place wagers with other women. The man was competitive. Sex was as much a game to him as baseball.

Silence stretched between them until Romeo cleared away the sandwich wrappers. He tipped up her chin with one finger, forcing her to look at him. "If not Readers for Life, join me at the Athletic Club in two weeks for a short cocktail party and presentation. High school athletes will be awarded scholarships. Great human interest."

Two weeks away. No excuse to decline came to mind. She sighed, weakened. "One date, then you'll leave me alone?"

"The question is: after one date, will you be able to walk away from me? You may become so hot and bothered, I'll start to look good. I am good, Em. Damn good."

She was sure he'd be as legendary as his tattoo.

"*Out.*" She pointed to the cubical exit.

Romeo left with a satisfied grin on his face. He looked as if he knew he'd worked her up, that her body was now warm and restless.

His empty chair still held his presence. Strong, dominant, and very male. His scent lingered, sunshine and citrus. All a maddening reminder that Romeo Bellisaro left his imprint with every visit.

She picked up the chair and carried it to the cubical across the hall. Distance only made her heart grow fonder. Romeo was still real to her. Larger-than-life and too sexy to forget.

Her frustration built. A small part of her wished she'd accepted his invitation to Readers for Life. She'd passed on the event to spend an evening with a pint of white chocolate raspberry ice cream and a DVD of *The Notebook*.

No doubt a big mistake.

She'd suffer for her decision. She had no idea how much until the following morning.

She was back at her desk by six a.m., flipping through the morning edition of the paper. She scanned Sports. Slowed on Features. Her coffee soon grew cold. A zucchini muffin was forgotten by her fax.

She stared at the About Town section until her eyes hurt. A full-page photo of Romeo Bellisaro looked right back at her. Romeo and Afton Patterson. There were four photographs in all and twenty inches of newsprint. The Readers for Life Fund-raiser was proclaimed a huge success.

Amid the backdrop of evening gowns and tuxedos, Romeo looked perfectly at home, one of Richmond's elite. No forced smile, no stiffness. He could talk sports with men and charm the women. Em was sure everyone had dug deeply to donate to the library.

The thought of Romeo and Afton tightened Em's chest. She had no claim on the third baseman. After that one kiss, she'd restricted their time together.

She'd wanted a simple friendship. No strings, no ties. No more kisses. Nothing, however, was simple where Romeo was concerned. The man complicated her life. Tied her stomach in knots. Stole her identity. She'd known when she'd limited their activities that countless other women would line up to make themselves available.

She could have been at the fund-raiser by his side instead of reading about it the day after. He'd invited her. And she'd declined. Her stomach shouldn't hurt over the fact that Romeo received more column space in Features than the entire Rogues team did in Sports.

"Sweet article." The new Features editor stopped by her cubical. "I hope you don't mind that I stole Romeo from Sports. Every eye was on him at the library fund-raiser. The man can work a crowd."

Emerson glanced down at the photographs. "Looks like he worked Afton Patterson."

"They were pretty tight, drinking champagne

and dancing together." The editor dipped her head and lowered her voice. "I caught them in the parking lot right after the event. Afton had loosened his tie and jammed her hands *deep* in the pockets of his dress slacks. She was feeling for more than change."

More than Emerson needed or wanted to know. She immediately closed the paper. And the Features editor moved on.

Em had two weeks to get it together. To ready herself for the Athletic Club. But a week later, she knew she'd never attend the event with Romeo. Not after the syndicated news broadcast his picture across the wire. A photograph that spoke a thousand words: Boston hotel lobby; near the elevator banks; Romeo and Afton so wrapped together, Em couldn't tell where he ended and she began.

An article had followed. Afton had arrived by private jet to watch Romeo play against the Red Sox.

She claimed to be his number-one fan.

Romeo didn't offer a disclaimer.

Emerson had sat in her cubical, feeling numb and disheartened, until the afternoon cleaning crew nudged her to move her chair so they could vacuum around her desk.

Later that evening, when she'd wrapped up an interview with Jon Sloan, quarterback for the newly franchised Richmond Outlaws, she boldly asked him to escort her to the Athletic Club event. She'd taken him by surprise. The man had actually blushed. Emerson had found Sloan's shyness almost as charming as Romeo's confidence.

It was time to get on with her life. To move beyond the third baseman. Get out and date other men.

Even if her heart wasn't in it.

Romeo Bellisaro would have passed on the Athletic Club event had team owner Guy Powers not insisted his players attend. He'd arrived in a badass mood. Emerson Kent had canceled off their date in a phone message.

He'd played her message a dozen times. Her voice had sounded forced, not smooth and self-assured as was her normal manner. She hadn't even given an explanation. She'd just canceled.

He stood now, near the bar, surrounded by both professional and high school athletes. The younger jocks were all vying for college scholarships. Guy Powers backed new blood. That was the only reason Romeo had come.

He looked about the room. Sportsmen from all the Richmond teams had made an appearance. The Outlaws were well represented. The newly organized football franchise had won its first four games of the season. Members of the Renegades basketball team were there, too. Five of the starters stood head and shoulders above the growing crowd.

A crowd that suddenly included Emerson Kent and quarterback Jon Sloan. Romeo felt as if he'd been punched in the gut.

He watched as she smiled up at Sloan. The same smile that sucked air from Romeo's lungs and had spurred him to kiss her. The smile that left him hard as wood and walking stiff.

He hadn't spoken to Emerson since his road trip. Her choice. Not his.

"You been dumped?" Psycho McMillan's bluntness made him blink as the right fielder passed Romeo two fingers of scotch.

"Dumped and blindsided," Romeo admitted. "I had no idea Emerson would show."

"And with Jon Sloan."

Romeo's gaze fixed on the quarterback. The man's hand rested low on Emerson's spine. He was too damn familiar for Romeo's liking.

Psycho tugged on his gray tie, which he'd worn over a black T-shirt scripted with *Guess What I've Been Up To?* He wasn't one for dressing up. Guy Powers had given Psycho a look that indicated the right fielder would be fined for improper attire. Wouldn't be the first or the last time. Psycho had his own rules. He preferred to pay fines rather than conform.

"Your reporter doing football now?" asked Psycho.

"Looks that way," Romeo said angrily.

He didn't know how to fix what he hadn't thought broken. Even though she'd resisted, Romeo had believed Em was into him. Her body reacted to his nearness. Her scent was warm and aroused. She had all the trademarks of a woman who wanted a man.

Perhaps he'd read her wrong.

"Seen Chaser?" Psycho asked.

"He bowed out," Romeo told him. "Man's got marriage on the brain. He's buffing new tile floors in Jen Reid's kitchen tonight."

"Buffing, huh?" One corner of Psycho's mouth curved into a smile. "Beats the hell out of small talk."

Romeo wasn't feeling sociable. Anyone approaching him quickly veered away from his scowl. He sipped his scotch. Stared at Emerson Kent. He caught every tilt of her head, the way her eyes smiled, her hand gestures. The twist of her dress over her hips when she shook hands with someone. The sweet curve of her calves. Her poise in spiked heels.

The realization of how much he'd missed her was as startling as the look on Em's face when she caught sight of him. She went wide-eyed and pale, then turned her back on him.

Her body language said it all. Romeo wasn't welcome in her life. She'd yet to give him a reason why.

He recalled their kiss at Hollywood Harts. How she'd shattered and gotten scared. How she'd held him at arm's length from that point on. She was a woman who hated losing control.

Romeo, on the other hand, got lost in his partner during sex. All inhibitions were left at the bedroom door. He appreciated a woman's body as much as he enjoyed baseball.

Em was both woman and baseball to him. He'd

felt a real loss when she'd stopped traveling with the team. Now it seemed she'd stepped out of his life and into someone else's. She was decked out in a little black cocktail dress with gold link straps that left her shoulders bare. She looked damn hot.

Beside him, Psycho nodded left. "Afton Patterson's got her eye on you. She sure came on strong in Boston. Heard you had to call security. She's one scary bitch."

"The woman can't comprehend 'not interested.'"

"You're off the market. That makes women nuts."

Romeo cut Psycho a look. "Who says I'm off the market?"

"Anyone watching you watch Emerson Kent."

Heat circled Romeo's collar. "That obvious?"

"You're a goner, dude." Psycho finished off his scotch. "I'm out of here. Two-drink limit and I've had three. Guy would fine me for a fourth."

Romeo glanced at his watch. "We've been here less than an hour. Powers requested ninety minutes."

"Guy introduced me to a high school senior who plans to steal my position when he graduates from college. Kid's a kiss-ass."

"You're unmanageable." Romeo set his glass on the bar. "I'm good to go."

"Not just yet." Psycho pointed toward Emerson. "The lady's on the move. Looks like she's headed to the restroom. On my way out, I'll distract Sloan while you sneak up behind her."

"What makes you think I need to sneak?"

"The shocked look on her face when she saw you. She won't meet you head on."

Psycho was right. Romeo read her as a bundle of nerves.

He waited until Psycho shook hands with Jon Sloan before he took off down the hallway toward the ladies' restroom. He stood outside the door and collected his thoughts.

He'd never gone after a woman the way he had Emerson Kent. He might never do so again. He was out of his mind to want a woman who didn't want him back.

Within minutes, she swung through the door, almost colliding with him. She nearly jumped out of her skin. Her breathing stopped and her hand flattened over her heart.

He'd surprised her, all right.

Panic crossed her face, then a split second of pain. He'd expected her nervousness, but not the hurt. Something was off. Way off.

"Having a good time?" he casually asked.

"I was, until I saw you."

She wasn't her usual self. "I won't keep you long."

"You've no right to keep me at all."

She looked as though she might scream or knee him in the groin. "You broke our date to go out with another man? Why, Emerson?"

She took a moment to answer. "Jon and I have a lot in common."

"So do we. We share America's favorite pastime."

"Baseball season is almost over." Her words cut

him. "The Rogues are holding their own. You don't need my column to take you to the playoffs. Another reporter has been assigned to the team."

His lip curled. "So you can do football and Sloan?"

"Crude, Romeo. I expected more from you."

More *what*? Manners? Indulgence? Wasn't going to happen. He leaned in, and she backed against the wall. Her rejection made him crazy. Not Psycho crazy, but borderline nuts nonetheless.

"The Rogues will take our division, then go on to the World Series," he predicted. "When we win, Em, I don't give a damn who you're dating. I'm coming to collect on our bet."

He left her in the hallway, her eyes wide, lips parted. Motioning to Psycho, he hit the door. The two men walked out together. Romeo refused to look back.

Emerson Kent couldn't catch her breath. She felt miserable, crushed. Totally devastated. She hadn't planned on talking to Romeo at the Athletic Club event. When she'd found him waiting for her outside the restroom, her heart had slammed so wildly she'd felt faint.

Suddenly tired, Emerson closed her eyes. She wanted to lie down and sleep. For a solid week. Maybe a month. Maybe until next baseball season.

"Emerson, you sick?" Jon Sloan found her leaning against the hallway wall. "You're pale. Trembling. What can I do?"

After her brush with Romeo, she'd needed the support of the wall to hold her up. She forced a smile. "Take me home please. I've been working a lot of hours. I'm asleep on my feet," she lied.

Jon tucked her under his arm, lent her his support. "Happy to oblige."

The quarterback saw her safely home, then departed. Emerson entered her condo and stopped dead in the darkened foyer. A light flickered from the sunken living room. A light she hadn't left on before she'd gone out for the evening.

She picked up an umbrella from a stand near the door. Quietly, she pulled her cell phone from her purse, started to dial—

"I'm not a burglar, Em."

Romeo. She dropped the umbrella, moved toward the steps. She licked her lips. "Who let you in?"

"Psycho. The man has skills. Picking locks is just one of many."

What was he doing on her couch? All sprawled out and looking at home. He'd removed his charcoal suit jacket, loosened his silk tie. The top two buttons of his dress shirt were now open.

A copy of the week-old *Banner* was spread out on the coffee table. The newspaper that included the photographs of him with Afton Patterson.

The copy where she'd drawn devil horns and a goatee on Romeo's face. And blackened Afton's teeth.

She wanted to die. "Breaking and entering is a crime," was all she could manage.

"Arrests require fingerprints. Psycho works clean. Police couldn't raise a print."

Her heart felt squeezed by a fist. "Why are you here?"

He rattled the newspaper. "To tell you I look better in a mustache than a goatee."

Heat rushed to her cheeks. "I was being childish. I shouldn't have marked up your picture."

"Childish . . . or jealous?"

Definitely jealous. "Afton Patterson wants you."

"So do a lot of other women." His words held a straightforward honesty she had to respect. "Doesn't mean I want them back."

"Afton was in Boston."

"Uninvited in Boston," he stated. "She came on to me, was so persistent I paid hotel security to stand outside my door. The lady had a passkey."

"You didn't sleep with her?"

"I haven't slept with another woman since I met you."

It took several seconds for his words to sink in. During those seconds, he ran his hand through his hair, then looked her straight in the eye. "Psycho had the wild notion we weren't done talking. That more needed to be said."

"How much more?"

"Enough so that if I walk away, I walk away clean, with no regrets."

She'd regret his leaving. "You scare me, Romeo. When I'm with you, I lose me."

He pushed himself off the sofa. Stood tall. "I never wanted you lost, Em, only to find me."

Her breath hitched. Even with his blond hair mussed and his shirttail wrinkled, the man was hypnotically gorgeous. "I wish you weren't so good-looking." *And so damn hard to resist.*

"You're the first one to complain."

"You make my stomach go soft."

"You make me go hard."

"You're very physical."

"You're mental, Em. You think too much."

She bit down on her bottom lip and opened her heart. "I do like you."

"Then relax and let us happen." He moved to the bottom stair. Six steps separated them. "Meet me halfway, Emerson Kent." He took one step up.

She was too emotional to move. If she walked into his arms, she wasn't sure if her heart would burst with happiness or tears.

"I've had women after me all my life. I've never committed to anyone. Not until you." He took a second step. "Halfway, Em." He paused, hesitant. "Unless there's someone else?"

That set her feet in motion. "No one else."

Romeo blew out a breath. "Halfway . . ."

She met him in the middle of the staircase.

He stood still on the wide step, staring down at her. "Want me?"

"Want you bad," she admitted.

"Bad is very good." He slid one finger beneath one of the gold link straps on her dress and drew her to him. He traced that same finger down her cheek, along her neck, and over her bare shoulder.

She shivered. Was she ready for this man?

He took the decision out of her hands. "I'm not staying the night," he said softly. "Your body wants me, but your mind's not yet convinced.

255

Kate Angell

Talking is what we do best right now. The sex will
come later." A slow smile spread across his lips,
looking sexy and promising. "When we win the
World Series, I plan to kiss your panties off."

THIRTEEN

Kiss her panties off.

Romeo's words stayed with Emerson. Hot flashes claimed her whenever she thought of the third baseman.

Her mind was on him a lot.

The division play-offs had begun, and the Rogues hung in the race as a wild card. Em sat in the press box, covering every game. They might be all banged up, but the players' hearts beat strongly.

Psycho McMillan had T-shirts made up. White with a black inscription: *I Didn't Come Here to Lose*. The players wore the shirts beneath their jerseys.

Emerson had started traveling with the team again. Whether it was a home or an away game, once play ended, Romeo found her. Either at her condo or her hotel room. They talked, about their childhoods, friends, life in general.

Their minds connected on many levels. She smiled over the little things they had in common: organic cereal, Tide detergent, a preference for rye bread. Museums, concerts, and sporting events interested both. They liked cold weather. Bunny hill skiing for Emerson and downhill racing for Romeo.

To his credit, Romeo never pushed for sex. Never even brought up the topic as they lay in bed, her head on his shoulder. Talking was all he wanted. Until after the World Series.

The anticipation nearly killed her.

Beside her now, Romeo stretched his big body. He'd slept bare-chested, his pajama bottoms low on his groin. His *Legendary* tattoo was visible. "Day off, Em. Any plans?"

She pushed herself up on the sleigh bed, arranged pillows behind her head. Then tugged down her red silk nightgown, which had crept up her thighs. "I'm open to suggestions."

"Tomorrow we play the Raptors for the division title. A five-game series. My entire focus will be on winning. Today, I want to do something mindless. I want to totally clear my brain of the game."

"We could hit the American Folk Art Festival at Gallery 001. There's an exhibition by Jacob Kass: Painted Saws. The Features editor is out with the flu. I agreed to cover the event."

"Saws?" Romeo rubbed his eyes. "I said mindless, Em, not mind-numbing."

She rolled onto her side, placed a palm on his broad chest. When she felt his muscles jump, she smiled to herself. "You believe in the American spirit. Appreciate nostalgia. Kass's work depicts a simpler, trouble-free time."

"Depicted on dangerous tools."

"How about the Mystery Playhouse, then?" she suggested. "The Butler's Been Murdered Brunch."

"Too much thought. I'd have to track clues."

"There's a pumpkin-carving contest at Memorial Children's Hospital," she said. "I saw it on the Rogues' calendar of events."

"Psycho will be there. He carves Leatherface from *The Texas Chainsaw Massacre*. The scariest pumpkin you've ever seen. The kids love it."

Em would have nightmares. "Halloween's coming up fast."

"Right after the World Series."

She circled his nipple with one finger. "The Rogues will win."

"You believe this because . . . ?"

"You have to collect on your bet."

He kissed her then. A light kiss that had her leaning in as he slowly pulled away. He curved his hand over her hip and squeezed. "Sex can be mindless."

"So can saws."

"You want saws, I'll give you saws." His breath blew warm against her neck. "If they sell souvenirs at the Folk Art Festival, I'll buy Psycho a chain saw to do his pumpkin carving."

An hour later they found a lot more than chain saws at the exhibition. There were hand saws, circular saws, ice saws, sickles, corn cutters, and carpenter squares. Romeo went through the entire exhibit, then doubled back for a closer look. Emerson stood beside him, taking notes as he read about Jacob Kass's career as an artist following five decades as a master letterer and painter of commercial vehicles in Brooklyn. Only after retirement did his art embellish milk cans and frying pans, then eventually saws and other cutting tools.

Kass brought a bird's-eye realism to his work. Emerson's favorite, *Back to the Barn*, started near the handle of a grass scythe. The overhead view pictured a man herding a half dozen cows along a dirt road. Farther along the blade the road receded and the view expanded to take in farm buildings and cultivated fields. Near the point, faraway hills appeared under clouds streaked pink by the setting sun.

A composition of a New York subway station spiraling around a circular saw blade captured Romeo's attention. A slice of life with cosmopolitan appeal.

Emerson had planned to see the Jacob Kass exhibit with or without Romeo. It was twice as nice that he'd attended with her. She had all the information she needed for a great article. She would honor the man's life.

Souvenirs came in photographs of Kass's work. Romeo bought Em a matted depiction of *Back to the Barn*. She thanked him with a kiss once they were seated in his Viper.

A kiss that moved beyond *thank you* and straight to *want me*. Parked in an alleyway between a brick wall and a gray SUV, Romeo teased her lips and made her moan.

His erection ran the full length of his zipper. With a heavy sigh, he channeled his sexual energy into the Halloween event. "Time to carve a pumpkin."

"I don't touch pumpkin guts," Em told him.

"Psycho does."

Psycho McMillan was on his third pumpkin by the time Em and Romeo arrived. Set up in a lounge on the fourth floor, dozens of children too sick to attend Hollywood Harts had rolled their wheelchairs around a table. Several nurses accompanied them, and all eyes were glued to the rebellious, knife-wielding Rogue, who was capturing Casper the Friendly Ghost on an enormous pumpkin. Psycho held the kids spellbound with his contagious laugh and wax vampire teeth.

Every time he smiled, someone shrieked or giggled.

Standing off to the side, Emerson noticed a thin woman taking it all in. The same woman who had been at Jacy's Java the day Em met Romeo for an interview. It seemed ages ago, but in reality it had been no more than six months.

While Romeo hugged and chatted with the kids, Emerson approached the blonde. "Emerson Kent," she reintroduced herself.

The woman smiled. "You're Romeo's reporter."

"And you're Psycho's designer."

"Keely Douglas," the blonde said. "Psycho had a playdate with the kids and asked me to come along."

"Romeo wanted a day away from baseball," Em returned. "We attended an exhibit at the American Folk Art Festival this morning."

"Psycho watched cartoons until noon. His way of distancing himself from the game. Scooby Doo did the trick."

"The guys face a lot of pressure."

"All that stress will evaporate with a win. And the Rogues will win," Keely said confidently. "Today's about kids who may not see their next Halloween. Romeo and Psycho make a difference in their lives."

"They sure do." Emerson watched as Romeo selected a fat, misshapen pumpkin from those stacked against the far wall. He handed it to Psycho, who sliced off the stalk with a boning knife. Psycho then passed it to the little boy next to him to clean out the seeds.

"The gutting spoon, please," requested the boy.

Psycho threw back his head and laughed. "Use your hands. Spoons are for sissies."

The boy stared wide-eyed at Psycho, then back at the pumpkin. He squirmed, and the girl next to him squealed.

"You'll never earn your vampire teeth if you can't gut a pumpkin," Psycho told them.

As if to prove himself worthy of the teeth, the boy closed his eyes and stuck his hand inside. His face pinched and "yuck" escaped as he withdrew a handful of seeds and pulp from the inside. He immediately dropped the guts into a big bowl, shaking off his hand.

Psycho patted the boy on the back. "Way to go, Adrian." Reaching in to an athletic bag at his feet, Psycho rewarded Adrian with the wax teeth.

Adrian stuck them in his mouth and smiled a vampire smile.

After gulps and grimaces, Sarah, the little girl seated beside Adrian, earned her teeth as well. As did every child at the table. In no time, vampire smiles had everyone laughing.

Emerson turned to Keely. "Psycho's got a big heart."

"There's a good man in that bad boy," Keely agreed. "Earlier, he blindfolded the kids, put grapes in a bowl, and told them they were touching eyeballs. He did the same with strawberry jelly and called it blood. The kids went nuts. Psycho treats them as if they weren't sick. These children may be fragile, but they deserve to have fun at Halloween."

Both Psycho and Romeo brought fun. Emerson watched as Romeo pulled up a chair beside Sarah. He supported the little girl's wrist as she took a grease pencil and drew a face on the pumpkin. From where Em stood, it looked like a bat. They went on to attempt a mummy and Darth Vader.

Em soon realized the children didn't care if the face on the pumpkins resembled any of their requests. For an hour or two, the kids were with their baseball heroes. That was all that mattered.

Snacks of orange Jell-O and peach slices arrived. They all took out their teeth except Psycho. As they were getting ready to leave, Sarah gifted Romeo with the pumpkin they'd carved together. Emerson saw his jaw lock and his throat work as he bent and placed a kiss on the little girl's cheek. And Sarah giggled.

Psycho and Keely followed Romeo and Em from the hospital. "You can take out those teeth anytime now," Emerson heard Keely tell Psycho.

Psycho turned a heated look on the blonde, snapped his teeth, and she blushed bright red. Emerson could guess their plans for the rest of the afternoon. Bed and bite.

After their good-byes, Romeo set the pumpkin in his Viper, then took Em's hand. They started walking. They crossed the parking lot and strolled aimlessly for close to an hour.

Neither spoke until they reached a public park where children ran, swung on swing sets, and climbed on a metal structure that resembled a mountain. Romeo leaned against the fence, staring at all the activity. At all the kids with long, healthy lives ahead of them.

"Sarah gave me her pumpkin." his words came out slowly. "When the World Series is over, I want to take a group of terminally ill kids on a vacation of their choice. I want to do this personally, outside of Make a Wish or any other foundation. I don't want it publicized. I'd like you to come with me."

Tears welled up in Emerson's eyes. She blew out a breath. Romeo Bellisaro was an amazing man. "Of course, I'll go."

He nodded, smiled. "We'll put our plan in motion. Private bus, train, or plane, we'll find the best transportation possible. Keep the kids comfortable. Contract a medical team. I want to hear Sarah laugh."

Sarah would laugh, Emerson knew. The little girl would be downright giddy to travel with Romeo.

The sun sank behind a cloud. Dusk was fast approaching. Romeo looked around. "Where are we?"

They'd walked for miles, keeping quiet company, not paying attention to their surroundings. "South of the hospital," she guessed.

"Think we can find our way back?"

"If not, we can always call a cab."

Ninety minutes and several wrong turns later, they caught sight of the hospital off in the distance. "Buy you an early dinner?" he asked.

Em shook her head. "Let me cook for you instead. We'll stop at Blockbuster, pick up a few movies. Keep it relaxed and in-house tonight." She plucked her cell phone from her purse, dialed, and spoke briefly. Disconnecting, she turned to Romeo. "My masseur will be at the condo shortly. Let Max work you over. A deep tissue massage takes you to a happy place."

That had been two hours ago, and now Romeo was feeling damn happy. The massage had removed all the stress from his body. Emerson's spaghetti and wine sauce filled his stomach. *The Gladiator* with Russell Crowe had captured his attention. The feel of Emerson curled by his side on the sofa felt right. As if he'd waited for just her fit all his life.

Tomorrow, the National League Division Series pitted the Rogues against the Raptors. They'd need to win three out of five games to advance to the Championship Series. Chris Collier would be the starting pitcher. A pitcher thought by many on the team to have seen better days. Yet Psycho backed the man. The enmity between the two seemed to have vanished overnight. Now Psycho could actually be heard supporting the pitcher.

Romeo had discussed Psycho's change of attitude with Chaser. Chaser wanted to let sleeping dogs lie. There had been no further comments made. Psycho never offered an explanation.

Game day arrived, overcast and spitting rain. Not a good sign for the superstitious, but damp, slippery grass didn't hinder the Rogues. Metal cleats and an indomitable spirit brought them wins both at home and in Ontario.

The Rogues took the series 3–1.

Afterward, the players lined up for the team trainer. From strained shoulders to torn Achilles tendons, they were doctored and taped. Only Psycho and Chris Collier declined treatment. Psycho was too focused to feel pain. Collier swore himself good to go.

The Rogues next played St. Louis in the League Championship Series. The Cardinals were last year's World Series Champions, and planned to hold on to the title.

The Rogues saw it differently. Romeo pushed himself to the limit. And beyond. Every muscle in his body ached. He dove for line drives, tagged players out at third, even those who played dirty and purposely ran him over in the hope he'd drop the ball. He held tight.

Psycho hit like a maniac. Home run after home run.

Chaser made major plays at home plate.

The guys were tired, sore, and worn, yet continued to push themselves hard. When they beat St. Louis, their celebration was wild. Then the struggle began once again as they faced the Minnesota Twins, the team with the highest overall ranking in Major League Baseball.

At team captain Risk Kincaid's suggestion, and for the first time in team history, the Rogues made a pact to stay out of the spotlight. They avoided the press, kept to themselves. Unity snuck into the locker room. Cemented them as a team.

When the World Series opened in Minnesota, the Rogues were ready. Romeo watched as a wild-eyed and very wired Psycho McMillan played his ass off. His energy fired the team, kept everyone playing at the highest level.

With the series at 1–1, the Rogues returned to Richmond. Fans at James River Stadium gave the team their full support. The Rogues took the next two games. One more win, and they'd take the World Series Championship.

Romeo chose to spend the afternoon before the Saturday night game with Emerson. He knew he wasn't good company. His thoughts were on the game and not on her. But she didn't seem to mind.

He'd sent her six dozen white roses and hand delivered a French blue nightgown embellished with lace and seed pearls. She'd bought an expensive bottle of champagne.

"I'll find you after the game," he told her as he was about to leave. "Be ready for me." He was that certain of winning.

Emerson arrived at the park two hours later. She'd chosen to sit in the press box, even though she wouldn't be taking notes. She'd asked to be taken off the story so she could watch Romeo and not worry about missing any details of the game.

Excited and nervous, she'd morphed from a professional journalist into a cheering, crazy woman rooting for her man.

The game got off to a good start. Chris Collier threw fastball after fastball. Minnesota struck out as many times as they connected for line drives. But eventually those drives got the Twins on base and in scoring position.

In the seventh-inning stretch, Minnesota led 5–4.

At the bottom of the eighth, the Rogues recaptured the lead. Now it was 6–5.

At the top of the ninth, the Twins drew their final bat. Three outs, and the game would end. Unless Minnesota tied or bettered the score.

Emerson forgot to breathe. She was concentrating so hard on the field, she swore her heart had stopped.

Chris Collier struck out the leadoff batter. The crowd exploded. Everyone was on their feet, waving their red, white, and blue rally towels.

The second batter smacked the ball to right field. A perfect rainbow. High, long, and soon to be gone.

Psycho refused to accept defeat.

He jumped, throwing his body halfway over

the cement wall to make the catch. His drop back onto the field seemed to occur in slow motion. He landed on his feet, then hit his knees. One arm cradled his rib cage; the other was held high to demonstrate his catch.

The stadium grew still, quiet as a morgue while Risk Kincaid sprinted to Psycho. Kincaid waved off the team, those who needed to know their wild man wasn't down for the count. He spoke to Psycho privately.

From the press box, Emerson felt Psycho will himself to his feet. Will himself into right field to finish the game.

The fans' response broke all sound barriers. The glass in the press box shook. The crowd's stomping and cheering sounded like an earthquake.

Chris Collier went the distance for the Rogues. The third batter took two strikes and three balls. Full count, and a sly smile slit the batter's lips. The impact of his swing sent the ball over the first baseman's head, a line drive directly to Psycho.

Emerson clenched her hands so tightly, her knuckles turned white. Psycho scooped the ball, ready to fire it to second, but muscle spasms seemed to grip his side. He bent to catch his breath. The runner advanced to second before Psycho could cut him off.

The next batter had power and precision. He also looked to right field.

Emerson saw Risk Kincaid shout at Psycho, but the right fielder shook him off. Clearly, Psycho wasn't leaving the game.

The batter broke the bat on Chris Collier's heat. The ball jammed between first and second. Psycho got to it quickly. He fired the ball to third.

The Twins player ran all out. He shot by Romeo and was headed home. Romeo relayed the ball to Chaser, who went for the tag at home.

The batter bulldozed the catcher.

Both men went down.

Chaser lost his mask.

The Twins player's batting helmet flew off.

The stadium held its collective breath.

Out . . . or safe?

It took the ruling of the home plate, first, and third base umpires to hand the Rogues their win. With that decision, fans screamed and fireworks exploded.

Emerson's eyes welled up and tears streamed her cheeks. Through it all, she watched the Rogues hug, jump up and down, and go crazy. They sprayed champagne over themselves and the crowd. Shook hands with every fan they could reach.

Em watched as Psycho and Chaser split away from the team.

Chaser tore off his catcher's gear and trotted to the sideline seats south of the Rogues' dugout. Among fans who were slapping him on the back, he lifted a tall, slender woman right out of the stands. In front of the television crew and all those present, he kissed her soundly. He'd chosen to share his win with her.

Psycho followed suit. One arm was curved around his ribs, the other around Keely Douglas as he pulled her from her seat and set her on the field. Keely laid her hand on his chest, her fingers splayed over his ribs in a gesture that was both protective and caring. Just then the team trainer pointed toward the locker room and Psycho obliged with Keely at his side.

It took Emerson a moment to realize her own Rogue was coming for her. Escorted by security, Romeo now climbed the stairs to the press box.

The door swung wide, and his "Privacy, please" sent the reporters and news crew scrambling. "Watch my back," he said to security before the door closed on the outside commotion.

Emerson's breath stuttered. Before her now stood the sexiest man in Major League Baseball. All tousled hair, grass-stained jersey, and enormous grin, as if he'd conquered the world.

He had. The Rogues had won the World Series.

Soon, he'd kiss her panties off.

She looked into his eyes, and fell into his arms. His kiss was charged with adrenaline and need. He couldn't get close enough to her. He curved his hands over her shoulders, then bracketed her ribs, finally cupping her bottom. They were as close as they could get, without being naked.

Naked would come shortly.

"The press, celebration in the locker room, autographs. I'll be home as soon as I can," he promised.

Several more kisses and another squeeze to her bottom, and he was called back to the field for the trophy presentation.

Kate Angell

The fans remained at the ballpark for hours after the Rogues cleared the field. Fireworks and music sounded until midnight. Emerson sat quietly and took it all in, needing to embrace the win along with the crowd. The Rogues had brought it home.

Around one a.m., she returned to her condo. She read in bed until Romeo showed up at two. She met him halfway on the stairs to her bedroom. She could tell he was hyped, happy, and wanting her bad.

He scooped her up and carried her back to bed. She lost her nightgown between the top step and her feather mattress. Only her French blue panties remained when he laid her down, then covered her. The press of his midnight-blue Armani suit felt rich against her skin. His sunshine and citrus surrounded her.

He slipped off her red reading glasses. Set them on her bedside table beside the Easy Ryder Magnum XL condoms. "A box, huh?"

"You're the legend."

"And I'm here to deliver."

She traced his silver and plum paisley tie with one finger. "Nice suit."

He loosened the Windsor knot. "Even nicer once it's off."

They bumped together, tugging at his clothing.

He shrugged off his suit jacket.

She set her hands to work on his shirt buttons, rolled the dress shirt off his shoulders.

He ripped off his belt.

She went for his zipper.

272

He rid himself of his slacks, socks, and shoes, then rocked back on his knees, fully naked and aroused. Emerson stared. The man was even more muscular than she'd expected. Curly golden-blond hair dusted his well-developed chest, rippling over his skin as his muscles moved.

He was a man in his prime, full of strength and heat, and born to give pleasure. The sexiest man in baseball had a major league hard-on.

"All for me?" Her fingertips grazed his sex.

"See anyone else in the room?"

"Good, 'cause I'm greedy."

He took her hipbones between his broad hands and pulled her toward him. Her knees bent on either side of his hips. The tips of his fingers nosed down, tripping lightly across the silken band of her panties. Easing his thumbs beneath the elastic, he stripped them down. The caress of silk was arousing.

He took his sweet time working his way up her body, going for her most sensitive areas first.

He licked his way up her inner thigh. Kissed her where she was most vulnerable. Then came the touching. So much touching. The man was good with his hands. Every move he made was sexy.

His fingers slid over and inside her. Desire tickled between her thighs. Her hips rolled and her stomach fluttered.

He pressed his mouth to those flutters, delivered a butterfly storm of kisses to her belly. His fingers splayed over her ribs, as heated as rays from the sun.

He tongued her navel, scraped his teeth over one hip. Kissed his way up her body, over each delineated rib to the warm curve of her breast. He took her nipple into his mouth, rolled it with his tongue.

He nipped the pulse point at the base of her throat.

Nuzzled her neck and ear.

Soft shadows from her reading light settled over his body as his long legs pushed her own apart. He rested on his elbows and looked down on her. Smiled.

"You ready for me, Em?" he breathed against her mouth.

"Ready since our first interview."

Lust and surprise lit his eyes. "You had me fooled."

"I didn't want to lose control. Until now."

"Lose it tonight with me."

He penetrated her then, and she gasped at the suddenness of it. She arched her back, and bonded her body to his male length. Pleasure pulsed from her breasts to her belly and in between her thighs—pure, raw, endless.

When he finally kissed her, she was lost. Completely, totally, and forever taken.

He controlled his body. And hers.

She accepted his heat with the naturalness of breathing. He moved inside her, deep circular motions that changed the angle of each thrust. The intensity, the ecstasy, the sheer power of the climax rose from deep inside her as he drove for his own release.

Her nails dug into his back, scored his skin.

She craved, throbbed, went mindlessly mad.

The tension in Romeo's body strained his every muscle. She could feel his body lock, jerk, and come at the exact moment lights brightened, then burst behind her eyelids.

She surrendered to the pulsing of a thousand nerves.

Time shifted, left her weightless. By degrees, her frantic breathing slowed.

She and Romeo lay motionless for long minutes, lacking the energy to roll apart, yet sustained by the warm tangle of arms and legs and remnants of pleasure.

The man was legendary.

He was also still hard inside her.

She looked into his eyes, questioningly.

He gently brushed back her hair, which had gone wild during sex. "I want you again," he said.

"Again?" She'd yet to blink away the bright lights behind her eyelids.

"Again and again." His mouth took hers in deep French kisses.

Their tongues once again tangled, as did their bodies.

Hot kisses and hotter hands brought them to orgasm a second time. Emerson was so spent and exhausted, she rolled onto her side with a sigh.

They spooned, her bottom kissing his belly.

His arm curved over her hip, his hand full on her breast. It was the gentlest of touches, yet so full of expectancy, her body shivered. She would have this man once more, as soon as she recovered.

"Emerson." His words whispered against her shoulder. "There's something I need to say."

She looked over her shoulder, caught his eye. Emotion etched his features. "Tell me."

"I've had sex with a lot of women."

She'd known that.

"Sex is best with someone you love."

Love . . . the word stole across her heart, caused her pulse to quicken.

"We waited seven months for sex," he slowly continued. "I can wait seven more if it takes that long for you to love me back."

She turned fully, faced him. Her soft breasts brushed his hard chest. His sex was wedged between her thighs. "I love you now."

His throat worked, his smile breaking on a release of breath. "Love is good. Marriage even better."

The man wanted to spend his life with her. Joy shot through her chest and acceptance tingled her toes. "I'm yours, Jesse Bellisaro." He would be Jesse to her from this point forth. Romeo was his past.

"You won't be sorry," he promised.

In keeping with that promise, he rolled her on her back and kept his legend alive.

FOURTEEN

"Get dressed, Cody McMillan."

Keely Douglas had called him by his given name. She must mean business. Psycho turned his darkest look on her. She rolled her eyes, unafraid. "Get out of bed," she ordered.

Hard to take orders from a woman standing in the doorway in nothing but a tangerine boa. Even if the boa did drape over her breasts and cover her crotch, he still knew she was naked. He wanted her naked in his bed.

Keely, however, insisted he make himself ready to welcome his guests. Those guests invited to celebrate the completed restoration of his Colonial.

He didn't have a welcoming bone in his body.

He held out his hand. "Come talk me into getting up."

"Do it on your own."

He jackknifed from the bed, stood tall. "I could attend nude."

"Not everyone would appreciate you as I do."

Kate Angell

"You had to invite Becky, didn't you?"

"Both Rebecca Reed Custis and the Richmond Historical Society."

"Shit." The day had doom and gloom written all over it.

"Romeo, Chaser, Risk Kincaid, and Chris Collier will be here."

"Yippee."

"And the gang from Wally's."

Psycho's eyes went wide. "Becky and the bar crowd. You're mixing prude and rude."

"It will all work out fine." She hesitated. "I think."

He understood her concern. Becky had bulldozed Keely into the open house. Keely, however, didn't have the oil painting she'd promised for the mantel. Only with Colonel William Lowell's portrait hung over the fireplace would the Colonial be fully restored.

Keely feared having to tell the truth.

Psycho had her back. She just didn't know it yet. He'd wanted to share his purchase, yet had chosen to wait until the painting was officially under his roof.

His trust in Chris Collier had solidified with the delivery. The Winslow Homer had arrived late yesterday afternoon while Keely was chin-deep in a bathtub of bubbles.

From the bubble bath, he'd talked her into his bed. Sex had replaced all thoughts of the painting. There had been no time to tell her about the masterpiece. All his words had gone into sweet

278

talk. How good she tasted. How he burned inside her. How much he liked her deep blue eyes.

Surprising Keely would be the high point of his day. The painting would be the best birthday gift she'd ever received.

She'd be grateful and loving. His hardheaded woman would go all soft in his arms. He wanted his "thank you" delivered in the metallic-blue boa tonight. It glowed in the dark.

Psycho scratched his belly. "You wearing a T-shirt and jeans?"

Her cheeks turned pink. "I bought a dress."

"What do you expect me to wear?"

"A suit."

No way in hell. "Door number two."

"You make my life difficult," she said. "I'd hoped you'd clean up and make as good an impression as your house."

"I don't do good impressions."

"You could if you tried."

"I try for no one."

"Not even for me?"

"Don't ask, and you won't be disappointed."

She crossed her arms over her chest, and the tangerine boa fluttered. Just enough to expose her right nipple and a hint of the blond curls between her thighs.

He looked down at his groin. *Batter up, and no relief pitch in sight.*

Catching his gaze, Keely covered herself the best she could. She tilted her head, her expression suddenly somber. "How are your ribs?"

He'd fractured three during the World Series. His leap onto the right-field wall had nearly punctured a lung. He remained sore, but on the whole, he was healing nicely. "Two weeks, and I'll be working out."

She looked down at her feet. Her toenails were painted hot pink. A thin gold link bracelet wrapped one ankle. Her most recent birthday present. "Now may not be the best time," she said slowly, "but I've been meaning to ask for a letter of recommendation. Rebecca has set me up with an interview for a second restoration. A Colonial on Rhode Island. The owners requested a letter from you. I've got a plane ticket to Newport on Friday."

Rhode Island? Friday? The thought of her leaving paralyzed him. "You haven't finished training the dogs."

"Boris and Bosephus can sit, roll over, and come on command. You may never get more from them."

"What about me?"

"Untrainable." Her smile was soft, but didn't quite reach her eyes. "A woman would be crazy to try."

"Damn crazy," he agreed.

"You hired me when I desperately needed a job," she said. "I'll always be grateful."

So grateful she'd leave him.

She turned then, the curve of her shoulder and her round little bottom walking out of his life. Anger and hurt slammed together in his chest, followed by an explosion of pain. He wanted to punch a wall. Throw back his head and howl. Go after her.

He remained where he stood. He'd never chased a woman. Had never wanted one to stay in his life.

But that was before Keely.

The skinny blonde with the deep blue eyes made him feel and need. Two emotions he'd survived without for thirty-two years.

She made him laugh.

He made her blush.

She satisfied him in bed.

He reminded her how fun birthdays could be every day of the week.

It had been an even trade-off. Until today.

He hated the fact that she'd move on and restore someone else's house. As if Colonel William Lowell's home wasn't enough to keep her happy. Son of a bitch.

Across the hallway, Keely Douglas dressed carefully. She'd spent two weeks' salary on a designer sweater dress in mauve cashmere. A scalloped gold chain looped her waist. She knew she looked sleek and stylish. The matching sling-back pumps gave her confidence. She'd done a damn fine job on Psycho's Colonial. It was time to showcase its beauty and heritage.

The only problem she faced was telling the truth. She wasn't related to the Lowell family, even on the bastard side, but she hadn't been able to think of a graceful way to admit she'd made the claim up. Her only hope was that her ability as a designer would outweigh her lie.

She crossed her fingers. Added a silent prayer.

Once downstairs, she checked on the caterer set up in the formal dining room. The King Midas Room, as Psycho referred to it, because the walls were gilded. The cut crystal, china, and vintage table linen gave off a burnished glow in the candlelight.

The doorbell soon rang. Keely greeted the arrivals in the foyer. She directed each person toward a buffet fit for a king. She accepted compliments on the chandelier dripping in prisms, and the bronze lions guarding the antique fire screen. More than one person sat and enjoyed the entry bench upholstered in sky-blue silk toile.

Every other minute, Keely looked toward the fireplace. She'd arranged red amaryllis and peonies in a silver punch bowl next to an antique painting covered by a black silk cloth. She'd bought a portrait of a cairn terrier captured in oils. It was a fine piece, but the little dog couldn't replace Colonel William Lowell on the mantle, no matter how proudly it posed.

She dreaded the moment when she'd have to unveil the terrier and announce that her ancestors did not branch from the Lowell family tree. The start of a headache hit her square between the eyes.

Rebecca Reed Custis arrived on the arm of architect Franklin Langston. Dressed in a dove-gray suit, the woman looked exactly as she had the first day she'd marched on Psycho's Colonial, demanding he honor the Confederate colonel. In Keely's eyes, William had been honored.

The remaining Daughters and members of the Richmond Historical Society followed Rebecca inside. Placing her hand over her heart, Rebecca spoke for the group. "An immense amount of thought has gone into restoring Mr. McMillan's Colonial. You are to be praised, Keely Douglas-Lowell." There was a soft round of applause before Rebecca introduced Keely to those guests she did not yet know.

The older woman went on to endorse Gloss Interiors. Keely's imaginary design firm. Everyone commended Keely on the success of the project. Silently they applauded her patience in dealing with Psycho McMillan.

Rebecca then led her group into the living room. In giving her tour, she pointed out her favorite slipper chair in cranberry velvet; a rococo sofa and the Elizabeth Randolph writing desk. The rosewood piano. Along with a bull's-eye mirror with an eagle perched on the top.

Romeo Belissaro and Chaser Tallan showed up with their fiancées. Jen Reid, Chaser's lady, had driven both couples in her classic turquoise '65 Thunderbird. An engagement gift from Chaser. Keely had heard that her El Camino had died a quick and painless death at James River Stadium. And never was revived.

Romeo checked Keely out as thoroughly as he did the foyer. "Place looks amazing," he finally said. "You've never looked better."

His compliment made her blush. The man stood tall and handsome beside his reporter. The diamond on Emerson Kent's finger cast as many prisms as the entrance chandelier.

"Thanks for coming," Keely said.

"Psycho's gone Colonial. Wouldn't miss this for the world," Chaser stated. "Where is our man of the hour?"

"Debating what to wear."

"Or not to wear," guessed Romeo.

Her shoulders slumped. "I requested a suit, but he—he—"

No one was listening. Every eye had suddenly shifted to the staircase. Utter stillness invaded the foyer.

"Holy shit," she heard Chaser mutter. "Psycho . . ."

Keely had never been more afraid to turn around.

Her fists clenched and her temper spiked.

Just once she'd have liked him to play by the rules.

She was going to kill him.

She spun about, ready to do battle . . .

Only to expel a breath in disbelief. Psycho McMillan descended the stairs in a black suit. His expression was sharp, severe, on the attack. There was more snarl than smile to the man as he hit the bottom step, daring anyone to make a comment on his formal appearance.

Someone whistled behind Keely, followed by "M-mmm, Psycho Rogue cleans up nice." The gang from Wally's Bar had shoved in behind Romeo and Chaser, and it was Mona who'd cut through the silence. Her second wolf whistle put everyone at ease.

The awkwardness was replaced by warm smiles and slaps on the back. As the crowd fanned out to other rooms, Keely faced Psycho. His gaze touched her with heat and intensity, nearly burning the cashmere off her body. She shifted on her high heels and folded her hands over her stomach to contain the flutters.

"The open house is a success," she finally managed.

"So I see."

"Most everyone has arrived. Many brought housewarming gifts. I've put them in the family room."

"Good place for them."

"Risk and Jacy Kincaid are running late, because the cappuccino machine at her café broke down. She's waiting for an electrician. Chris Collier and Sophie Hart send their regrets. Apparently·someone named Fancy caught a cold."

At the mention of Fancy, Psycho's lips twitched. "Fancy's a pig."

"Oh . . ." She'd run out of news. Psycho's short responses indicated he hadn't much to say either.

While she'd love to comment on his transformation from nudist to major player, he wouldn't want flattery.

The word *virile* came to mind when she took in the way his black turtleneck defined his chest. As did *tailored* and *tempting*.

He was startlingly masculine and totally lethal.

He hadn't shaved. Late afternoon stubble roughened his jaw. The ends of his overly long hair curled against his collar. He was both handsome and hunted, Keely thought, as two women from Wally's came to claim his attention. Women who knew Keely only as Psycho's designer. They had no idea she'd loosened his hips during seasonal play.

"I'd better see to your guests." She excused herself.

The afternoon progressed in a haze. The Daughters continued to sing Keely's praises. Their compliments lifted her spirits, but she knew the crash of emotion was but minutes away. No oil painting. No further acceptance. She'd be shown the door.

As the time for the portrait's unveiling approached, she felt Psycho's gaze on her. Psycho was not a man to show his feelings. Yet his look stamped her his.

Air. She needed air. Slipping behind Romeo, she wove along the fringes of the crowd toward the dining room. She was feeling light-headed. Absorbed in her many duties, she'd forgotten to eat both breakfast and lunch.

She filled her plate with sherried crab and steamed spicy shrimp, then snuck out the back door. She circled the new stone patio, wanting to check on the two Newfoundlands. Boris and Bosephus greeted her with excited barks. Keely quieted them with a bite of crab.

"Dogs have gourmet tastes." Psycho approached her, so dangerously handsome her heart quickened. "Seeking solace?"

"I like it out here. Just me and the dogs. They're better company than most people."

He rested his arms on the fence, scratched Boris's head. "You'll get no disagreement from me."

She cut him a look. "How are you doing?"

One corner of his mouth pinched. "How do you think I'm doing? I'm a private person, Keely."

"It hasn't been all that bad."

"One hundred people have invaded my home. I've lost two hours of my life."

Keely wished time would stop. In ten minutes, she'd be facing the greatest humiliation of her life.

Rebecca Reed Custis was a clock-watcher. "Keely Douglas-Lowell!" the older woman called from the patio. "Do unveil the painting, dear."

Keely inhaled slowly. "Guess I'd better go," she said to Psycho.

"I'm right behind you." He pressed his palm to her back. It felt big and warm through the cashmere.

Once inside, she squeezed through the crowd gathered near the fireplace. Psycho held back, standing off to the side. His expression was now unreadable.

Keely looked at all those gathered. Her heart beat in her throat as she fixed in her memory the people that had become such a big part of her life. She'd been unemployed and down on her luck when she'd first knocked on Psycho's door. Seven months later, she was being praised for a phenomenal restoration. She felt successful. Right up until this moment, she'd never known life could be so good.

Rebecca Reed Custis linked arms with Keely. She beamed with southern pride. "It's time to return Colonel William Lowell to his rightful home."

Keely's hand shook as she reached for a corner of the black silk cloth. She wished she had a magic wand. One wave, and the colonel would replace the terrier.

She closed her eyes to shut out the expressions of disappointment once the dog was revealed.

One tug, and she'd freed the cloth.

Silence. Pure and utter silence. Followed by an upbeat buzz of appreciation. The guests liked the dog? Keely peered through veiled eyelids. Blinked. Stared at the painting. Nearly fainted. The colonel's portrait hung on the mantel.

"Such a handsome man, our William, pictured astride his warhorse Ranger." Rebecca was the first to speak. "His painting's come home."

Who brought the painting home?

Amid applause and genuine smiles, Keely located Psycho on the edge of the crowd. He raised a brow, his smile slow, knowing. The man had saved her from the most humiliating moment of her life.

Tears came quickly to her eyes, spilling onto her cheeks. He'd known she'd lied. Yet he'd saved her butt.

She cut through the crowd until she was standing before him.

He took her hand, led her to the family room. Then closed the door on his guests. No one would dare disturb them.

Among the mountains of housewarming gifts, she found her way to the black leather couch and sat on one end. She swiped at tears that continued to fall.

Psycho located a box of tissues and handed it to her. "You impressed them, Keely Douglas-Lowell."

"I'm not a Lowell," she sniffed.

"You know it and I know it. Becky never has to know the truth." He jammed his hands in the pockets of his slacks. "There's little historical documentation on William's brother, Marshal. The man never married. Somewhere in his deep dark past, he probably bedded a tavern wench and fathered illegitimate children. We'll assume he did."

She looked up at him. "You'd protect me?"

"I have your back."

"Why?"

A simple question, yet the answer would complicate his life. In a very good way. "I didn't want you to feel less of a person because you couldn't produce the painting."

"Where did you find the colonel?" she asked.

"In Williamsburg. His portrait was delivered yesterday. Happy birthday, Keely."

Her throat worked. "I don't know how to thank you."

"Nudity, boas, the foam finger come to mind."

She gave him a weak smile.

He continued. "You saved my ass in April when the Daughters marched on the house and demanded it be restored. I saved your butt today with the painting. We've come full circle."

She licked her lips. "You've gained everyone's respect and approval."

He shrugged off his sport coat. Rolled his shoulders. "I don't care what people think of me, Keely."

She stared at him, confused. "Yet you allowed the restoration, the open house, bought the oil painting."

He ran his hand down his face, rubbed the back of his neck. "All for you."

"Me?" Her voice was no more than a whisper.

"You." He looked her square in the eye. "The skinny blonde with the torn jeans, cheap sunglasses, and mismatched flip-flops. You with the crooked part in your hair and incredibly deep blue eyes. You, who steal the bed covers and the last whole wheat bagel. You, who fit in at Wally's Bar as well as with the Daughters. No woman wears a boa like you do. You look damn fine naked."

Her eyes had welled up again and her lips had parted.

"The dogs are going to miss you, Keely." He scratched his jaw. "And so will I."

"You could ask me to stay."

He'd always asked women to go. He'd held the door wide, showed them the exit. The pain in his chest hurt like a son of a bitch, and it wasn't from his fractured ribs. He desperately wanted her to stay, but was equally worried she'd refuse him.

He'd never had a reason to commit. Until now. "Stay, and be naked with me for the rest of our lives."

"Lives, as in longer than tomorrow?"

He saw her hope, her need, and felt in that instant he could conform just a little for her. There were, however, a few things he couldn't get around. "I don't do big weddings."

"Courthouse works for me."

"No more suits."

"No nudity before the justice of the peace."

"Small reception."

"The Bat Pack's fine."

His gaze warmed. "I can do a honeymoon."

"No privacy like your own home."

"I do love you, Keely Douglas-Lowell."

"Keely Douglas-*McMillan*." She was off the couch and in his arms in a heartbeat.

He closed his eyes, breathed in her hair, held

her so tightly she gasped for air. He kissed her then, and she kissed him back. A full-body press that included tongues and touching and a whole lot of moaning.

Their clothes soon hit the floor. She looked into his eyes and smiled. "You looked so handsome today."

"Your cashmere made me stiff."

On the couch, in the chair, then down on the oriental carpet, Psycho McMillan promised Keely Douglas a future of love and great sex. When night shadows crept around them, Keely rose and peeked out the door. The Colonial was empty of all guests.

"It's you and me now." Psycho came to stand behind her.

"You, me, and the colonel," Keely corrected.

Outside, the Newfoundlands howled. "You, me, the colonel, and the dogs," Psycho added.

She turned, stroked his *Stands on Command* tattoo. "Someday, some little Psychos."

"If you can do crazy."

"I'd do crazy for you."

Her commitment brought peace and calmness to his life.

The Rogues had won the World Series.

And he'd won Keely Douglas.

He'd scored big on both counts.

He planned to savor his wins.